ANGELA M

CAT
IN A
BAG

WK

WIDOW'S KISS

Copyright © 2017 Angela M. Sanders

Printed in the United States of America.

First Printing, 2017

ISBN 978-0-9904133-8-7

Widow's Kiss
P.O. Box 82488
Portland, OR 97282

www.WidowsKissBooks.com

To Aunt Pucci, kind reader and great gal

The Joanna Hayworth Vintage Clothing Mysteries

The Lanvin Murders
Dior or Die
Slain in Schiaparelli
The Halston Hit

The Booster Club Capers

The Booster Club

CAT
IN A
BAG

CHAPTER ONE

Not much broke the routine of the Carsonville Women's Correctional Facility, so the weekly 12-step meeting for shoplifters was a treat. Inmates from embezzlers to streetwalkers to Adele, the prison's lone art forger, attended en masse. A few actual shoplifters showed up, too.

If Adele planned things right, this would be her last 12-step meeting. Ever.

"Please," the facilitator said. A new one, Adele noted. "Be seated. We're already five minutes late."

The spring morning's light sliced through the barred windows in a pattern that might have graced a Rembrandt, only this scene was closer to an illustration in a Depression-era confessional magazine. Bit by bit, the chattering quieted as women in blue cotton shirts and matching elastic-waist pants dropped into folding chairs.

"I'm sorry the regular facilitator can't make it." The woman glanced at her watch. "Let's get started. I'm Deborah, and I'm a shoplifter."

"Good morning, Deborah," the women said in unison.

"I understand that last week you talked about step eight, forgiveness. For homework, you made lists of people you wronged. Forgiveness is a big topic. Let's continue today."

Adele sat near the room's edge. The group leader had an innocence about her, not like the other leaders hardened through years of social service work. With her delicate features and short hair, she might be Adele's sister. Adele touched her own head, shorn into a pixie only the day before.

"Who'd like to begin?" the facilitator asked.

A small, plump woman toward the front raised her hand. Her metal chair scraped the linoleum floor as she stood. "My name is Shirley, and I used to rob banks."

"Not a shoplifter?" Deborah asked.

"Not regularly."

"You do know this is a meeting for shoplifters, right?"

"What?" Shirley said. "You want me to steal something so I can come back to the meeting? I could go down the cellblock and boost some tampons."

"Of course not, Shirley," Deborah said. "Maybe we could hear from a shoplifter first, that's all."

The inmates looked at each other. Adele figured maybe a third of them had some kind of theft in their backgrounds. One woman, a kleptomaniac, raised her hand.

"Yes?"

"My name is Claire, and I'm a shoplifter. I steal other things, too. I mean, not just in shops."

"No kidding," one of the inmates murmured. Just about everyone in Claire's cellblock had lost a comb or bottle of shampoo at some point.

"Go on, Claire," the facilitator said, her voice full of sympathy. With her translucent skin and blue eyes, she looked as if she'd stepped from a Flemish painting, Adele thought. The drab walls added to the effect. All she needed was a vase of parrot tulips nearby and a bowl of fruit with a fly on the peach.

"I still struggle," Claire said. "I think I have it under control, then something happens, and I get angry—"

"—And you can't help but steal something," the facilitator finished. "Tell me more."

"I really like hair products," Claire said. "For our homework, I made a list of people and places I've stolen from." She unfolded a piece of paper. "It started when I was in second grade. Judy Berman's mom had packed her a deviled ham sandwich, and I…."

For the next hour, inmates rose one by one and recited the wrongs for which they sought forgiveness. Listening to them, it appeared that Carsonville County's entire stock of goods regularly shifted hands. Adele suspected some of it was invented. Did an inmate really steal two goats and dress them in cheerleading outfits and send them to tryouts? That story about the microfilms of Latvian submarine blueprints was hard to swallow, too. Adele had her own wrongs to right, which meant today's plan had to go smoothly.

She glanced at the wall clock. Each click of the minute hand seemed to take hours. Catching herself balling her hands into fists, she flattened her palms on her knees.

"And that wraps it up," the facilitator said. "Thank you, everyone, for sharing."

The room began to empty, but Adele hung back. A guard at the door watched as inmates filed back toward their cellblocks. Next on the schedule was an hour of free time, then lunch. She folded the chair next to hers and carried it to the rack in the corner.

"The bathroom is in there?" the facilitator asked.

Adele nodded and watched as the door clicked behind her.

"You coming?" the guard asked Adele.

"I have clean-up duty this week." She hoped the guard hadn't noticed the tremor in her voice. Forging paintings was her business, not assault and battery. She stacked the used paper cups and glanced over her shoulder. When the guard stepped into the hall to chat with another warden, Adele sucked in a breath and shoved her way into the bathroom.

The facilitator was washing her hands. She met Adele's gaze in the mirror. "Did you—?"

Adele shut the door behind them. "Sorry," she whispered and tied the facilitator's scarf around her mouth. The woman's eyes widened, but she barely struggled as Adele fastened her wrists and ankles with the cord she'd made from shredded socks and hidden in her bra. It was a moment's work for Adele to strip her of her dress and tote bag. Adele clipped the visitor's ID badge to the dress's collar and slipped on the therapist's oversized sunglasses.

The guard was still chatting with her colleague in the hall when Adele emerged from the bathroom and shut the door behind her.

"I'm ready for you to escort me out," she said, mimicking the facilitator's girlish tone.

"Where's that inmate, the one with the short hair?" the guard said.

"I'm not sure who you mean." Adele kept her smile steady. "She must have left. There's no one else here."

The guard glanced behind Adele at the empty room. All was quiet beyond the bathroom door. Adele was sure her thumping heart must be audible above the prison's humming HVAC system.

Finally, the guard turned. "All right. Let's go."

✲
✲✲

The sedan pulled up to a stucco building that sported a few Italian-inspired arches in front but went full-on institutional toward the rear. "Villa Saint Nicholas" was inscribed over the portico. Sitting near the front door in a worn Adirondack chair was an elderly man in a baseball cap, cane at his side, shuffling cards.

"Where are we?" Adele asked.

"Home, my child," the car's driver said. He'd introduced himself as "Father Vincent," and he looked like a priest: fatherly bearing, white collar, and black raiment with a tasseled belt. But he piloted the car like he was born with a hand on the gearshift.

"For a while, anyway," added the car's other occupant, a middle-aged redhead named Ruby. Her T-shirt featured the silhouette of a small dog with the words "Cheers to Chihuahuas" printed above it.

"Oh," Adele said. She leaned back. The scheme had gone off exactly as planned. She'd stridden to the visitors' parking lot and headed for the sedan with the red silk rose in its back window, as instructed. Father Vincent and Ruby had popped up from their hiding places, and, an hour later, here they were.

"You girls get out here, and I'll take the car back to the motor pool before anyone misses it," the priest said.

That would explain the Department of Property Assessment parking pass in the window.

"We'll get you settled," Ruby said.

Freedom, Adele thought as, for the first time in three years, her feet hit ground not owned by the county. She was free. The air smelled better out here, bursting with oxygen. On the drive to town, every gas station and fast food restaurant fascinated her. The naked street trees, their boughs barely tipped with the green of spring, engrossed her more than the color plates in the book of Redoute's paintings of roses she'd studied in the prison's library. She'd forgotten how vivid the colors on a political billboard could be or how fascinating the jangle of shapes in a backyard strewn with tricycles and tools.

As they entered the building, even the disinfectant's tang was somehow fresher. Now she could dig her hands in the dirt, eat ice cream all day, and, best of all, paint. No one could tell her what to wear or when to go to bed.

Ruby glanced her way. "Sorry you won't really be at liberty here."

"But I—"

"If we're caught harboring a fugitive, the whole place will go down." Ruby patted her arm. "But you understand that."

Adele's enthusiasm was only slightly dampened. She was still out of prison. That was the main thing.

They passed a small office off the entry hall, and Ruby waved at a muscular, tattooed man leaning back with his feet on the desk. His novel featured an embracing couple on its cover. "Hi, Warren."

"That the new tenant?" The man set his novel aside and swiveled his legs to the floor, but he didn't stand.

"I'm Adele." She stuck out a hand.

He didn't move.

Ruby lifted her chin. "Warren, we talked about this last night. I don't expect you to be happy about it, but you could at least be courteous. Adele is our guest for as long as she needs us. You know the deal."

"Pleased to meet you," Warren said, still avoiding eye contact.

"Warren is the Villa's manager. He keeps an eye on the entrance, does a little plumbing and electrical. Used to be a prison warden."

What an odd place this was. Was it only last week that she'd put out the word to Uncle Larry that she needed his help? Through

Larry's note in the prison library's copy of *Carpet Care Through the Ages*, she'd learned that something called the "Booster Club" had taken her on, and that today was the day for her breakout. All she had to do was follow their instructions regarding the 12-step group facilitator—poor woman, hopefully she was all right—cut her hair into a pixie, and look for the sedan with the red rose. She winced at the memory of the facilitator's shock when Adele had gagged her.

Now, here she was, free, but with nothing but this strange group's benevolence. Not even a toothbrush.

"What room, Warren?" Ruby asked.

"We'll put her on three. The room toward the alley." He folded his arms in front of his chest. "Remember, blinds closed. No one can know she's here."

"You hungry, doll?" Ruby asked Adele as they passed through the corridor. She pushed the button to call the elevator. "I bet the food in prison was awful. With Cook, you're in for a treat. I'll take you to settle in and come up with a sandwich in a few minutes."

"Where are we?"

"The Villa Saint Nicholas. A retirement home."

Adele turned this over in her mind a moment. "He doesn't like me. Warren, that is."

"Don't worry," Ruby said softly. "He'll come around."

The elevator stopped with a jerk at the third floor, and Ruby and Adele walked down a dimly lit hall to an even dimmer room toward the building's rear.

"Wait here a second." Ruby flipped on the lights and closed the blinds. "There. Safe now. I'm afraid it's not the most cheerful room. It was Candace's until last November, when she passed, bless her soul. Her eyesight was failing, so she didn't mind this atrocious wallpaper."

Adele took in the flurries of Southern belles and straw-hatted gents playing banjos on sternwheeler boats. "Maybe the dim light is best."

Ruby shook her head. "Such a shame for a gifted counterfeiter to go blind. You do forgeries, too, am I right?"

"Fine art, mostly eighteenth century," Adele said, but she was only half listening. As long as she was safe, she didn't care where she slept. It was the mission that mattered. The amends. She had work to do.

"Hon," Ruby laid a hand on Adele's arm. "I know we don't have a lot of time. Larry filled us in about your trouble. I'm sorry."

Adele's gaze dropped to her hands. "Thank you for everything you're doing. I don't know why you're helping me, but—"

"It's Larry the Fence's doing. Uncle Larry to you, I guess."

"He asked you, and you said yes?"

Ruby sat on the bed's edge. "It was a little more complicated than that. The Villa's clientele are special. You aren't the first inmate they've seen, and you won't be the last. Just about everyone here has done time."

"They're criminals? This is a retirement home for crooks?"

"They had to agree to give up their professions before moving here."

"I see." Adele let her hand sweep the desk's top. Real wood. Battered, but so much nicer than the particleboard and metal in prison. "You don't live here, do you? You couldn't be old enough." Adele put her age at fifty, maybe, with canny makeup and hair meant to lower the estimate ten years.

"No, I'm just a friend of the Villa. I have a past, too, but these days I do hair. And the occasional prison break-out, I guess."

Adele smiled. Ruby seemed a genuinely kind person, but kindness and foolhardiness weren't the same thing. "Why are you helping me?"

Ruby pulled at a ridge of the chenille bedspread. "Your uncle said he'd make sure the Villa was relicensed if the Booster Club helped you out."

"Relicensing must be tough." It had to be, seeing that they'd already gone to so much trouble, and the job wasn't half over.

"Like I said, the Villa isn't your typical retirement home. They, well, they fly under the radar in a lot of ways, and I'm not talking simply about the building. Although it's perfectly safe," she added quickly. "But the residents don't need inspectors marching in and out. Your uncle said he could help with that."

"I see."

Ruby rose and touched Adele's sleeve. "We'll get you squared away. Don't you worry. I'll be right back."

After Ruby left, Adele took her place on the bed. Other than the bed, the small room held a maple dresser and desk, both scarred from decades of use. She rose to open the door across from the bed. The bathroom. She sighed in contentment. Her room might not be much bigger than the cell she'd shared just this morning, but now she had a bathtub. Her own bathtub, too. Someone had thoughtfully set a toothbrush and toothpaste on the sink and a fresh stack of towels on the back of the toilet.

She lifted the blinds an inch and peered out. No sirens, at least. She jumped at the sound of the door opening behind her. Ruby set a plate with a grilled cheese sandwich and a pickle on the dresser. "Here you go, honey. I'm cutting the hair of a few of the residents downstairs. You rest in the meantime."

Adele had been too nervous to eat breakfast. She didn't know if she could eat the sandwich either, but she'd try. After a tentative bite, she devoured it. This was no simple white bread and American cheese number. Gruyère, if she wasn't mistaken, and tangy Dijon mustard.

She wiped her mouth with a linen napkin, pushed the plate aside, and yawned. Ruby was right. A nap sounded great. She pulled up a quilt and lay back on the bed.

Until last week, she'd expected to be in prison another five years. Then she saw the prison's doctor for debilitating headaches she couldn't shake. At the memory, Adele rubbed her temples. The doctor had recommended a CT scan. The next day, she was called back to the infirmary and sat across the desk from the stolid-faced physician. "I'm afraid I have some bad news," he said. She had an inoperable brain aneurysm. She shouldn't count on living past spring.

He'd taken off his glasses and rubbed the bridge of his nose but wouldn't look her in the face. "I'm so sorry. There's nothing I can do."

So, she was going to die. She hadn't panicked or cried or cursed fate. Before she'd even left the room, she knew what she had to do. The knowledge had settled as quickly and surely as the smudge on the bottom of the CT scan she'd just seen. She had to get her paintings off the market before anyone figured out they were fakes, and, worse, what she'd done to them. She got in touch with Uncle Larry. He'd told her the Booster Club would help. The Booster Club. With those words on her mind, Adele fell asleep.

A knock on the door woke her. "May I come in?"

With a jerk, Adele sat up. Where was she? The room was completely dark, unlike the prison's relentless fluorescent buzz even after lights out. She let out her breath. The retirement home. She clicked on the bedside lamp. "Sure. Come in." When the door opened, her jaw dropped. It was the 12-step group facilitator from the prison.

The woman broke into a smile at Adele's shock. "Oh, come on. Don't you think I would have fought back a little harder if I hadn't known? Deborah Granzer." She shook Adele's hand. "I'm sorry I won't be able to stick around to see the Booster Club through the job. I'm leaving town tonight."

"Oh." After three years of incarceration — the same routine day in, day out — she'd practically lived another three years since morning.

"I'm afraid I'll be out of touch for the next week or so, too," Ruby, right behind Deborah, said.

Deborah clapped her hands together. "So. Have you met the others?"

CHAPTER TWO

In the Villa's cafeteria, Gilda stuck the last brown rosebud into the floral arrangement and stood back, one hand on her hip, and the other on her walker. She squinted at the bouquet. Could be worse. She crammed a dead fern on the arrangement's edge.

"Not bad," Bobby said. He'd come in from outside and continued to shuffle cards while Gilda worked. "Who's that one for?"

"Some cheating yahoo," Gilda said. "Why don't these roses come with thorns? It would be so much better that way." She hummed a few bars of "Frankie and Johnny" as she put the finishing touches on the arrangement.

Ever since Gilda had come up with the idea to make a little cash with Bad Seed, a business delivering dead floral arrangements, she'd loved imported South American roses. They died on the stem without even opening, their brown heads bent as if in shame. Lilies were a waste of money. When they were over the hill, they simply dropped their petals. She had better luck with hydrangeas.

Voices from the hall drew nearer. "This is our cafeteria. The Villa's residents hang out here a lot. Never play cards with Bobby, by the way." It was Ruby, leading a frail-looking girl by the elbow.

"What?" Bobby said once they entered the room. "What did I ever do to you?"

"Card shark," Ruby said in a stage whisper. "We'll meet in here because of the television. Keep an eye out for news of your escape. Grady tends to monopolize the television room."

Warren leaned in the doorway. Deborah followed Ruby and closed the cafeteria's blinds enough that some light came through, but no one would be able to see in. The sounds of bouncing balls and children's laughter came from the school next door. Ruby clicked on the television, and a *Perry Mason* rerun filled the screen.

"Everyone, this is Adele Waterson." Ruby turned to Gilda and lowered her voice. "Deborah's dropping me off at home. Are you sure you can handle it?"

"We talked this over earlier, remember? We'll be fine." Just because it had been a few years—okay, decades—since most of the Villa's residents had been in the business didn't mean they couldn't help a girl out before she died. Now that she was out of the joint, it would be easy. Wasn't that what the Booster Club was for? At least, that's what Larry had argued when he'd made his case last week. His niece wanted to take care of a few items before she died. Why shouldn't she have that chance? In exchange, he'd fix things with the licensing board.

Warren had led the camp against helping the girl. "You think relicensing is a problem," he had said, "what about getting caught harboring a fugitive?"

Gilda smiled at the girl. She was a delicate thing, the niece. Maybe prison had done that to her. As a rule, members of the bent community had a survivor's look about them. They were the hearty shrubs at the back of the flowerbed, not the blooms that held the place of glory in a vase on the sideboard. Maybe they weren't showpieces, but they grew with minimal water and no fertilizer.

Of course, art forgers were different than your run of the mill

criminal. Gilda had only known one, a specialist in Post Impression-
ism, and he'd died of cirrhosis of the liver when she was a teenager
and only just beginning to trawl the nightclubs. She'd heard the
stories of mistresses and artistic snits and empty bottles of Scotch
whisky. This one was a different sort of artist. She was an observer,
not the drama-spewing center of attention. You could see it in her
wide eyes and how she shifted her gaze from person to person.

Gilda set down a fistful of babies' breath and pushed her walker
to the new girl. "Hi, honey. Ruby, you and Deborah go on home.
No problem."

Ruby and Deborah left to a round of goodbyes and kisses on the
cheek. "You're sure it's all right?" Ruby said, hand on the doorknob.

"We've got it, no problem. You girls drive safely," Gilda said. She
steered Adele toward a chair along the cafeteria's far wall, where she'd
be out of sight of the street.

Most of the Villa's other dozen residents had eventually sided with
Larry the Fence. It was great to pass retirement with other people
who knew the life, but, face it, you spend a long time being old. And
this was a "creative" bunch. They got bored. Talking about the old
days, the old heists, the old crowd didn't excite. Finally, just after
dinner, they'd voted to take on the Booster Club's mantle and help
Larry's niece make her peace before she died.

"How do you like your room?" Gilda asked.

Adele's gaze took her in as if she were appraising a fine sculpture.
"It's nice. Thank you for having me."

"Then I'll introduce you around," Gilda said. "This is Adele. We just
sprang her from Carsonville Women's Prison." She nodded toward
the television. "They'll have an APB on her soon—"

"Yes," Adele said, her voice small.

"Speak up, hon," Bobby said.

"I said, yes, thank you."

"Adele, these are your new housemates until we get things straightened out for you. Don't worry about remembering everyone all at once." She touched the priest's shoulder. "You've already met Father Vincent. Besides living here, he drives us around town, takes us to appointments."

The priest nodded. "Pleased to be helping you."

"I heard Ruby mention Bobby to you. He's the one shuffling cards," Gilda said.

"Got to keep my hands busy."

"And speaking of keeping his hands busy, the man whittling next to Bobby is Mort."

"What's his specialty?" Adele asked Gilda.

"Ruby told you about the Villa, did she?"

"Confidence man," Mort said. "The whittling's just a hobby."

"He's good," Gilda said. "He did the bust above the fireplace." After her longtime partner and Villa founder Hank had died, Mort carved his likeness, down to the horn-rimmed glasses and slight underbite. It brought them both comfort.

"Thank you." Mort continued cleaning his pocketknife, keeping an eye on the girl all the while.

"Then we have Red" —she pointed toward the white-haired woman— "Mary Rose, and Grady. I assume you've already met Warren, the manager, on your way in. The others are napping or out, but you'll get to know them soon enough."

Adele seemed to be taking it all in. "What is the Booster Club, anyway? I asked for Larry's help, and the next thing I know, I'm here. Not that I'm not grateful," she added quickly.

Gilda had always thought Deborah was fine-boned, but this girl would look like a 12-year-old from a distance. Tiny chin, tiny wrists. Lovely cheekbones, though. Maybe later she'd lend the girl some blush and a lipstick. "The Booster Club is a do-gooders group."

"Sort of a fraternal organizational for the underclass," Father Vincent said. "We have particular skills, and we use them for society's good."

"Yes. The Booster Club's membership is fluid. It started with a few of the younger folk—you met Deborah and Ruby—and we helped when we could. This job's all ours."

Adele's eyes were wide as a kindergartner's on the first day of school. "And everyone here is bent? This is an old folks home for criminals?"

Gilda waved a dead rose at her. "Don't tell me you're too good for us."

Adele let out a long breath, then smiled. Then laughed. The girl looked as if she hadn't laughed in a long time. She leaned back. "No, I'm…." All at once, she was serious again. "What kinds of projects have you taken on?"

"You know the old firehouse, the one that's now a family shelter? That was the Booster Club," Gilda said.

"I read about that in the paper," Adele said. "We all wondered if the woman who lost it at the end—"

"Ellie Whiteby," Gilda said and shook her head.

"—would end up at Carsonville Women's with us," Adele finished.

"She went to a psychiatric ward. She fought the firehouse tooth and nail, and it left her unbalanced," Gilda said. "After the firehouse, the Booster Club started an adoption program for inmates' companion animals. Ruby's idea. She fosters Chihuahuas."

Gilda watched as Adele's gaze traveled the room, pausing a

moment on Warren before returning to Gilda. The girl swallowed. "I'm here because last week I learned that I have a brain aneurysm. If it bursts—"

"Kaput," Bobby said. "Larry told us."

"The doctor at the infirmary gave me a few months at most to live, but I could die anytime."

"Infirmary doctor, pshaw," Father Vincent said. "We'll have Doc Parisot look you over."

Due to helping patients get cheap medication from Canada and the bad luck of stumbling over a few FBI agents, Dr. Parisot no longer had a medical license. He kept up his training through attending conferences under a variety of aliases, and he treated everyone at the Villa in the ground floor doctor's office. Grady had dubbed it the "sick bay" when he was into *Star Trek*, before soap operas took over his TV schedule, and the name had stuck.

"It doesn't matter. I've come to grips with it. Sort of." Her voice softened at the last few words.

"Look. The television," Warren said. "Turn it up."

"We interrupt programming to bring you breaking news. A woman has escaped from Carsonville Women's Correctional Facility. She is not known to be armed, but she could be dangerous. She may have been assisted in her escape." Adele's mugshot appeared on the screen. Her delicate skin showed purple under her eyes. "If you see Adele Waterson or know her whereabouts, contact the number at the bottom of the screen." After a moment, the screen switched again to black and white, with Perry Mason gesturing toward the judge.

Warren turned down the volume. "Well, that's it, then. 'Assisted in her escape.'" He shook his head. "If she's caught, it will be the end of the Villa."

"Don't get so dramatic," Gilda said. All those years reading potboilers must have messed with the boy's mind. She'd been in a lot tighter situations and made a clean go of it, no problem. Nevertheless, she glanced toward the parking lot in front. Father Vincent was careful about "borrowing" and returning cars without leaving anything incriminating behind. Surely he hadn't been followed. She couldn't help but notice Father Vincent stealing a glance out front, too.

"Maybe we could start tonight, even," Adele said, perhaps emboldened by the television report.

"Speak up, girl," Grady repeated.

"She said we might get started tonight," Gilda said. Then, to Adele, "That's Grady. He's a little hard of hearing but great with computers."

"Oh." The poor girl looked overwhelmed.

"Like I said, don't worry too much about names for now." She pulled out a chair and sat. "I'm free once I've finished this floral arrangement. What do you have in mind? Larry said you had a few things to settle."

"Perhaps a difficult family relationship?" Father Vincent said. "I've helped many families reconcile over the years."

"A few debts to pay off?" Mary Rose said. "We don't have a lot of money, but with your uncle's help I bet we could work it out."

"Maybe she has something fun she wants to do," Red offered. "You know, go bungee jumping or something."

"No. I want to get back my forgeries and destroy them."

The Villa's residents were silent a moment. Even Bobby stopped shuffling his cards. Only Mort continued carving. He was making a boat for Mary Rose's grandson and had whittled a captain's wheel at its prow.

Finally, Father Vincent spoke. "What?"

"Huh?" Grady said after adjusting his hearing aid.

"That's what you wanted, for the Booster Club to steal back your paintings?" Warren shook his head. "This was not part of the deal."

"Darling," Gilda said. "We're not equipped for fine art heists. Larry said nothing about this."

Adele's voice grew stronger. "I need those paintings destroyed."

"Oh, no." Warren shook his head. "Absolutely not. We can't take the risk."

"You don't understand," Adele said. "People see these paintings. They think they're looking at masterpieces, but it's all a lie. It's wrong."

"Those paintings aren't hurting anyone. Folks are probably enjoying them," Gilda said. Something about Adele's insistence struck a false note. After years of playing people for money, Gilda's B.S. detector was finely calibrated. The girl didn't have a con's slick demeanor, but she was hiding something.

"Not as much as they would if they were real. Plus, it's disrespectful to the artists. Their paintings are their legacy. People shouldn't know them by forgeries."

"Aren't they dead? The artists, I mean?" Gilda said.

"Not as long as their work survives." Adele clenched her jaw. Gilda knew this look. Cook did the exact same thing when they were trying to get her to get the cheaper store-bought eggs instead of shell out for the pastured eggs at the farmers market. There was no arguing.

"How many paintings are we talking about?" Bobby asked.

"Only eight," she said. "That's all."

"Only eight," Gilda said. "You want us to steal eight paintings, probably all in high-security areas, for you?"

Adele didn't even blink. "And destroy them."

Gilda shook her head. "Hon, look around. There's a lot of

experience in this room, but not quite as much agility as, say, fifty years ago. Stealing a valuable painting takes planning, skills, money…." She looked up. "Does your uncle know about this?"

Adele stayed silent.

"So, you didn't tell him. Honey," Gilda said.

"We need Deanie," Bobby said.

"She could do it," Father Vincent said. "Didn't she lift two Boulangers from the Frick?"

"She's not in the business anymore, and you know it," Gilda said. He was right, though. Claudine—Hank's daughter—would have been the perfect cat burglar for them. She was young, fit, and had nerves of steel. There wasn't a safe made nor security system designed that she couldn't crack. But she wasn't available.

"I have an easy one to try first," Adele said.

"Doubtful," Mort said, still whittling.

"No, really. It's a small painting, an Italian landscape, at the Oak Hills golf club here in town. It was my first forgery, sort of a test run. It's not very valuable. It should be easy to lift."

"Easy for you, you mean," Grady said.

"Please," Adele said. The girl's hands moved to the base of her skull. Whatever it was she was hiding, Gilda noted, these paintings really did weigh on her mind. "Just listen."

"I'm sorry, but—" Warren started.

Gilda held up her hand. "Stop. Let the girl talk."

Warren's expression turned stone cold. He left the cafeteria. A few seconds later, his office door slammed shut.

"I'm not saying we'll do it," Gilda said. "But we'll listen."

CHAPTER THREE

"Ms. Millhouse," the orderly said, "you'll take care of yourself, right?"

Ellie bristled. "Whiteby. Ms. Whiteby." She wound a scarf around her neck and picked up her gloves. Before long, she wouldn't have to put up with John's sniveling concern and repeatedly calling her by her soon-to-be ex-husband's name. Just because she made a mistake and ended up in a lock-down psychiatric ward was no reason to serve her divorce papers. If it weren't for that damned Booster Club, she'd still be the toast of Carsonville.

Sure, from its white columns and Georgian gables, the Bedlamton Arms looked like a country club from the outside. The inside wasn't bad, either. The Gothic revival chairs in the hall were clearly fakes, not even real cherry, and the landscapes were second-rate, but at least they made a show of being the "relaxing home-away-from-home every busy executive needs." She'd paid her lawyer a king's ransom to get her sentenced here instead of a state-run institution. But it was its own form of prison. Without the right code for the security system, she couldn't leave its grounds. Heck, she couldn't leave her own room at night.

"Sorry, Ms. Whiteby. It's just — it's just that I'd lose my job, or worse, if they knew I was helping you."

She smiled sweetly. "You're the only one I can trust, John."

He tugged at the collar of his white jacket. "And someone escaped from the Carsonville Women's Correctional Facility this afternoon. It's all over the television. You've been so good to me. I don't want anything to happen to you."

"Like I said, I'll be back soon." She softened her voice and even patted his arm. "I simply need to wish my darling daughter well on her birthday. Then I'll rush back to you and the comfort of the Bedlamton Arms. You'll see."

He shifted feet. "Are you sure? Couldn't you just send her a card?"

"A card is not the same as a mother's kiss."

"Why the large bag, then?"

"Oh, John. I see you doubt me." She sat on the bed and patted the brocade bedspread next to her. "Sit. Think about your own experience growing up. Your parents were never there for you, were they?"

He looked at his shoes.

"Everything you have, you earned the hard way. Not every neglected child could have made it to be an orderly at a fine institution like this one."

"They call us valets," he said.

"But you know your real function." They exchanged glances. This was the first time Ellie had been so straightforward about the home's real purpose. "I want to make sure that my little Sylvia—"

"I thought you said her name was Sherry?"

"That's her nickname," Ellie added quickly. "Chérie. You know, 'dear' in French." When he didn't respond, she said, "I want to make sure Sylvia has your fortitude, your strong attitude."

To her horror, John took her hand and squeezed it. He'd touched her. She fought the urge to grimace. "I understand," he said.

She pulled her hand away and stood. "So, the codes?" Afraid her voice had been too harsh, she added, "John, dear?"

His gaze searched the room, then, apparently making a decision, he reached into his breast pocket for an index card. "Here."

Ellie released her breath. "Thank you. You won't regret this."

"You will be back, though?"

"Have I ever lied to you?"

Her regency-style clock — bolted to the mantel and soldered shut — tick-tick-ticked. At last, John sighed and stood. "I'll carry your bag."

They padded down the darkened halls, the floors redolent of lemon wax. The other residents would be sleeping by now, locked into their rooms. She and John came to the rear service entrance.

He handed her the satchel and punched a code into the keypad near the door. He held it open for her. "I'll wait up for you."

"Oh, please, I'd feel so much better if you got some rest. You'll do that for me, won't you?"

He shyly tucked his chin and nodded. "Bye, Ms. Mill — I mean, Whiteby."

Ellie walked serenely until she passed out of the building's light, then picked up her pace. Pausing behind an ornamental shrub, she pulled her black shawl up over her hair so that her body was a long shadow. She'd planned her break for a night when the moon was new, and the home's grounds were so black she could almost feel it. She was still too close to the main building to turn on her flashlight. Any false move could trigger the alarm and trip floodlights.

As planned, she kept to the path. Her nightly regimen of calisthenics in her room gave her the endurance to keep moving, despite the heavy bag. Within twenty minutes she was at the service gate. Only now did she dare use the flashlight, and even then she kept it sheltered in her shawl. She set down her bag and pulled out the index card John had given her. The exit code was marked in careful block letters.

She glanced behind her. The house was the size of a child's plaything in the distance, but would someone be able to hear the gate's motor? She had to risk it. She held her breath as she punched in the code, and the black metal gate slid open, nearly silent on its oiled track.

If she'd been another person, she would have pumped her fists in the air for victory. Eleanor Whiteby didn't partake in these kinds of antics. She calmly pressed the release button to close the gate and walked away from the Bedlamton Arms. Forever.

She slung her bag over her shoulder. Keeping to side roads, she walked through the countryside. The new moon gave scant light, and the night was rich with the scent of wet earth. Twice she passed raccoons rustling in the bushes, and once she almost collided with a porcupine.

Her three months at the Bedlamton Arms had felt like three years. Instead of running a business empire, as she had before, she'd spent her days in a zombie-like schedule of individual therapy, crafts, lunch, group therapy, and "taking the air." No wonder lobotomies weren't fashionable anymore. They didn't need them with deadening routines like those.

She'd used the routine to meet her needs the best she could. During crafts, for instance, she'd fashioned a set of picklocks, and during group exercise, she'd built her physical endurance. And, of course, she'd befriended John the orderly.

After a few miles, houses sprang up here and there, their occupants deep in sleep. Then the density of houses thickened, and soon she was within Carsonville's city limits.

Dawn still a few hours away, Ellie dropped an envelope into the first postbox she found. An anonymous letter, of course, to the Bedlamton Arms's management. They should know they had a traitor on staff.

CHAPTER FOUR

Alone at last, Adele thought. Alone and free. Well, sort of.

She closed her bedroom door behind her, then opened and closed it again, just because she could. Gilda had lent her a filmy, mint green peignoir with marabou trim to wear, but another resident, Red, the lovely white-haired safecracker's widow, had set a flannel nightgown on top.

Adele knew she wasn't allowed to open the window, but surely just an inch wouldn't hurt. She celebrated her freedom with a deep lungful of spring night air before closing it again. The moist air eased the throb at the base of her skull. She carried the flannel nightgown to the bathroom.

At dinner, Gilda had made sure Adele had stayed out of sight, close to the cafeteria's inner wall. The Villa's cook had prepared a delicious risotto with mushrooms and fragrant herbs she couldn't name, although anything would have been manna after the awful food at Carsonville Women's. The company was different, too, despite the fact that they all had rap sheets.

First, Mort had come around and taken everyone's cocktail orders, followed by a platter of clams casino. Father Vincent put Dean Martin on the stereo, although Red complained they always listened to the Rat Pack, and how about some Loretta Lynn for a change?

"They let you have cocktails?" Adele asked.

"We're old, child. Not dead," Father Vincent said as he accepted a tumbler of Scotch whisky.

"The usual," Red told Mort. "Soda water with lime." She directed this to Adele. "Heart trouble. I have to keep an eye on my blood pressure."

A short, round woman named Mary Rose settled in with a Manhattan and told Adele that she was also a forger, only her specialty had been sausage. For years, she'd sold meat wholesale under a national brand name— "Rhymes with Timmy Bean"—but it was so good that before long no one would buy the real stuff. The national firm found out and sent her a cease-and-desist order.

Conversation turned to Adele's request to round up her forgeries. The Booster Club was skeptical about the Oak Hills golf club painting. It wasn't easy to convince them, and Gilda seemed a bit too quiet, as if she knew Adele hadn't told her the whole story. After half an hour of her best arguments—her head throbbing the whole time—one of the Villa's residents agreed that it might be "interesting" to consider. Father Vincent ventured that he knew at least three routes home from the golf club, including one that passed a parking structure in which he could shake any tail. Bobby pointed out that golf clubs have kitchens that need health inspections, and county IDs were as easy to fake as Boy Scout cards.

In the end, they had decided to give the heist a go. If Adele wasn't mistaken, extra excitement pulsed through the Villa's residents. Red and Mort danced to the Glenn Miller Orchestra, and Cook joined them for dessert.

After dinner, the redhead, Gilda, had patted her arm and sent her upstairs to "rest after such a stressful day." Gilda was a sweet lady.

She seemed to be the Villa's de facto den mother, and she was always humming a tune or shouting orders. While the dishes were cleared, Adele had caught Gilda looking into the distance with a sadness that vanished seconds later when she'd asked if anyone would like coffee.

Full and happy, Adele turned down the sheets on her bed—real sheets! A feather pillow!—and opened the bathtub's taps. She stripped and dangled a toe in the water. Perfect. Gilda had offered to lend her nail polish, and maybe she'd take her up on it. A Monet pink would suit her.

As the tub filled, Adele lowered herself into the water and leaned back. Even if the police busted in right now and hauled her off, it was worth it for this moment. Anxiety would come to visit later, for sure, but right now was pure bliss.

The tub was nearly full, and she sat up to turn off the tap. Adele's eyes snapped open. The water didn't slow. The tub was nearly overflowing, and she couldn't stop it.

She yanked the tub's stopper and leapt from the water, pulling on the flannel nightie as she darted from her room and down the stairs. The manager. She needed to find the manager.

She skidded to a stop in front of his office and gasped, "Warren."

He tossed a fat novel onto the desk and sat up. "What?"

"The bathtub. I can't make the water shut off."

Warren froze for a second, then shot up the stairs, Adele at his heels. He burst into Adele's room, the tub's taps rushing in the background. He reached behind the tub and twisted two oval-shaped knobs just as the water rippled at the tub's lip.

Adele fell against the wall and caught her breath.

Warren perched on the tub's edge and again folded his arms. "You still want a bath?" He said. The tub was slowly draining. She had the feeling he struggled to control his anger.

She looked at her feet. "No. That's okay."

"I'll fix the taps in the morning. Faucet probably needs a new sleeve. But look here" —he touched the oval valves— "If this happens again, all you have to do is turn these. There's no need to come get me."

Adele pulled up the flannel nightgown's collar. "I'm sorry." Her voice was quiet. She averted her eyes from Warren's stare. He didn't like her and resented the risk she brought to the Villa. He'd made that clear. And now this. "You don't want me here."

He stood and leaned against the towel rack. He was a big man. All muscle and shaved head. Plus, he looked to be in his early thirties, just a bit older than she and a lot younger than anyone else at the Villa. She plucked at her flannel sleeve.

"It's not you," he said. "It's this whole situation. Everyone here has some kind of background, and chances are good that they haven't paid their full time for it."

"Yes?"

"These are good people."

Adele nodded. She got that.

"We don't need anything that points a finger here, you see? Especially with the relicensing."

"Yes," she said.

"I don't know why they're so uptight about the inspection. We'd be fine without your uncle's help. I can take care of things here."

"Clearly." He seemed to be calming down, but still tense. He wouldn't meet her eyes. With the curve of his shoulders under his T-shirt and his prominent brow, he could be the modern-day equivalent of a laborer in a Work Progress Administration mural. "I don't want to draw trouble to the Villa, but I have to make things right."

"Before you die. I heard you telling the others."

"Brain aneurysm. Right here." She touched the base of her skull. "I asked Uncle Larry if he could get me out, and I guess he found the Booster Club."

"I guess." He dropped his arms. "But, listen. You'd be doing us all a favor if you turned yourself in. Walk out tomorrow, find a phone downtown, and call the prison."

She looked toward the bathroom's pink tile floor but didn't reply. He wouldn't understand about her need to destroy the forgeries. He wouldn't know a Turner from a turnip. When she gathered the courage to look at him, his gaze was soft. Curious.

"But you're dying." And with that, he left.

CHAPTER FIVE

It was almost light when Ellie arrived at the Villa Saint Nicholas. She stood out of sight, down the block, and watched the sun wash pink over the stucco on the home's eastern wall.

She was going to take the Booster Club down. Before they came into her life, she'd been the toast of Carsonville: CEO of a successful development company, owner of the best salon in town, and president of the Carsonville Women's League. Roger, her husband, was from one of the city's founding families. If she'd wanted, she could have been the guest of honor at dinner parties every night of the week.

Then the Booster Club decided to turn one of her capital projects—a decrepit firehouse that should have been a sparkling new building full of condos and boutiques—into a shelter for homeless families. They'd tricked her. Her breath quickened with rage to remember it. When the judge had sentenced her to lockdown psychiatric treatment, her reputation had plummeted. People had even had the nerve to suggest she should have gone to jail. Now, no one would cross the street to spit on her if she were on fire.

Oh, yes, the Booster Club was going down. She'd thought out her plan to the last detail. Her months at the Bedlamton Arms had been productive. She'd scoured floor plans, net worths, laws, and timetables. She'd strengthened her body and sharpened her mind. During her regular bouts of insomnia, she'd run through the scenario like a movie until every second of the plan was embedded in her brain.

Except for one detail. She hadn't figured out where to stay. From her study of the city map, the Villa's neighborhood was mostly residential, and a look at a real estate website confirmed that its houses were occupied. She shifted her gaze to the school separated from the Villa by a chain link fence. This would have to be it, then. It was her last resort, but she didn't see an alternative. She picked up her bag and rounded the block.

Just an old pickup truck was in the school's parking lot. The janitor. She'd studied the school's floor plans and knew that, as was true for many mid-century buildings, an attic ran across the building's top. It would have to be her lodging for the few days it would take to carry out her plan.

The school's side door was unlocked. Inside, she heard a cheerfully whistled rendition of "Ain't We Got Fun," but the hall was empty. Directly to her right was a staircase. She leapt into it just as she saw a mop jab its way out of a classroom and into the hall.

She crept up the staircase, past some child-drawn nonsense about Earth Day plastering the walls. Two floors, a basement, and an attic, the floor plans had said. Thank goodness for the solid construction of these old buildings. Back when she'd worked in real estate, she never would have shelled out for terrazzo floors. But they didn't creak.

The stairs stopped at the second floor with no door to the attic. Ellie stepped into the dark hall. There was another stairwell at the building's opposite end. Keeping her black-clad body near the wall in case she had to duck into a classroom, she hurried down the waxed floors, her bag bumping against her legs.

Just as she reached the end, the janitor's whistling filled the stairwell. Ellie yanked herself into the nearest classroom and crammed her body behind a rack of coats just inside the door. Damned kids. The coat rack hung so low that she had to crouch. She held her breath as the rolling clatter of the janitor's mop bucket passed the door. She straightened her back, then crept to the door. All clear.

The door to the attic was at the top of this stairwell. Weeks of studying videos and practicing with the Bedlamton Arms's pantry lock — most of the other locks were keypad controlled — made cracking this simple doorknob lock a cinch.

And she was in.

The attic's only light was from a row of dirt-streaked windows, placed more for decoration than function. Although mice scat showed that no one had used the attic in years, at one point someone had made a sort of lounge at its center. Ellie left her bag at the door and swallowed a sneeze as she crossed the bare wood floors to an old couch and armchair. Not ideal, but it would do.

Using a corner of her shawl, she wiped the window. The school's eaves would hide her, and while this window was her eye into the world, it was only a tiny spot to anyone on the street. She was safely hidden. A smile spread over her face. Yes, there it was: the Villa Saint Nicholas.

Today was Friday. Tonight, when the school emptied, she'd break into the janitor's cupboard and clean the attic up enough to make it bearable for the few days she'd stay. The cafeteria would yield some kind of meal. She could wash herself in the teachers' lounge. In the meantime, she'd lie low. And deliberate the Booster Club's demise.

CHAPTER SIX

"Put them right there." Gilda pointed to a side table in the cafeteria.

The homeless man wheeled a shopping cart full of dead flowers to Gilda's worktable. "Got you six or seven arrangements already made. I found a new spot."

"Where?" Fred looked pretty good lately, Gilda thought. He was putting on weight, and his skin was clear. Must be staying sober.

"You won't tell the others?"

"It's just you, Fred." Gilda pulled a block of green Styrofoam from the cart. An entire white floral arrangement was stuck in it. Brilliant. All she'd have to do was set it aside until it worsened from limp to fried, and she'd be set with a readymade Bad Seed bouquet.

"I was digging in the Dumpsters behind the floral shops, like you said, see, and I thought, why not go to where they get bouquets all the time?"

"The church," Gilda said. "You went to the church."

"There are big weddings down at St. Stephen's nearly every weekend. I'd try the country club, too, but I can't push the cart that far."

"Have you had breakfast yet? Cook probably has some leftover sausages and pancakes." Gilda pulled a wad of cash from between her breasts and peeled off a few twenties. "Here. Have a seat. I'll see what we've got."

As Fred finished his meal, the recorded chimes of an ice cream truck neared. "Just in time for dessert," he said.

Gilda checked her watch. "Yep. Right on schedule. You should see the kids next door go nuts. I swear he drives by just to torture them."

When Fred's breakfast dishes were cleared and he'd left, Gilda set to work. It was her job to plan the Booster Club's first outing for Adele, and over her eighty years of life—forty-nine, if anyone asked—she'd learned that she thought best when her hands were busy. She had three arrangements to make today: one for a lascivious boss, and two for cheating husbands. Most of her clients were women. That figured. Women were subtler about revenge, she'd found. Men drank a lot and made scenes. Women hired lawyers and sent dead flowers.

"Hank—" She'd turned to share this thought with Hank before remembering that he was gone. Gone six months now, but she still reflexively turned to him.

Bobby, pausing his infernal card shuffling for a split second but keeping his eyes on the television, said, "Dead."

I know. Gilda didn't even respond. Outside, the trees were beginning to bud. Hank used to crack open his window upstairs at about this time to hear the kids playing at recess. It was her room now. By watching the kids, she had the feeling Hank could somehow see them, too. It was a small tie to him. She couldn't quite bring herself to remember him lifeless in the hospital bed. Leaving that room—and Hank—behind was the hardest thing she'd ever done.

She let out a quiet breath, and set the arrangements Fred had brought onto a tray to store in her closet for a week or so until they were dried out. She placed three empty vases on the table.

Last night, they'd talked over how to approach the Oak Hills golf club to boost Adele's painting. She'd described it as a small landscape—the painting itself was barely larger than a magazine, although the frame bulked it up—with a buxom milkmaid, a calf, and a copse of oak trees. Italian, she'd said. Grady had done some research, and even with no one's name on the piece, it was worth a cool seven thousand bucks.

Gilda still suspected Adele was hiding something from them. Why hadn't she told her uncle what she'd wanted to do? It didn't add up. The argument about respecting the great artists? That was hogwash. If she'd felt so strongly she was damaging their reputations, she never would have painted the fakes in the first place.

Gilda selected some twigs from a pile that Father Vincent had collected on one of his walks and stuck one in each vase. One of the twigs had a splotch of moss. Nice touch.

Booster Club, schmooster club. She shouldn't have let Claudine talk her into getting involved. She said it would be good for her to keep busy after Hank's death. Claudine could hardly play high and mighty about Gilda's grief since she had dropped by the Villa only a handful of times since then. Sure, she had a new job. But as Hank's daughter, Claudine was family. The winter months had come and gone with two visits. That was it. Claudine had sloughed off the Booster Club and Gilda along with it.

She let out a long sigh, but it barely eased the pain in her chest. Well, it shouldn't be much trouble to drive to some fancy golf club and filch a painting. The gang was kind of excited about using their old skills. Then, chore number one, check. Larry would be happy, and the Villa would be one step closer to getting its license renewed. As for the rest of the paintings, they'd take it as it came.

CHAPTER SEVEN

Ellie flipped to her other side, but it was no use. The couch was too lumpy for her to rest, even after a sleepless night. No wonder it had been exiled to the attic. She squinted in the dusty light, and the couch's springs complained under her weight.

For months she'd plotted how she was going to make the Booster Club pay for having her sent to the Bedlamton Arms. A thousand ideas had filtered through her brain: deadly accidents, poisoned casseroles, doctored hair dye. At last she had settled on a plan that would not only bring the club down, but would help revise the town's opinion of her. Once she revealed that the Booster Club was a bunch of crooks, she'd have the ultimate "I told you so" moment. The Carsonville Women's League would welcome her again instead of turning its back. The country club would save her usual table, place a vase of her signature orchids nearby, and lower the thermostat a few degrees to her preferred brisk temperature. As for Roger? Her soon-to-be ex-husband had proven himself a dud, anyway. She wished him luck with his new bride-to-be, some second grade teacher who was happy doing crossword puzzles with him all day. He'd get his once her lawyers were in touch.

She'd be back. Oh, yes.

Her plan was simple. She'd steal a particular rare and expensive item and plant it at the Villa. It had taken a few months of research to figure out just what item would be valuable enough and loved enough by its owner to guarantee swift police response, but she had succeeded. Get in, take item, plant it at Villa, leave anonymous tip with police. Couldn't be simpler.

Groaning, Ellie rose from the couch and moved to the window to examine Villa Saint Nicholas again now that the light was better. Her view took in the Villa's front entrance and parking lot. A man with a cane had settled himself out front and was shuffling cards. Another man, sporting a shock of white hair and a utilikilt, messed under the hood of a vintage Mercedes. She could even make out movement in what her study of the Villa's floor plans had told her was the cafeteria.

From the attic, her angle of vision was too restricted to see deeply into the cafeteria. She crouched to see if it would help.

"What are you looking at?" came a little voice behind her.

Ellie jumped and slammed her body against the wall, arms wide. Almost instantly, she drew herself tall and narrowed her eyes. It was a boy. Some brat with a shaggy haircut and a bandaid over one eyebrow. "How did you get up here?"

The kid, unfazed, pointed toward the attic door. Damn. She hadn't locked it behind her. Every detail was important, and she'd blown this one.

"You'll go back to class now, and you'll tell no one what you saw. Or you'll be really, really sorry. Understand?" Ellie packed as much venom into her voice as she could while still keeping it low.

The kid nodded and ran out the door. Ellie locked the handle from the inside and leaned against it. Shoot. If he told anyone, she was toast. They'd take her back to the Bedlamton Arms and put her in the Jane Eyre suite in the attic. Her meals would be slid under the door. Even John the orderly couldn't help her there.

But she couldn't sneak out now, either. Not with a whole elementary school in session and a hundred little monsters screaming on the playground.

So she waited. For hours. At every creak in the building's joists or trill of the old-fashioned bell, she stiffened. She prepared the dignified speech she'd give the police about how she was carrying out a citizen's duty. She hid her duffle bag with its vital contents in the attic's far corner. And she waited some more.

Sunlight rose over the building, slanted through the attic's windows, and sank. Car engines idled outside, then left. Every few hours she rose and stretched her muscles aching from the long walk and broken sleep. At last, the school was quiet. No one had come for her.

Barely breathing, Ellie unlatched the attic door to darkness and the piney scent of industrial cleanser. She stepped forward, and something clattered and rolled, causing her to leap back and bite off a curse.

The object stopped rolling at her feet. Ellie picked it up. It was a child's telescope with a note attached. "For you," it said.

CHAPTER EIGHT

Gilda waited under the Villa's front portico as Father Vincent pulled around an anonymous sedan.

"It's not hot, is it?" she asked as he helped her into the passenger side.

"Not exactly. I made friends with a mechanic at the county motor pool. This one's in for busted air conditioning. Told him I'd fix it if he let us have it a few hours. We won't need the air conditioning today, anyway."

"It's official, at least." With the government plates, no one would question their credentials.

"I aim to please." Father Vincent wore a button-down shirt and a violently colored kilt. He must have caught Gilda's stare, because he said, "What? When I'm in the car, no one will be able to see me below the waist."

Since taking the cloth, Father Vincent had also taken to skirts and kilts. He said his old priest garb had been so comfortable that he couldn't return to pants. Gilda had let out a few of her old hostess skirts for him to wear around the house. At the Villa, no one looked at him twice anymore. Not so in the real world.

"I guess it's okay." She clutched her purse to her lap and settled her cane next to her. "Mary Rose said we can pick her up at the family shelter. She's serving lunch this afternoon." Ever since Mary Rose had resurrected her sausage recipe for the firehouse shelter, she liked to be available for compliments.

Father Vincent drove them across the river. Gilda loved this time of year. Maybe it was working with all those dead flowers, but seeing the leaves itching to bust out gave her hope. Almost as soon as the observation crossed her mind, darker thoughts intruded. Hank wasn't here to see this spring. She smoothed a palm over the papery ridges on the back of her hand. Who knew? It might be her own last spring, as well.

It was definitely Adele's last spring. Poor girl.

Mary Rose waited on the sidewalk outside the shelter. Father Vincent pulled up, and Gilda rolled down the window.

"Ready?" Gilda asked.

"Yeah." As Mary Rose slid into the sedan's back seat, she flexed her fingers. "Ladle fatigue. Those street people have hearty appetites."

Gilda glanced in the rear view mirror to see Mary Rose shedding her smock and swapping out her tennis shoes for pumps.

"Did you bring a clipboard for me?" Mary Rose asked.

Gilda handed it to her, along with an ID to snap to her collar.

"Mary Rose Hinkley, County Health Inspector," she read. "I take it from the skirt that Father Vincent's staying in the car."

"It's just you and me. As the senior member of the team, I'll take the lead."

Twenty minutes later, Father Vincent pulled the sedan through the gate of the Duchess Heights complex. On the way to the golf club, the car passed two faux Tuscan villas, a mini-chateau, and four English manors before turning down Marquise Way. He idled at the long awning at the clubhouse's entrance.

"This is it," Father Vincent said.

"It shouldn't take long," Gilda said.

Mary Rose held Gilda's cane as she lifted herself from the car. Damn these legs. They used to dance across the best nightclubs in town, and now they could barely manage a flight of stairs. She turned an ankle to admire the curve of her calf. Maybe these legs couldn't skip up stairs, but they still looked good.

"Come on," Mary Rose said.

The golf club was in a new Tudor-style building with saplings in the parking lot. Everything was new out here. Built with new money and meant to feel old. People with the title of CEO making their homes on streets named after dead hierarchies.

"Me, first," Gilda told Mary Rose and stepped ahead to enter the lobby. True to the building's exterior, the lobby had the exposed beams and faux half-timbered walls of a Shakespearean cartoon.

"May I help you?" A woman looked up from a desk in the dark foyer. Gilda had halfway expected to be greeted by someone wearing a beefeater's uniform, but this woman had a platinum crew cut and hoop earrings as big as Gilda's fist.

"Yes." Gilda smiled sweetly. She knew how to look like a kind old lady when she needed to. "I'm Gilda, and this is Mary Rose. We're from the Carsonville County Health Department. Just a spot inspection."

The woman rose. "We had our inspection last month. I can show you the paperwork." She fished keys from a pocket and made her way across the foyer to a door built flush into the wall and made to look like part of the paneling.

"That won't be necessary," Mary Rose said. "We've seen all that." She patted her tote bag as if the club's paperwork were already there. "This is something different."

Gilda edged in front of Mary Rose. "It's a random mini-inspection. A formality. No need to be concerned."

The woman looked from Gilda to Mary Rose and back again. "What do you need?"

"Just a few minutes to walk through the facility."

The woman pushed her chair under the desk. "That's fine. I don't have a meeting until eleven. I'll come with you."

"Don't trouble yourself," Gilda said. "We'll poke our heads around and be out of here in a shake."

The woman was already at their side. She glanced at Mary Rose's ID badge. "It's no trouble, Mary Rose. The members will feel better if I'm with you. Shall we start in the kitchen?"

Gilda nodded at Mary Rose. "The kitchen is a good idea. Tell you what. To keep this shorter, we'll split up, and I'll look down here." She pointed her clipboard toward a corridor off the foyer. Adele had told them the painting was in the outer hall.

"That's mostly meeting rooms," the woman said. "Nothing the health department would care about."

Gilda raised an eyebrow. "What about vermin?"

"There's no vermin here."

"Then it will go quickly."

Mary Rose set off for a doorway marked "Dining Room," forcing the golf club's manager to follow her. Gilda turned in the opposite direction after only a second's hesitation. Mary Rose had the tote. If Gilda found the painting, she'd have nothing to hide it in. As Hank had always told her, every job had at least one surprise. Carrying off a heist meant thorough planning, but it also meant being able to think on your feet.

She gripped her cane and started toward the corridor. Gaudily framed photographs of the golf club's leadership lined its walls. No paintings. Gilda forged ahead, her ID badge swinging. The hall turned right, and she followed it.

Ah, here were a few paintings. A girl with a bonnet; a horse; a man hunting with two hounds. No landscape. Just ahead, a wide door labeled "Members Only" opened onto the corridor. That's where they'd keep the choice artwork. A man came out, his hair damp, and nodded at Gilda. Gilda smiled in return, and, as if she'd been there a hundred times, pushed open the door.

Heat and steam choked the air, and it took a moment for her vision to clear. When it did, she found herself facing three elderly men seated at a card table. The men wore nothing but towels. One man's mouth dropped open. Another man stopped scratching his heat-reddened chest, and his hand fell to his lap.

The fourth man, his comb-over plastered to the side of his face, said, "Gilda?"

Shoot. It was Wilfred, Carsonville's chief of police sometime in the Kennedy administration. They'd had a short but profitable relationship. Lousy kisser, Gilda recalled.

She smiled, then booked it for the exit. She couldn't move fast with her cane, but she had the advantage of being fully clothed.

"Gilda!" she heard from behind her. "What are you doing here?"

The hall she'd come from had lines of sight that were too clear. Just ahead, the hall turned right again and likely circled to the dining room. Maybe she'd find a back door.

"Gilda, stop!"

No time to investigate dining rooms or back doors now. Gilda leapt into the first nook off the hall and pressed her back against the wall. She mopped her forehead. "Laundry," read the sign on the door next to her. The architects probably put this nook here to keep mundane services out of the direct sight of the members. Two men, towels wrapped around their waists, passed the nook. Gilda caught a glance of pasty backs and sparsely haired legs.

"She's gone into the dining room, Wilf. We can't go in there like this."

"What the hell was she doing here, anyway? I thought she was in Florida."

"Probably someone else. Come on. We'll have to deal a new hand."

When the men had returned to the steam room, Gilda closed her eyes and let out a long breath. She had told him she was moving to Florida, Gilda recalled. That was her default too-da-loo. Boca Raton, she'd tell them. To live with her sister. Still, after all these years, he remembered her.

But she had no time to gloat. She was in a pickle—trapped, recognized, and she still didn't know where the painting was. Father Vincent would be idling the car out front. What next?

She opened her eyes. On the wall directly across from her was Adele's landscape. She screwed her eyes closed and opened them again to the soft colors of Tuscany in summer. Yep, that was it. She had no time to question her luck. She had to get the painting out.

The laundry room next to her was locked. A second after she released the doorknob, the door opened, and a small, dark woman peeked out.

"May I help you?" she asked.

"Spot inspection." Gilda flipped her ID badge. "County health department."

The woman opened the laundry room door, and Gilda circled the room, nodding at the whirling washing machines and humming dryers. The woman had been folding towels from a large canvas tub on wheels. Gilda picked up a fresh towel, sniffed it, and dropped it back into the tub.

"I'll borrow this for a moment." She pushed the tub out the door, leaving the woman to watch. "Confidence," Hank had always told her. "They'll never question you if you look like you know what you're doing."

When the door closed, she dropped the landscape into the laundry tub, fluffed a towel over it, and wheeled the tub toward the back of the golf club. Yes, a side entrance. Leaving the tub in the hall, she wrapped the painting in a towel and slipped out to a gravel path bordered by azaleas so new that the earth around them was still black with soil from the nursery pots.

It had been a while since she'd moved so fast with just the cane, but in less than a minute she was at the club's entrance. Father Vincent met her, the sedan's door open. Mary Rose was already in the back. Gilda tossed the painting toward her and collapsed into the seat. The door was barely closed when Father Vincent pulled away.

"You got it," Mary Rose said.

"Yes." It took her a minute to catch her breath. "Yeah. Got it. But I don't care what Larry the Fence or Adele have to say. We're not doing this again."

CHAPTER NINE

The Villa's residents huddled in the cafeteria.

"It was a disaster," Gilda said. "How was I supposed to know I'd run into the old chief of police in the locker room?" She pushed her dessert plate to the side. Adele had seemed surprised they ate so early, but she'd made short work of the coq au vin and drank Cook's Burgundy like her lips would never touch wine again.

"I don't understand what you were doing in the locker room, anyway," Mary Rose said. "It's not like the painting would be in there."

Gilda wasn't going to try to explain it. She adored Mary Rose. Truly, she did. It was just that the woman's mind worked in such a linear way. If it wasn't about ground meat, she wasn't much for creativity. "Bottom line, we can't lift the other seven. Too risky," Gilda said.

"We promised Larry the Fence," Father Vincent said. "He's arranging the relicensing."

"How much do you want to bet he didn't know what his niece wanted us to do?" Bobby said.

The others, including Gilda, nodded in agreement. Larry had been vague. Likely, he hadn't come to grips with the fact that his niece lived with a death sentence. He simply wanted her to be happy, so he hadn't asked a lot of questions.

"There's no way he'd expect us to hook eight valuable works of art,"

Mort said. "He's not nuts."

"We might have done it, back in the day," Red said.

"Even then it would have been a major operation. Months of planning." Gilda eyed the others. "We don't have time. Remember Adele's aneurysm. No saying how long she's good for."

"Good point," Father Vincent said.

"Plus we'd need teams set up across the nation," Gilda said. Heists like that took more than skill and planning. They took money. She looked at the hodgepodge of chairs—some spindle-backed, some from the fire sale when the Rumpus Room closed—and the gallery of artwork left by deceased residents. They were comfortable. She couldn't complain about that. But no one would confuse the Villa's cafeteria with the Ritz's lobby.

"Maybe there's something else we can do. Like, write letters to the owners and tell them their paintings are fakes," Mort said.

Gilda drummed her fingers on the table. "I don't see how we can do more. But Adele won't be satisfied. She wants them out of circulation. All of them."

Bobby cast a glance at the women. "Tell me when you've made up your mind. Care if I turn on the TV?"

"Can you use the television room, instead?" Gilda said. "Grady's soaps are over."

"Fine, fine." He took the ever-present deck of cards from his shirt pocket as he left.

"Today was a warning," Gilda said. "We've got the smarts, but it's been a while since we've carried out this kind of heist."

"I just don't get it," Mort said. "Those paintings aren't hurting anyone. People are enjoying them. Why rock the boat?"

"I know what Adele would say. Remember? She'd say it's not right.

A master's work shouldn't be aped and passed off as the real thing. We've been over this," Gilda said.

"I still don't get it. No one's hurt. What's done is done."

"I agree. I don't get it, either. But we're not the one with the dying wish," Gilda said.

"If we go after those other paintings, we might be," Mort said.

The faint sound of gunfire and shrieking tires drifted in from across the hall. Father Vincent rested his elbows on the table and leaned in. "I like Mort's idea, Gilda. Are you sure we couldn't just send them anonymous letters saying their paintings are fakes?"

"From looking at the first one, they're good copies," Gilda said. "If the owners figure out the originals were stolen, they'd at least get insurance money for them." She sighed. "I guess we could run it by Larry, see if it satisfies him."

Mort shook his head. "Too bad Claudine isn't still in the business."

Gilda turned to him. "What did you say?"

With a bit of planning and a good team, Claudine could have lifted the paintings as easily as Cook flipped a tarte tatin. But now Claudine was a detective for an insurance company. They paid her well to track down stolen diamonds and antique furniture, and she'd left the criminal life behind.

"I said, it's too bad Claudine isn't—"

Gilda sat up straight. "I heard you the first time." A smile spread over her face. "Here's the thing. Claudine *is* still in the business. I think we've got Adele covered after all."

"How can you promise that?" Mary Rose said.

"We've got Claudine. Just not the way you think."

∗

Adele stood uneasily across the desk from Warren. Between them was Adele's forged Italian landscape. With triumph, Gilda had handed her the painting and said, "Here you go." She'd turned around and headed for the elevator, presumably to fill in the rest of the Villa's residents on their victory.

Adele had barely looked at the painting. She was too embarrassed she might catch a hint of what was hidden in it. She'd wrapped it in a bathrobe and taken it downstairs. Warren would know how to get rid of it.

"Am I interrupting you?" she asked. "I hoped you could help me."

"You want to destroy it?" Warren said.

Adele studied his expression. Was he upset? She couldn't tell. "Definitely."

He tilted the painting toward him. "Are you sure?"

It had been more than five years since Adele had seen the painting. The one thing about her type of work was that you did the job and let it go. You didn't have the luxury of examining your work over the years, appreciating the skill or simply its loveliness. But here was the landscape again. It was a small painting, showing summer-leaved trees lining a blue river with a castello in the distance. In the foreground, a milkmaid in her apron but with no barn in sight played with a calf.

With each copied silken brushstroke, she'd felt closer to the original's creator. She'd imagined him sketching in a meadow, then working in a cold room with a thick ceramic bowl of coffee on the table next to his easel. He had scruffy black hair, she was sure. Dirt caked his fingernails. Taking a break, he might have walked past the academy with its students in fresh white shirts and new brushes paying homage to the master by copying him. In a way, that's what she had done.

"It's nice," Warren said.

Adele looked at him in surprise. Nice? "You like it?"

"It's Italy, isn't it? I can tell by the architecture." He pointed to the castello and flipped the painting over. "Can't people tell it's a fake by the canvas?"

"They could if I'd used a new one. I didn't. This was painted over a damaged painting that I scraped. It's as old as it should be—or nearly, anyway."

"What about the paints? Can they tell by that?"

Who knew he'd be so interested in art? "Some colors weren't used until later. Pure white and Prussian blue, for example. As long as I avoid those, I'm fine." The longer she looked at the painting, the deeper the ache grew in her chest. She wanted to paint again. She needed to paint. There had to be a way.

Warren lowered his head a few inches closer to the canvas. "So, you're saying forgery is easy to get away with."

"Yes and no. The best way to tell a forgery is to know the style of the work's artist. But the truth is that most dealers—and a lot of collectors—don't want to know. A dealer who gets a good deal on a rare painting doesn't want to question its origins too closely."

"These things come with papers, though, don't they?"

"Papers can be forged, too," she said. But it's the painting that's important, she longed to say. She clenched her fingers to her palms so tightly that her fingernails, short as they were, dug into her palms. Those fingers should be holding brushes. She had to at least paint again before she died.

"Hmm."

They looked at the painting. It had cost two weeks of study, another week of work, and, after the string of forgeries that followed, a prison sentence. A dealer had sold it for five thousand dollars and collected his twenty percent. Not even forty-eight hours had gone by before he was back in touch with the fence to ask if he had "discovered" any other paintings.

"Did the dealer do time?" Warren asked.

"He's still in business. Doing well enough to buy full-page ads in *Art News*."

"That hardly seems right. He's just as guilty as the rest of you."

"He'd claim he had no idea the painting was a forgery."

"Yeah, right." Warren snorted. He lifted the painting to eye level. "The milkmaid looks ready to jump out of the picture, doesn't she?"

Adele had to admit that the landscape was nice work. Nice enough to have set her on a path of eighteenth-century forgeries. The milkmaid's skin glowed the pink of a baby's buttocks, and the next few frames of the life the painting portrayed almost unrolled before their eyes. The milkmaid would laugh, she'd tease the calf, they'd run to the river.

A milkmaid and the Tuscan countryside weren't all the canvas showed. So far, no one had caught on, and Adele meant for it to stay that way.

"Do you have a pocketknife?" she asked him.

"Are you sure you want to do this?" Without waiting for the reply, he slipped a knife from his pants pocket. For the first time, she read kindness in his face.

She took it from him and turned the still-warm knife in her hands. She pulled at one of its blades. It stuck.

"Try the other one," he said. "I never use the small blade."

The larger blade opened easily. "Thank you." Her breath caught in her throat. She swallowed hard. "Here goes."

Aiming for the castello, she plunged the blade through the canvas and drew it straight toward the milkmaid. The canvas fought her every inch, but at last a gash as long as her hand rent the painting. *There.* She'd expected relief, but instead a vague sadness crept in.

Adele handed the knife to Warren. "Will you do the rest?"

CHAPTER TEN

Ellie stood. At last, it was safe to leave the attic. The children and school staff had gone, and the janitor wouldn't be in until morning.

Her first trip was to the restroom. Feeling her way in the dark, she descended to the second floor and found the door marked "girls." She cursed at how low the toilets were to the ground, and she crouched to wash her hands.

That important business taken care of, she went in search of food. The cafeteria had to be on the ground floor. She clicked on a penlight to guide her down the dark halls. She'd always been a good student. She'd won the spelling bee every year, performed an immaculate version of "Für Elise" on the piano at the holiday recital, and even won a gold medal at the regional badminton tournament. She'd walked the school's halls with her chin up.

But for some reason, kids hadn't liked her. Most teachers seemed a little put out with her, too. Her mother said it was because she was a better class of girl. The others were jealous. Jealous of her intelligence and her shined patent leather Mary Janes. Once Ellie had asked her mother for tennis shoes like the other kids wore, but the frozen stare she'd earned in reply had shut her up.

At last Ellie found the cafeteria. She wove through the small tables and chairs to the kitchen. The door was locked. She pulled and rattled its knob, but it didn't give. After a moment's thought, Ellie hiked up the rolling cover shutting the window that the lunch ladies used for passing trays of food to the students. The stainless steel counter was cool under her rear as she slid across it.

Once in the kitchen, she flipped on the bank of lights. It was safe here — no windows. The walk-in refrigerator had a seemingly endless supply of tiny milk cartons. But on the right was a large bowl with a dishtowel draped over its top. Ellie lifted the towel and dipped in a spoon. Sloppy Joes. Poor kids. Poor her. This was dinner.

She took the bowl to the counter, found a hamburger bun, and microwaved the combination.

As she stood at the counter and chewed, she reviewed her options. Should she leave the school? Now that she'd been busted by that kid, she wasn't safe. But where else could she go? The school had the best view of the Villa. Besides, the kid hadn't turned her in. He'd even left her a telescope, the poor sucker.

She'd stay. Tomorrow was Saturday. The school would be empty over the weekend, giving her plenty of time to carry out her plan. She'd have to risk it one more day in the attic.

Her next task was to scope out the school. She cleaned up the kitchen so that no one would know she'd been there and left the way she came. Down the hall was the administrative office. The office was dark behind its half-glassed door. She tried the handle, and it opened. The receptionist's desk didn't have much to interest her. She found a russet lipstick in an upper drawer and rouged her lips, rubbing them together with a satisfied smack. Behind the desk was a box marked "Lost and Found." She took two coats to help even out the attic's lumpy sofa.

A brass plaque marked the principal's office. Ellie tried this door, and it, too, opened. They locked up the kitchen but kept the principal's office open to the world? She surveyed the office with satisfaction. It was tidy, not a paper out of place, just as she preferred her own office. The temperature was even a bit on the cool side. Perfect. Ellie tried the desk drawers and found a fifth of bourbon and a cut crystal tumbler. She took a swig straight from the bottle. Urban camping at its finest. She recapped the bottle and tucked it under her arm to take upstairs. What was the principal going to do? Complain? On second thought, she grabbed the tumbler, too.

Now, fed and vaguely tipsy, Ellie nosed into a classroom but soon backed out. Even in the dark, she was too easy to spot through the bank of windows. Besides, there were so damned many toys in there, she could fall and break her neck.

Swinging the coats with one hand, she passed further down the hall. The teachers' lounge had to be here somewhere. That's where the good stuff would be. She tried a few doors—one was the custodian's closet, another the nurse's office—until she found it.

She flopped onto the couch. The window here was high up, so she allowed herself to turn on a table lamp. Coffee pot, cupboards, sink, small round table with chairs. Framed inspirational poster with seagulls and a saying she forgot even as she read it. Tissues. Old issues of *Rolling Stone* magazine.

She stood. Her office at the Shangri-La had been more interesting than this, and all it had was a bunch of nitwit cosmeticians staffing it. Even her business office downtown with its bland cubicles and CPAs was livelier. But that was her old life.

She yanked a lamp's cord out of the wall and took the lamp, along with the coats and booze, back up to the attic. The teachers could fight with each other about who'd stolen it. She made a second trip down to borrow a broom and some cleaning supplies from the custodian's closet.

The big round clock above the drinking fountain read nine o'clock. Before she made the attic habitable, she'd take another look at the Villa. With the light on in there, she should have a decent view.

She adjusted the toy telescope. A mash-up of old furniture filled the cafeteria, from the handful of recliners toward the end with the television and fireplace to the tables and chairs that made up the dining area. She couldn't see deeply enough into the room to examine the art on the far walls, but it had to be dreadful, too.

The residents didn't seem to mind the heinous decor. One man whittled. A couple others were watching TV. She wondered if the news was out about her disappearance from the Bedlamton Arms. Probably not. The Arms would keep that sort of information quiet. When Marcia Atkinson went berserk and chased after Dr. Loyly with an electric pencil sharpener and had to be taken upstate, not a peep had gotten out about it. For a second, she remembered the prisoner John the orderly had said escaped. Ellie wondered if she'd found somewhere to hide, too.

Now the old redhead with the walker was draping a shawl over a leopard print dress. Ellie remembered her from the fiasco with the firehouse. She had a phony Hollywood type of name. Yes, Gilda, it was. Out front, a man in a floor-length skirt walked toward a sedan.

She tilted the telescope. A light was on in one of the bedrooms, but its curtains were closed.

What was that movement? She pointed the telescope toward the street. Someone had parked down the block and was walking up with a large, flat parcel under his arm and a shopping bag heavy enough to cause him to stop and stretch his fingers. He paused where he would have turned to go into the Villa's front entrance, but he continued on. Yet, he clearly wanted in the Villa. Ellie could tell by the way he'd stopped and looked. Yes, there he was. He was going around back. He was dropping something off and didn't want the Villa's residents to know. Interesting.

Yes, interesting, but unimportant. It didn't have to do with her plan. Ellie set down the telescope and reached for the whiskey bottle. She'd be using that back door soon, too.

Tomorrow was phase one. She glanced toward her duffel bag with her materials. Just one more night to rest, watch the Villa, and gather her strength.

Armed with a list of paintings in Adele's precise hand, Gilda let Father Vincent help her into the car.

"You're sure it can't wait? I was having my Bible study," Father Vincent said. "Besides, she's probably asleep."

"The sooner we go, the better. It's barely nine o'clock now. The shank of the evening."

They pulled up to the perfume boutique that Hank, Claudine's father, kept as a front and that Claudine managed now. It occupied the ground floor of an old house bordering the commercial district. Claudine lived upstairs.

"You're going to have to tell her to come down," Gilda said.

"I can help you."

"No. There's no way I can make it up those stairs and then down again." Back in the old days, when she and Hank were getting to know each other, she took the stairs two at a time, even in heels. Now Hank was gone.

Father Vincent unbuckled the seatbelt and disappeared up the building's side entrance. A few minutes later, the rear of the Perfume Shoppe glowed yellow with light, and Claudine appeared at the side door. Father Vincent was at the car again, helping Gilda to her feet.

"It's been a while. How are you?" Claudine said.

Claudine favored her mother's side of the family, a line of quiet jewelers always sepia-toned in Gilda's mind. Claudine seemed to have been lifted from a black-and-white movie. As a twelve-year-old in front of her birthday cake, she brooded like Lauren Bacall. Even after all these years, Gilda never could tell you what she was thinking. Tonight she wore one of her mother's old dressing gowns, a 1940s number in ribbon silk.

"It's been too long. We've missed you at the Villa."

"I've been — busy."

"I see." Claudine had never been one for blabbing about her feelings, but something was different. Claudine used to visit every few days, weekly at the least. She was family at the Villa. Nearly everyone had known her since she and her brother André were kids. Now, they were lucky to see her every few months. Claudine had a new job, but Gilda suspected it was more than that. "Well, don't be a stranger. You have someplace to sit?"

Claudine moved a gilded chair next to a display of Jean Patou's Joy. The warm waft of amber and wood that had permeated the boutique's walls over the decades enveloped Gilda. Claudine pulled up another chair. "Father Vincent? Can I get you a seat?"

"If you girls don't mind, I think I'd like to finish my devotions in the car."

Gilda watched him, his Indian skirt rustling behind him, head outside.

When the side door closed, Claudine said, "It's a surprise to see you."

"A good one, I hope."

"Of course." Claudine's expression betrayed no emotion.

Gilda pursed her lips and pulled Adele's list from her handbag. "It will be a good one, I tell you. I've got your promotion right here."

Claudine sat and took the list. "Paintings and addresses. What is it?"

"The Booster Club is working on another case. We're helping an art forger take care of a few things before she dies."

"Adele Waterson, isn't it?"

Gilda raised her eyebrows. "How much do you want to know?"

"You sprang her from prison? I saw on the news that she'd escaped."

"Ruby and Father Vincent did most of the work. She's dying, and Larry the Fence wanted her to have the chance to get a few things done before she croaked."

Claudine watched with her cat-like gaze. Inscrutable. "What does she want with these?" She waved the list.

"She wants them destroyed." At Claudine's open mouth, Gilda added, "But we don't have to replace them with the originals. It has something to do with respect for artists."

"Really?" The faintest glimmer of a smile played on Claudine's lips. "I remember Adele, barely. Only met her once. She tended to stay in the background. She was working with Punch's gang before they moved to L.A. Larry the Fence's niece. She's dying, you say?"

"Doc Parisot's coming by tomorrow to look her over. Grady can help get her records off the computer." Grady might be the Villa's oldest resident, and his brain might be preoccupied with daytime

TV, but he was a hacker extraordinaire. He'd even been approached to work for the National Security Agency. These days, the hacker community thought he was a Belarusian teenager named Britney. "Adele has a brain aneurysm that could kill her any time. Larry said if we sprang her from prison and helped her out, he'd make sure the Villa was relicensed."

"Did he know what Adele wanted you to help her with?"

"I doubt it." She raised her chin. "We got one of them, though. From the Oak Hills golf club. I had to run into the men's locker room, and you'll never guess who—"

"It's best I don't know anything about it." Claudine shook her head. "A prison bust and a heist. You should be more careful."

"We did it for good reasons." When Claudine didn't reply, Gilda fastened her gaze on her and stared for the count of three. "Your father would have loved it."

Claudine's eyes took on a faraway look. Hank used to get this look, too, when he was planning a job. The familiar cavern of emptiness opened inside Gilda.

"I know." Claudine picked up a tester of Joy perfume and sniffed it, her mind clearly far away. "They're going to want to know how I got this list."

"Oh, come on. They didn't hire you because you were a cop. They wanted you for your background. For tips like these."

The girl simply watched her.

"Can't you say you 'found' the list somehow?"

Claudine looked at the paper. "They know Adele escaped. Everyone does. It wouldn't take Einstein to put two and two together."

"So they figure it out. What does it matter?" Gilda scooted her chair closer. Light sparkled from a faceted display bottle filled with purple water. "Adele's dying. What's the point of tracking her down? They'll be grateful they don't have to insure all those paintings."

"They don't insure them all. Other companies would be involved. Plus, if the owners can prove that their paintings were stolen, the insurance company will be out solid cash. A lot of it."

"The originals were stolen. This list makes the insurance company look smart, like they're on top of things. Trustworthy."

Claudine examined her fingernails, but Gilda knew she wasn't inspecting the manicure's condition. "All right. I'll do it. I'll say I got the note anonymously. You're sure it's correct?"

"Absolutely." Their business was over, but Gilda remained seated. Before Hank died, conversation would have segued to Cook's menu or gossip in the community. Now, Claudine seemed ready for her to leave. "Will we see you at the Villa anytime soon?"

Claudine's expression stayed immobile. The girl barely even blinked. "I've been busy."

"I see." Gilda backed up her chair and clutched her cane to stand.

"Wait a minute," Claudine said. Graceful as a panther, she rose and slipped behind the counter. She returned with a pink box wrapped in a ribbon. "Dad wanted me to give this to you on your birthday, but I think you should have it now. He told me when he was at the hospital. When he…." She looked at her hands.

The throb of emotion rose in Gilda's chest. She didn't need to unwrap the box. She knew what it was. Shocking by Schiaparelli, in the real perfume form. They didn't make it anymore, but somehow Hank had always come up with a bottle for her birthday. She dabbed at her eyes.

"I miss him," she said.

Claudine enclosed Gilda in her arms. "So do I."

CHAPTER ELEVEN

Gilda was unprepared for the drama she found on her return to the Villa. Every light blazed from the second floor and part of the third, and the murmur of voices reached her even in the lobby. Only Bobby remained downstairs, shuffling his deck of cards.

"What's this?" Gilda pointed her cane at the ceiling.

"Warren and Adele are at it. Started a few minutes ago. Warren's sure she'll be the end of the Villa."

"Why? I thought we'd been through all that."

"Can't say. I'm staying far away."

Gilda took the elevator to the third floor, where a throng of people in bathrobes and slippers choked the hall outside Adele's door. Parts of phrases in Warren's deep voice — "you can't deny it" and "no gratitude" were a few she heard — were answered by words so soft that Gilda couldn't make them out.

"Clear the way," Gilda said, poking her cane into one resident's rear end. The residents parted. She pushed the door open further.

Adele sat on the bed with her head bent and arms hugging herself. Warren, hands on hips, towered over her. A whitewashed canvas leaned on an easel near the window. That was new.

"Now, what's going on in here?"

"She's been in contact with someone on the outside," Warren said.

"Keep your voice down. We're all adults here," Gilda said. "Adele, is this true?"

The girl didn't move. She stared at the easel and barely blinked.

Gilda turned to Warren. "Tell me more."

This was apparently what he was waiting for, because his arms dropped to his sides. "I was—"

"Just a minute." Gilda turned to the hall. "You can all go back to what you were doing. I'll fill you in at breakfast."

"This has to do with all of us," Mary Rose said. She clutched a hot water bottle and had on only one slipper.

"She's right, you know," Mort said.

Gilda realized in all of these years, she'd never seen him in night-clothes, and here he was, in a bathrobe. She glanced toward his legs. Nothing else, either. All that walking to the woodpile for whittling material kept him in good shape. "They're not going to talk with everyone hanging around. Go back to bed." She shut the door without waiting for a reply. "Go on," she said to Warren.

"I was checking the Villa's perimeter" —Warren still clung to a few of his warden habits— "and I saw a guy leaving by the back exit, the one that lets out from the stairwell. He ran off before I got to him. It didn't take long to figure out where he'd been." He fastened a steely gaze on the back of Adele's head.

"And?" Gilda said.

"I came upstairs and found this." He waved at the easel and a box of art supplies.

This was bad. Adele was a fugitive. If anyone caught her at the Villa and started poking around, they'd be scattered to Medicare facilities throughout the region. Horrible. Adele knew better than to contact anyone. And art supplies? She couldn't be forging again, could she?

When Gilda found words, her voice was cold enough to send chills down her own spine. "Adele? What do you have to say for yourself?"

She turned toward them. Her eyes, wide and moist with tears, must have taken up half her face. "I just wanted to paint."

"Paint what?" Gilda said. A moment passed in silence. The crowd outside must have left, probably for a pick-up poker game in the TV room, or maybe to adjust the odds of Adele's continuing residency at the Villa.

"I don't know," Adele said.

"I didn't hear you," Warren said.

"I said I don't know." Adele turned her body toward them and pulled her legs up under her chenille bathrobe. "All I could think about when I was in prison was that I wanted to paint. You don't know how awful it is to see the seasons change or note someone's expression or pass a stack of books in all their different colors and not be able to put it on a canvas."

"She called someone." Warren yanked the phone's cord from the wall. "I don't know why I didn't do this earlier."

"It was the art supply store. That's all. I sent the bill to Uncle Larry. Besides, I know the guy. He'd never turn me in."

"I wouldn't be so sure," Gilda said. Honor among thieves was a noble concept, but in her experience it was a lot more rare than crime movies led one to believe. Adele's friend might be willing for now to keep his mouth shut about Adele. It was a short step to deciding to make some money off this information. He could bleed the Villa long after Adele was in her grave.

"You say you just want to paint. Right. You get out of the joint, and, boom, you're churning out the forgeries," Warren said. "We keep things clean in the Villa. We have to."

"Mostly," Gilda amended. Adele was here, after all. Not exactly legally.

"No, I'm not forging." Adele's eyes had dried, but they were still wider than a puppy's. "I don't have anything to copy. See? No photo, no nothing. Besides, you don't just slap an eighteenth-century painting on a brand new canvas."

"Maybe you're doing modern ones now." Warren's legs were planted shoulder-width apart. A fighting stance.

"She did say she wants her forgeries destroyed," Gilda told Warren.

"Her parole officer wouldn't want her painting. I'm sure it's a condition of her release."

"She doesn't have a parole officer," Gilda pointed out. "Skipped that step." Warren was right, of course. Being caught with Adele on the premises was bad enough, but being caught with Adele and the tools of her trade was worse.

"You know what I mean." He stepped forward, and his words came out loud. "I can't stay here with her in the building. We're risking everything."

"I understand." Gilda made a decision. "Warren, you go back downstairs. Hush people up. Adele and I are going to have a talk. I'll come see you later. You can decide then if you want to leave."

Warren cast a wary glance at Adele, and, with the phone curled under one arm, opened the bedroom door. "Okay. I'll wait up to hear from you."

To Adele's dismay, when the door closed behind him, Gilda stayed. The older woman sat on the bed's edge and rested her cane against the mattress. Adele had always assumed that one day she'd be an older woman, too. Her hearing or — she shuddered — vision would dim, joints would ache. She'd slow and drill down on her perspective on life. Her hand reached for the base of her skull. She'd never even reach her thirtieth birthday.

"It's just the two of us girls now," Gilda said. "I want the truth. You've been very selfish, you know."

She'd let the Villa's residents, so generous, down. "I know."

"Why?"

"I wanted to paint so badly, but I shouldn't have taken the risk. It's crazy. You've all been so kind to me. Maybe I" — her gaze traveled from the Southern belles on the wallpaper to the scarred dresser to the blank canvas— "I don't have much time. Is that an excuse?"

Adele let Gilda pull her hand into her own. She had expected it to feel dry and papery, but Gilda's skin was as soft as silk velvet. "An explanation, maybe. Not an excuse. None of us here have a lot of time. You get used to it as the years pass."

Adele dropped her head. "I'm sorry."

"Can we trust you?"

She nodded.

"I mean it. Can we trust that you won't put the Villa at risk by calling outsiders?"

"Yes." Adele looked up, pleading. "I promise. No more. I'll apologize to Warren, too."

"Good." Gilda's expression softened, and she dropped Adele's hand. "Do I seem foolish to you? Old and out of touch?"

"No." Her voice quavered.

"I don't believe you. I was your age once, too, although not as quiet."

"I'm so grateful to everyone here, but—"

"But what?"

"You're all strangers. I guess" —she took a deep breath— "sometimes I don't know how to act or what to say."

Gilda studied her a moment. Adele felt like she was being absorbed for a portrait. "We're just people, you know. A little older, that's all. Stand up for yourself." Her voice took a practical edge. "Never mind. I talked to someone who used to be in the Booster Club about your paintings. She works as a detective for an insurance agency now."

"What is she going to do?"

"Find out where your forgeries are and collect them. If she can." Gilda leaned forward. "Honey, as much as we'd love to, we can't gather up your paintings on our own. It's a stroke of luck that we know someone sympathetic on the inside."

"Thank you," Adele said. "This is better than I'd hoped. Will she give them to me?"

"My guess is that her company will destroy them, or…."

"Or what?"

"Or use them as evidence to prosecute you. Not that it matters now," Gilda added quickly. "As long as you don't get caught."

This was so much better than Adele could have hoped. She imagined the paintings toppling into an incinerator, one by one, and she relaxed back onto the bed's headboard. The little something extra Adele had added to the forgeries would vanish with each canvas. "Thank you," she repeated. "I mean, thank you so much."

Gilda might have blushed under her coating of ivory foundation. "Never mind. What are you doing with this painting?"

Adele smiled one more time in gratitude. "I'm not sure. I have a lot of ideas."

She wished she'd brought her sketchbook. They'd let her have one in prison, but she'd been forced to leave it behind. In it, she'd started a hundred projects. Some were studies of a stray leaf in the exercise yard or the strands of hair that escaped another inmate's ponytail. But what she really loved to paint were people. People's faces, especially when they didn't know they were watched, told volumes about fear, love, and hope. Their faces were better than movie scenes. Gilda's face, for instance. She wouldn't mind painting that. She went to the easel and absently uncapped the green pigment.

Outside, the wind had picked up, and the flagpole's line in the schoolyard clanked as its clasps hit metal. Gilda studied the back of the canvas, propped on an easel, illuminated only by the desk lamp. "You don't have anything here to use as a subject. Do you do it from memory?"

She'd already reached for the fine brush, the one she used for outlining. "Could I — could I paint you?"

Gilda drew back. Adele had seen this reaction before. People wanted to be painted, but they never thought they were "proper" enough somehow.

"Oh, honey. In this get-up?" She patted her leopard print housedress.

Adele talked. She knew words would relax Gilda, and her character would once again seep into her expression. Portraiture could be difficult. People put on masks at first. Usually, with time, the mask melted into a person's real spirit. Gilda was at heart an entertainer, and Adele knew she couldn't hide her personality for long.

Adele's hand moved quickly. Just green now. Color would come later. Her fingers remembered what to do. "I feel like I'm making a thought tangible when I paint."

"That's marvelous." Gilda's stiffness softened.

"Not really," Adele said, absorbed more by the transfer of her vision to the canvas than by her words. "My work is commercial. Not artistic."

"I don't understand."

"I mean I'm good at copying things, but I don't have the artistic temperament and imagination." The words came out so easily that she barely heard them.

"What?" Gilda stood, her expression now tightening to anger. "Who told you that?"

Adele's hands felt thick and clumsy. She set down the paintbrush. "It just…is."

Gilda lowered herself to the chair again. As fast as it had come, her anger morphed to concern. "When did you start to paint, honey? Tell me about it."

"Oh." Adele's hands reached for the brush again. As she painted—quick strokes here and there, her eyes darting between Gilda and the canvas—the high of creating settled over her like a goose feather duvet, warming her through her bones.

"You've been painting for a long time?" Gilda asked.

"What?"

"Since you were a kid?"

"I've been looking at things like an artist as long as I've been able to see, I think. But I didn't start drawing until I was twelve years old."

Her parents had always been fighting, it seemed. Yelling, smashing plates, slamming doors. The best way to survive was to keep her mouth shut and her eyes open. So, she'd watched, and she saw the world beyond its surface. The pieces of crockery fell in crazy angles, each casting a lip of shadow on the linoleum. Outside the apartment's window, a little boy held his mother's hand and laughed.

"Too young when they married," Uncle Larry had told her. It had nothing to do with her, he'd said. Finally, he took her to his home, and she hung out with him in the TV repair shop where he did business as a fence. Sometimes, when clients stopped by, she took bottles from the back of an old console television set he'd converted to a bar and made drinks. She watched the clients, too, watching them hopeful, then shrewd, then, at last, satisfied as they stuffed cash into their wallets.

Uncle Larry had been the one to notice her drawings on the back of his yellowing repair receipts. He'd given her pencils, then watercolors. Finally, he financed her tuition at art school. And now he wanted to make her happy before she died.

"I was an artist, too. A chanteuse," Gilda said. "That means singer in French."

Adele made a noncommittal noise as she continued to paint.

"Can I see?" Gilda asked.

"I've barely started."

Gilda rose from the chair and pushed to her side of the canvas. "Oh, darling. This is amazing. In ten minutes, you did all this. It's not that there's detail, it's something about the shape. It feels like me."

Adele had always been told she had a gift for sketching. Her detail, her ability to capture a split second nuance one teacher told her was "unseen — no one does this anymore." And she loved to do it. When she painted, her style was looser, but it still held the lifelike, yet candid, feel of her sketches. But, so what?

"It's nothing, really. Just a parlor trick."

Gilda put her hands on her hips. "That again. You're dismissing your own talent. You didn't come up with that on your own. Someone told you."

"Just because I can replicate something doesn't mean there's any art in it."

Gilda shook her head. "Where did you hear all this? This is not a photograph." She gestured at the canvas. "This is a moment in time, seen by you."

"No one cares about that anymore. I've been to art school. I know."

Gilda returned to her chair. "It was a professor, wasn't it?"

Adele's eyes widened. "How did you know?"

He was a professor all right. Handsome with his dark hair and straight figure, but his bent nose kept him from being model beautiful. So smart, too. He could talk about art for hours, and he knew so much. He'd pointed out how Rauschenberg was a fraud working to please the populace, and how Mondrian's genius wasn't fully appreciated. She'd venture an opinion, and he'd gently laugh and correct her. He told her she had a gift for mimicry, but that wasn't the same as art. She couldn't disagree. A quick glance at any art gallery put her in her place. At best, she was out of style. At worst, unimaginative.

At first, she'd been hurt. Then she was honored that he'd wanted to help her, despite her lack of talent. Besides, he'd praised her for being a good listener. He'd needed her.

"Damned teachers. You were a child. He was wrong to take advantage of you. I'm right, aren't I? You had an affair with him."

Blood rushed to Adele's cheeks. "You haven't met him. He used to hang out with famous artists. He wrote art criticism. He even has a painting in the Carsonville Art Museum."

A look of understanding came into Gilda's eyes. "I've met men like him. I don't know these people you're talking about, but this much I can guess: he's twenty years older than you. He told you that you had a lot of talent, then cut you down. He regularly got into the pants of his prettier students. For chrissakes."

Adele squeezed her fingers one by one.

"Honey. I don't have to tell you that I've seen this before. There's a certain breed of men no better than vampires, suckling on young girls to feed their egos. Not all men, though," Gilda said. "There are some good ones, too."

A lump lodged in Adele's throat. "He told me I was no good. As an artist. Said I'd never amount to anything."

"He said that?"

"Not in those words, but that's what he meant." She'd read it in his expression when he pointed at the curve of an eyebrow she'd drawn and pronounced it "precisely rendered" in a dry tone. He'd flipped through her sketchbook with a microsecond's pause at a page here and there, then handed it back with a stiff smile.

The wind filled their silence. Gilda drew a breath. "Jerk."

"After a while, he lost interest in me. I dropped out of art school." Adele squeezed a fist as if she could squeeze back the painful memory. "At first, I took a job in a bookstore. But I was obsessed with painting. It was all I could think about. When I had a few minutes, I drew. But I always hid it. Then Uncle Larry found one of my drawings. When he couldn't get me to go back to school, he hooked me up with Patch."

"Patch, the fine art fence. I never met him myself."

"Yes. He set me up in my own studio. He asked me if I could paint a Pissarro from a photograph."

"And you did." Gilda's expression was sympathetic.

"I don't want you to think the art professor was bad. I owe him a lot. He taught me that I don't have it in me to be a true artist.

Then, Patch taught me that I was a good forger. Forging is all about mimicry, like Oliver—that's the professor—had said. That I could do. That way, I could still paint."

"How'd you get busted?"

Adele abandoned the painting for the moment and sat on the bed. "It was one of Patch's gang. The one who got through the security systems. He was picked up on another job, and he traded his knowledge for a few years off his sentence."

Gilda looked alert. "What's his name?"

"He's not around here anymore. He did his time and got out of town before Uncle Larry caught up with him."

"I see." Gilda stood. "I get it. You won't be calling anyone else, right? You'll stay put?"

She nodded vigorously. "I promise."

"Then I'll fix things with Warren. Don't you worry about it. And I'll be back tomorrow so you can work on my portrait." She was halfway to the door when she turned around. "That jerk professor."

CHAPTER TWELVE

The next morning, Adele fiddled with a stray tongue depressor as she waited in the Villa's infirmary, or "sick bay," as the residents called it. Breakfast had gone all right — Gilda had calmed Warren and the other Villa residents as promised — but having another doctor look at her was a waste of time. She knew her days were numbered, and that number was low.

The doctor in the prison's infirmary had barely been able to look her in the eye when he told her she had a brain aneurysm. He'd made her sit down. He said it wasn't the first time he'd had to deliver this kind of news. He'd even offered to give her a few extra days in the infirmary, where the beds were softer and showers nicer, if she'd wanted.

A soft knock at the door told her the Villa's doctor had arrived. She straightened. "Come in."

A thin, basketball-player-tall man ducked his head and entered. His stethoscope swung as he bent to offer his hand. "I'm Doctor Parisot. I hear you have health challenges."

"I'm going to die," Adele said. "If you call that a challenge."

"We all are."

"Any minute? The doctor told me that one day I might get up to put on a sweatshirt for yard exercise and, poof, I'm dead." Despite her flippant attitude, her voice trailed off.

Gilda appeared in the doorway, the hall lights illuminating her hennaed hair. "You okay, honey? You want me to stick around, or should I wait in the cafeteria?"

She clearly wanted to stay, and Adele saw no reason to hide her physical condition from her. "Come in."

Gilda moved to the corner and turned her walker around so it made a seat. Dr. Parisot took the stool next to the examining table. Seated, he was much shorter. His height must be in his legs, like a spider.

"Now, tell me your situation," Dr. Parisot said. "What's wrong?"

Adele smoothed her skirt over her thighs. She was too small to wear anyone's pants except Grady's, and he wasn't keen on that, so they'd given her one of Candace's dresses. She felt like she was in a tent, and she was the tent pole.

"I was having headaches, and they kept coming back. I figured they were migraines, and maybe the doctor could do something. I went to the infirmary, and the doctor asked me a few questions, but everything checked out fine. So they put me in a CT scanner."

"I see. And?"

"It showed I had a brain aneurysm. Right here." She placed a finger at the base of her skull. "He said it could rupture anytime, and I'd die. Just like that."

Gilda's walker gave a squeak. She must have flinched.

"He told you not to over-exert yourself, I hope."

She nodded again.

"You're not a smoker?"

She shook her head.

He drummed his fingers on the chair's arm. "Who diagnosed you?"

"It was at Carsonville Women's. Dr.—"

"Bradley," Dr. Parisot finished. Adele nodded. "Not particularly bright, but he's thorough." The doctor turned to Gilda. "Get Grady. I want to see that scan."

Adele expected Gilda to leave. Instead, she yelled, "Grady!" All those years as a singer must have really developed her lungs.

Mort appeared in the doorway. "I'll find him. I think he's saving his spot in the TV room."

A moment later, Grady hunched in. "You called?"

"How's the hearing aid, Grady?" Dr. Parisot asked. "You're wearing it, aren't you?"

"It buzzes," he said. Grady's head barely reached Dr. Parisot's chest. Where the doctor seemed to sprout upward, Grady had sunk into himself over the years.

"You've got to get used to it. Play with it. It'll be worth it in the end."

"Sure, doc. What do you want?"

"He needs some records on the computer. For Adele," Gilda said.

"Yeah. What?"

"We need Adele's CT scan from prison. Can you call it up on a laptop and bring it here?"

"Sure, no problem. What's the date on it?"

"Last week," Adele said, glad she could contribute something. "Tuesday."

Grady jotted a few notes on the edge of a *TV Guide* he'd taken from his back pocket. "Fine. Give me five minutes."

"It's in a HIPAA-protected database," Dr. Parisot warned.

"Three minutes." Grady shuffled away.

"Adele is Larry the Fence's niece," Gilda said. "We're helping her out in exchange for straightening out the Villa's licensing."

The doctor sat back. "No kidding. Larry's niece, huh? What's he like? I've heard so much about him."

"Gentleman and a hustler," Gilda said.

"Uncle Larry is a good man." He'd brought Adele here. He'd put her in the care of these kind people. She looked at Gilda, who was in turn examining her tangerine-colored manicure. The theme song from *Gunsmoke* sounded next door. An issue of *Home Security International* on a side table was folded open to an article on wireless burglar alarms. A coupon for denture cleaner was its bookmark. The Villa's residents might not be Navy SEALs, but they had hearts of gold, and they were doing their best for her.

"I'm back," Grady said.

"Like a bad penny," Gilda said.

The old man set a laptop on the desk and opened it for the doctor. He clicked through a few screens, squinting, then tapping more keys with his knobby fingers.

Adele knew better than to hope he'd find that the infirmary's doctor was wrong. The blotch where unmarred brain tissue should have been was unmistakable.

"Can you enlarge that?" the doctor asked. A moment later, he said, "Next screen, please, lateral view." After a few minutes of examining the scan and her other health records, he sighed and closed the laptop. "Thank you," he said to Grady. Then, to Adele, "I'm afraid the infirmary's doctor was right. Classic aneurysm. The artery is unusually stressed. Let's check your pulse."

His fingers could have circled her wrist twice over, but they were surprisingly soft.

"Your blood pressure is low, at least. How about the headaches?"

"They come and go."

"Keep the stress down." He fidgeted with the end of his stethoscope. "I'm afraid—"

"Afraid what?" Gilda asked.

"It's a serious lesion. I've never seen anything so severe in so young a patient." He shook his head. "I'd put her remaining time in days, maybe weeks, if she's lucky. Not months."

They talked about her as if she wasn't there. "I—"

"Is that it?" Gilda interrupted. "There's nothing you can do? Give her some pills or something?"

He looped his stethoscope from his neck and set it on the examining table. "I wish I could tell you differently, but I'm afraid, no."

"Nothing at all?" Gilda said. "It's not like she has a lot to lose. Maybe there's something experimental?"

Adele looked around the sick bay. It might well be where she'd die. The room had little to recommend it—white walls, generic cabinets, linoleum floor—but it was part of the Villa, and so was strangely comforting all the same. It could be worse. Warren hated her, but the rest of the Villa's residents were sweet. She could paint and take baths. This week's menu included a spring vegetable fricassee and pasta primavera with handmade noodles.

"There is one thing, but I don't see us pulling it off."

"What?" Gilda said before the doctor had finished his sentence.

"There's a neurosurgeon in town who specializes in correcting brain abnormalities that other surgeons wouldn't even attempt. Name's B. E. Lancaster."

"What's the B and E stand for?" Gilda asked.

"Don't know. He lives here in Carsonville, but he has a national reputation. I saw him give a paper at a conference last fall in Orlando. Masterful." The doctor drifted off for a moment. "He has an innovative approach for accessing the hippocampus. I—"

Gilda snapped her fingers. "What would something like that cost?"

Adele's spark of hope fizzled. She was a prison escapee. She could paint forgeries for decades and not come up enough money to finance brain surgery. She didn't have decades. Maybe only days. And that's assuming the surgeon would even see her. "Never mind. As long as my forgeries are destroyed by the time I die, I'll be satisfied."

"I couldn't even tell you the cost," Dr. Parisot said. "His surgeries are probably scheduled out for months, too. By then…."

"By then it will be too late. I understand," Adele said. Somehow, knowing it was settled, she felt strangely peaceful.

"You don't care, do you?" Gilda asked her.

"Of course I care. I just…."

"You're just too worn out to care at this point," the older woman finished. She examined Adele before rising and turning her walker to locomotion position. "We'll see about that."

✫✫

"Did you get my present? The telescope?"

Ellie's eyes snapped open to see the grimy-faced kid from the day before leaning over the couch. Gray-shrouded sun leaked through the windows behind him. She bolted upright. "It's Saturday. What are you doing here?"

"I live close by. I brought you some breakfast." He clutched a toaster waffle. His mouth hung open slightly as he breathed.

"Where's your mom?" If she came looking for her brat, Ellie's cover was blown.

"At work."

She relaxed slightly. The child still held out the waffle, complete with chunks of margarine clinging to its edges. Her hips and shoulders ached from the night on the couch. She rubbed her lower back. "You eat it. I'm not hungry."

The boy crammed the waffle into his mouth in large chunks, as if he hadn't eaten for days. When he finished, he watched Ellie. Snot crusted under his nose, and his hands were greasy.

"Why did you bring me the waffle?" Ellie asked.

"You're a princess trapped in the attic because no one loves you. I don't want you to die here."

An unfamiliar quiver rose in her chest, then died as soon as it had tried to break free. "Maybe I'm here because I want to be."

The kid surveyed the attic, then shook his head. "They made you go here." He sniffled and wiped his face with the sleeve of his sweatshirt. "You could go anywhere. You wouldn't be here."

As if she needed the reminder. "Go home." She turned her back. She didn't hear his footsteps. After a moment, she swiveled to find him staring at her. "Why are you still here? I told you to go home."

"I'm not leaving you here by yourself."

"Why? What do you want?" She sat straighter. "How did you get in, anyway?"

He stared, mute.

"Tell me. The school doors are locked." She knew. She'd tested every one of them last night.

"There's a window to the basement that I can open. Don't worry. It's kid-sized. No bad man will get you."

"Go home. Get yourself cleaned up." She had the vague notion that children didn't wander the streets on their own. She'd have to secure that window. "Didn't your mom tell you not to talk to strangers?"

The kid might as well not have heard her at all. He stood like he'd been carved there.

"Jesus Christ." It was still early. Couldn't be much later than eight in the morning. "Anyone else here?"

The kid shook his head.

"Follow me." Ellie opened the attic door and headed down the stairs, the kid at her feet. She pushed open the restroom door.

"But this is the girls' bathroom."

"Get in there." He backed inside. The kid might not be too bright, but he was obedient. She pulled a wad of paper towels from the dispenser, set the taps to warm, and cleaned his grimy face. "Give me your hands." A few minutes later, skin appeared from under the dirt. Too bad she didn't have a full immersion tank of soapy water. "Come on."

She continued another floor down, to the cafeteria. She jimmied up the roll-down window and hoisted the kid to the counter. "In."

"Where are we going?"

"What does it look like?" Inside the kitchen, Ellie turned on the lights. "Yesterday was leftover Sloppy Joes. It wasn't bad."

"Friday we had spaghetti." The kid's eyes held definite interest now.

It crossed Ellie's mind that the spaghetti might have been his last solid meal. She examined the walk-in refrigerator and pulled out a carton of chocolate milk. The boy eagerly took the carton and popped open its lid. While he sucked it down, she found hamburger patties in the freezer and a can of corn on the shelf. The rest of the spaghetti must be in the Dumpster.

"Can I have another milk?"

Ellie pulled two more cartons from the refrigerator. "Here."

The kid went to work on the milk while she microwaved a breakfast of hamburger and corn. The boy had pulled himself up on the stainless steel counter and sat cross-legged, surrounded by empty chocolate milk cartons. She handed him a plate and a fork, and he tucked in.

She hadn't had much experience with children. She didn't have any of her own, and she preferred not to touch those who crossed her path. But here was this miniature human sitting across from her. Like any human, once he got what he wanted, he'd be gone. He clearly needed to be fed. Get enough corn and beef into his system, and he'd go home.

She'd promise him more food if he came tomorrow, as long as he kept quiet about her. Given the way he attacked his disgusting breakfast, he'd listen. If all went as planned today, by that time she'd be gone.

"Finished?"

The brat's stomach actually bulged under his too-small sweatshirt. He nodded.

"What's your name, anyway?" She didn't know why she asked. It didn't matter.

"Josiah," he said. A kernel of corn clung to his lip. "Princess, I love you."

CHAPTER THIRTEEN

Gilda made her way to the cafeteria and found Bobby examining an ad for a safe. The Villa kept a subscription to *Banker's Monthly* for old time's sake.

"You wouldn't believe how they work it now," he said. "All digital. I'd hate to be a box man in this day and age. Damned things would probably break on you, anyway."

"Claudine used to crack them."

"She's a youngster, and most of her safes were older wall models. Besides, they always left her the combination."

Before Claudine had dropped out of the heist business, she had mostly done insurance jobs. Clients who wanted the insurance payoff more than the item insured got in touch with Larry the Fence, who in turn called Claudine to arrange a "burglary."

Bobby tossed the magazine aside. "What happened upstairs? With the girl?"

"That's why I came down. We need a convo." She settled in one of the armchairs and picked up the house phone. "You stay put. I'll get Grady and Father Vincent down here. I bet Red and Mort are in their rooms. You see Mary Rose lately?"

After a few minutes, the group was gathered near the unlit fireplace at the cafeteria's far end.

"All right," Gilda said. "Here's the situation. Adele's going to die, just like she said. Her aneurysm could pop at any minute. Doc Parisot says there's a surgeon in town who might—just might, no guarantees—be able to fix it."

Each member of the group nodded. They knew what was coming next. They knew no legit surgeon would operate on an escaped prisoner without an incentive.

"You want us to take on another gig," Red said. "You really want to risk it?"

"I know the Oak Hills golf club heist was a close call," Gilda said.

"Close?" Mary Rose said. "It was danged near a total bust."

"This one's at a private home."

"Always easier," Mort said. "Especially during the work day."

"Besides, you don't have to do anything," Gilda said to Red. Red was at the Villa chiefly thanks to her time as her husband's shill. Not a particularly taxing livelihood.

"I have to live here. And that won't be easy if the place is shut down and everyone is in prison."

Grady watched them all. "You want me to dig or not?"

Once again, Gilda took charge. "Listen. Consider this an investment. We fix up Adele's brain, and Larry the Fence will be in our debt forever. Besides, it might not be so hard."

"Warren won't like it," Mary Rose added.

"There's one more complicating factor. Doc Parisot said Adele doesn't have much longer until the blood vessel in her brain gives out. If we go for this, we'll have to move on it right away. Like, this afternoon."

"Is that enough time to plan?" Father Vincent said.

"We won't know until we have an idea of what we're up against."

Gilda sat back. "How about this? We'll vote. All in favor of testing the waters to get the surgeon's help, say aye."

"Just having a look-see, right? Not actually going through with it?" Mary Rose asked.

"That's it. We're voting on having Grady poke around a bit, that's all."

Everyone said aye, except Red, who stared in her lap.

"The ayes have it. Grady, you can get started."

Grady opened his laptop. "Name?"

"B. E. Lancaster," Gilda said.

"What do the initials stand for?"

"Can't say."

"Never mind. Found him." Grady's knobby fingers worked the keyboard. "And that's Bruce Eric, by the way."

The phone extension in the cafeteria rang, an old-fashioned trill. "Never mind. Warren will get it. Check everything — money, police records, any hinkiness at all. Look at his medical school transcripts."

"Don't tell me my work," Grady said.

Gilda's mind always went to blackmail first. That had been her specialty for years, and it was a solid cash producer. She'd never been one of those blackmailers who'd squeeze the victim dry. She made one ask and moved on. If you were going to blackmail, you had to have a sterling reputation at it. She was good enough at her craft to finance a sweet apartment on the park blocks and a couple of nice vacations a year, even after her gig at the nightclub ended.

Warren popped his head into the cafeteria, his finger holding a spot in his novel. "Call for Bad Seed on line one."

Gilda sighed. "All right."

"Nothing," Grady said.

"At all?"

"Not a thing. Clean as a whistle. Subscribes to a hydroponic gardening magazine and buys a season subscription to the opera every year. Otherwise, zilch."

"What kind of vehicle does he drive?" Father Vincent asked.

"Late model minivan."

The father sat back in disgust.

Gilda took the phone, but before pushing the blinking button for line one, she said, "Then we look at assets. What has he got that he'd do anything to get back?" The back-up plan. Blackmail was cleaner. You steal something, and you can get caught. No one liked the risk. But Adele's life was at stake. "Bad Seed floral arrangements." Her voice was now remarkably sweet. "Did bad deeds? Send them weeds."

"Nice house in a nice neighborhood," Grady said.

"We ain't stealing a house," Bobby said.

"Any paintings? Maybe family jewelry?" Gilda covered the phone's receiver as she asked. She took notes for the floral arrangement with her other hand.

"Hold your horses. I'm checking his insurance file now."

Gilda couldn't help tapping her toes. "That's right. Only forty-nine-ninety-nine, and I can have it delivered tonight. No, it's extra for the special three a.m. delivery with doorbells and knocking."

"Okay, I think we got it." Grady turned his laptop around so the others could see the screen. He'd found something. Something the surgeon valued. Something they could steal and hold hostage in exchange for operating on Adele.

"Goodbye." Gilda hung up the phone. "Wait for me."

The screen showed a blue-canopied bed with a velvet cushion over the mattress, but something was wrong with it. Gilda couldn't quite put her finger on what it was. The bed's draperies were the rich blue of a late summer sky, yet somehow faded. Gilded carving adorned the posts supporting the canopy, and small feet held up the bed. It must sit painfully close to the ground.

"You want us to heist a bed? I guess I could borrow a moving van—" Father Vincent began.

"No, no. It's a little one. Here. Look at this photo." Grady clicked a few more keys and showed them the photo again. This time it sat next to a footstool and was barely wider than it—maybe two feet across and slightly higher with the canopy.

"A doll's bed? This doctor keeps a doll's bed?"

"That ain't no doll's bed," Grady said. "It's from the eighteenth century, and it's insured for a cool million bucks."

They waited for Grady to deliver the punchline. His consumption of soap operas had given him a flair for the dramatic.

"This here is Marie Antoinette's dog's bed."

Now that Josiah had gone home, Ellie began to put her plan in place. At last, it was time.

In the girls' bathroom, she opened her satchel. She smoothed her hair into a tidy bun and pinned it into place. From her bag, she withdrew a maid's uniform with its starched apron and laid it over the sink while she shed her black dress. She folded the satchel into the tiny pouch that contained it when it was empty and pinned the pouch under her skirt.

A few minutes later, indistinguishable from any efficient house-keeper, she left the school through the back entrance. On the street, she stepped behind a tree at the sight of someone—that older redhead with the walker—coming out of the Villa. She held up her chin and stepped to the sidewalk again. No one at the Villa would recognize her. Even if they noticed she bore a passing resemblance to Eleanor Whiteby Millhouse, they wouldn't give it a second thought. Eleanor was at the Bedlamton Arms. As far as they knew.

Ellie walked under old elms to the bus stop a block away. No one was out on this Saturday afternoon, it seemed. No one but a cable van creeping down the street. On impulse, Ellie turned to watch it. The van stopped outside the Villa. Even old folks need TV, she thought. Let them enjoy it while they can. If things went as planned today, the only television they'd be watching would be in the state penitentiary.

CHAPTER FOURTEEN

Father Vincent alit from the cable installation van in front of the Villa. Mort waved from the passenger side and rolled down the window.

"I want to come along," Gilda said.

"We'll take care of it. You stay here and rest," Mort said.

"What, 'stay here and rest'?" She pushed her walker closer. "Why shouldn't I come with you? I'll keep to the van. I won't be in the way."

"What if something happens?" Father Vincent said.

"Like the police," Mort added.

"Mort and I can deal with it better if we're alone. You stay here."

Good grief. Gilda pushed her walker to the side and grabbed the cane from its frame. "I'm coming with you, and that's that. If one of us goes down, we all go down."

Father Vincent and Mort exchanged glances. If they'd thought Gilda didn't see them, they were wrong. She yanked the van's side door open and looked among the tools and wire for a place to sit. That big spool of cable would make an okay seat. She navigated a stepladder and settled herself on the spool. "There."

Mort turned from his seat and shook his head. "If you insist." He took a pocketknife from his pants and a block of wood from his jacket to continue his habitual whittling.

"You look cute in that uniform, Mort," Gilda said. "Gray suits you. What's that patch say?"

"Al," Mort said. "Short for Albert. I like it. Has class."

The van's side door slammed shut, and Father Vincent climbed into the driver's seat. "Bud doesn't need the van back until three. The brakes are spongy, but it was all I could get spur of the moment. Grady has everything under control?"

"Said he'll disable the connection in twenty minutes, then reconnect exactly fifteen minutes later."

"Perfect." Father Vincent started the engine.

Gilda wouldn't be replacing her furniture with cable spools any time soon, but the ride wasn't too bad. She sang, "How Much is that Doggie in the Window?" to the engine's drone. When they made the turn to cross the bridge, she had to grab the back of a seat; otherwise, it was a relatively smooth trip with the rumbling engine obscuring whatever conversation Father Vincent and Mort were having up front.

At last they rolled to a stop. Father Vincent cut the engine. Gilda pulled her spool to a spot where she could see out the front windshield to a street lined in thick old trees and brick houses with white shutters. The van was one of the few cars on the street. Most of them — BMWs and Mercedes, Gilda bet — were coddled in garages.

Father Vincent opened the rear doors and set orange pylons behind the van. "I'll pretend to fool around outside on the ladder."

"Got it." Mort slid from the van.

Gilda squeezed to Mort's empty seat and watched him walk up the stone path to the door and press the brass doorbell. After a moment, Mort's words floated back to her.

"I'm Albert from Bombast Cable. May I speak to B. E. Lancaster?"

Beyond Mort was a small, bearded man in workout clothes. A towel draped his neck.

"This is he," the man said. "I'm not interested."

He began to shut the door, but Mort stuck his foot against the doorjamb. "I'm not here to sell you anything. I understand you have a service outage."

Mort was very convincing. Gilda had to hand it to him. He glanced at his watch. Undoubtedly checking against Grady's timing.

"I don't know what you're talking about. Everything's fine."

"I'd better not return to the station until you've checked. Service was reported as down. Since we're here, we may as well be sure."

Mort disappeared into the house with the bearded man, the door shutting behind him. Father Vincent loitered on the street. A moment later, Mort reappeared at the front door and gave Father Vincent a thumbs-up. The van's roof rattled as the ladder slid off. Gilda watched Father Vincent take the ladder to the house's side, in the driveway.

Now came the hard part: waiting.

Ellie rapped on the door. She should have been feeling fear, or at least anxiety. Instead, joy infused every step she took closer to her goal. It was as if she'd had a recurring dream, a good one, but had awakened each night for weeks before the final payoff. Now the dream was real. And so would be the payoff.

B. E. Lancaster opened the door. She recognized him at once from photos she'd studied. Even in workout clothes, he was tidy and precise, despite the beard. Before she'd looked up his photo in the business journal, she'd known a lot about him already from his wife, Mitzi, at the Carsonville Women's League. Mitzi would be at the club playing bridge right now, as she did every Saturday afternoon.

She knew B. E. Lancaster snored, for instance. He ate wheat germ with nondairy creamer for breakfast; had an electric ear and nose hair trimmer in each of the house's bathrooms; and raised hydroponic tomatoes in his sunroom. More annoying, she'd heard Mitzi drone on about how he ignored her to study heirloom tomato varieties and surgical procedures. Once Mitzi had caught her husband gazing at her. She'd told Ellie her heart had swelled with love. Then she'd learned B. E. was only determining where he'd put the saw to slice open her skull if she had pituitary gland abnormalities.

Above all, Ellie had heard about B. E.'s prized possession: the Marie Antoinette *lit de chien*. It was heavily insured and set up in its own display room. Mitzi wasn't allowed to go nearer to it than the hall. Once she'd bought a ceramic pug to set in it, and her husband had freaked out that anything should touch the same hallowed cushion that some queen's dog had drooled in.

"He doesn't appreciate me," *blah blah blah*, Mitzi had complained. But Ellie had got one good tidbit out of it. The man would do anything for his dog bed.

"Can I help you?" B. E. Lancaster looked her up and down.

"Dr. Lancaster? I'm the housekeeper the service sent over. Dorothy" —she almost choked. What was the last name she'd chosen for its efficient, generic sound?— "Josiah." Her mouth dropped open. Shoot. Why did she say that?

"We didn't send for a housekeeper. We have a regular gal who comes Wednesdays."

"Mrs. Lancaster requested us, I believe. For a special deep cleaning."

"This place is turning into Grand Central Station." He stepped aside. "Come in."

As she entered the foyer, Ellie had the feeling of being back in her old life before the Bedlamton Arms, her old life of waxed floors, pots of white orchids, and flutes of crisp champagne. Lancaster didn't offer her the suck-up smile she would have merited then. He turned his back on her and walked toward the basement, sure she'd follow.

"Down there's the closet with the mop and what-have-you. My wife will be home in an hour. If you have questions, save them for her. I'll be pruning my tomatoes."

"Thank you, Dr. Lancaster." Ellie made a show of rattling around in the cleaning closet. For a basement, it was nice. White carpeting—her favorite—and a huge TV and sectional sofa.

Enough sightseeing. She had work to do, and quickly. From the closet, she chose a feather duster and climbed back to the ground floor. A Bach cantata drifted from the house's far end. She continued up a flight, where she knew the dog bed was from Mitzi's prior wailing.

A peek through the door ajar at the back of the house showed the master bedroom. Other than a heap of workout clothing at the foot of the bed, the room was immaculate. Ellie's keen gaze estimated a good fifty thousand dollars of furniture in here, including the eighteenth-century gilded mirror. Mitzi had better taste than her drab club dress showed.

The next room was also a bedroom. It had the dark, stiff look of a guest room. She closed its door.

This had to be it. This door, also closed, had to open to the dog bed shrine. According to Mitzi, the room featured a large portrait of Marie Antoinette, a blue velvet platform holding the dog bed, and a leather armchair where B. E. could gaze upon it.

Ellie's joy spun to a fevered pitch. Her fingers itched to toss the bed into the black bag folded and pinned under her skirt and carry it away. In a few hours, when the Villa's residents were napping, she'd hide it in the basement's furnace room, clearly marked in the floor plans she'd studied. Then she'd call the police.

Hand on the doorknob, Ellie turned and pushed. Marie Antoinette's rouged face gazed down from her portrait. The armchair, the impression of B. E.'s buttocks clearly marked, was where she expected it. The blue velvet platform took pride of place.

The dog bed was gone.

This had been a straightforward job for Mort and Father Vincent, Gilda knew. Mort didn't have much experience with break-ins, but as a former con man, he was good at bamboozling people with small talk. Father Vincent was primarily a getaway guy, of course. Back in the sixties, before he'd entered the seminary, he'd helped on a few heists.

Not that this was a heist. At least, not formally. Mort would have checked the cable connections throughout the house, including in the study where B E. Lancaster kept his prized dog bed. He'd have handed the bed through the window to Father Vincent at about the same time that Grady reconnected cable service. In a minute, they'd drive away and set up the dog bed for ransom. Done. Even if B. E. Lancaster had been smart enough to jot down the cable van's license plate number, he'd find it was for a wrecked convertible in the junkyard.

At last, the van's rear door opened. Gilda squeezed back to her spot on the spool and took the package, wrapped in a plastic garbage bag, from Father Vincent. A moment later, Mort jumped into the van and belted himself in. Father Vincent, the ladder replaced on the van's roof, settled into the driver's seat.

"How did it go?" he asked Mort.

"No problem. Grady's timing is impeccable."

"A housekeeper knocked while you were inside. She didn't cause you any trouble?"

"Nah. I thought the place looked pretty clean already," Mort said.

"Sure it does. Because they have a cleaning service," Father Vincent said as he pulled the van away from the curb.

"With one less thing to dust," Gilda said.

CHAPTER FIFTEEN

The Villa felt empty without Gilda's singing and Mort's chatter while he whittled and Father Vincent's travels in and out to the parking lot with his tool kit. So much the better to paint, Adele decided.

She left her door open and cracked the bedroom window to let out fumes from her oil paints. Gilda's portrait was coming along well. She'd been afraid her touch might have become heavier and less precise while she was in prison, but her old easiness with the paintbrush had come right back. So had the delicious sense of absorption.

She was adding blue shadow under Gilda's jaw when Warren appeared at the door. "I can smell your paints halfway down the hall."

"I'm sorry." She set down the palette. "I opened the window an inch, but I didn't want to open it too much, because—you know."

"I know. We don't want anyone seeing you. I brought a fan." He lifted a small electric fan. "There's an outlet behind you."

She stepped aside while he perched the fan on a chair. "You know what they're doing for you, don't you?"

"No. Are they out now? The Villa seems so quiet."

"They're stealing an antique dog bed from a brain surgeon. They'll return it after he operates on you." Warren faced the window.

Adele was certain he avoided looking at her on purpose. "I didn't ask them to do that. I had no idea."

"You don't have to ask. These are good people." He placed his hands on his hips. "They shouldn't be carrying off spur-of-the-moment heists like this. Not at their age." He bent to the fan again and plugged it in.

"I'd tell you I'm sorry—and I am—but it doesn't seem to do much good. You've decided you don't like me, and there's nothing I can do about it." He opened his mouth to reply, but Adele cut him off. "Can we simply agree to tolerate each other until this is over?"

He pushed a button, and the fan whirred to life. "Fine."

It wasn't exactly a truce, but she'd take it. "Good."

As he turned to leave, his gaze fell on Gilda's portrait. His expression morphed from disapproval to wonder, and he lifted eyes to hers. "You painted that?" he said.

"Of course. You know I paint. You saw the Italian landscape."

"Sure, but…." He stared at the canvas. "That's incredible. It's Gilda, but so lively. You know what I mean? It's not like a photograph. It's as if it holds three expressions at once."

"I love to paint, but I don't pretend to be very good." She spoke tentatively at first, but when she saw he seemed genuinely interested, her words picked up passion. "It's been so long since I've been able to focus on my own work. Even if it's just for a few days, I can't tell you how happy it makes me."

Warren studied the portrait for another minute. "Listen, maybe I've been a jerk. I'm sorry. I've gotten so attached to these guys that anything that threatens them puts me on alert."

When Adele was a girl, her family had a mutt—a Labrador retriever crossed with a Rottweiler crossed with lord-knew-what—that barked and growled at anyone who knocked. The mailman would drop packages at their door and hurry down the corridor. The dog was a sweetheart, though. He slept next to Adele's bed, and he wagged his tail when she dressed him in a tattered velvet coat from her grandmother's house. Warren was like that dog. All his bark came from a good place.

Adele touched his arm. "That's okay. I understand."

He reached for her hand, and then withdrew. "Cook left me some tomato soup. She cans the tomatoes herself in the fall. Would you like to have lunch with me? We could make grilled cheese sandwiches, too."

"All right." They made their way to the cafeteria, then through to the kitchen, Warren in the lead. "I haven't been in here," Adele said.

They stood in a kitchen far smaller than Adele would have imagined the Villa required. A full battery of pans hung over a restaurant-style stove, but that was the room's only institutional touch. The cupboards were wooden, their handles threaded with drying herbs and ropes of garlic. Rag rugs lay in front of the sink and range.

"Cook is foraging for morels today, so we have the place to ourselves." He motioned toward a small pink armchair next to a wooden gate-legged table. "Have a seat. That's Cook's chair for when she takes breaks." Warren busied himself at the stove.

"What's in there?" Adele pointed toward a heavy wooden door.

"The larder. The Villa has a lot of strange nooks and crannies. I'll give you a tour some evening, if you'd like."

Soon they were sitting over fragrant soup and grilled cheese on thick-cut bread, all served on white crockery. "Do you eat here every day?" Adele asked.

"Most weekdays. Cook sets up the laptop, and we watch *The Andy Griffith Show* together."

"I love that show! Don Knotts is a genius."

"Have you seen *The Ghost and Mr. Chicken*?"

The next hour was spent in a way that Adele never would have guessed—in easy conversation and laughter with Warren. She discovered they both liked board games and shared a fondness for crazy eights; loved early mornings; and didn't like meat on the bone. When Warren relaxed, Adele saw it through his whole body. His face smoothed, his shoulders settled.

"Tell me," he said after they'd discussed the finer points of car camping. "Why are you so set on getting back your forgeries?"

She hadn't expected this turn of conversation. Furthermore, she wasn't ready to tell him everything. She considered her words. "Painting feels as necessary to me as breathing. Except that breathing is something you do without thinking. You can be an expert breather pretty much straight out of the womb."

"What does this have to do with the forgeries?"

"I'm getting there." She pushed her soup bowl to the side. "To forge a painting well, you have to get inside the artist's mind. By recreating his work, you become him—or her—in a way. For instance, once I did a forgery of a George Stubbs painting of a horse. When I finished the painting, I felt like I understood the artist. Even though he was a cranky and horse-obsessed man, I felt I could sit with him for a, a"—she wasn't sure exactly what eighteenth-century society horse portraitists ate—"pint of ale or something and really talk."

"Like what?" Warren asked. "How did you think you knew him?"

"Well, he loved animals, so he had to be a good person." Adele thought of Warren's tattoo of Goldie the pit bull. "And he was a scientist. You could tell he knew every tendon in a horse's body, as if he could see below the flesh. I also had the feeling he was the sort of guy who liked precision and would correct your grammar."

Warren's expression softened, but only for a moment. "What does that have to do with you wanting your paintings back?"

"It's a way of respecting these artists I came to know." She hoped this would be enough for him, but his gaze was sharp.

"Oh." He waited as if he expected her to elaborate, but she didn't. At last, Warren rose. "I suppose I'd better clean up before Cook gets back."

She stood, too. "Thank you for inviting me down for lunch. It was — great."

"So, we're friends?" He held out his hand. It was warm and strong.

"Friends."

CHAPTER SIXTEEN

"There it is," Father Vincent said. He'd just removed the dog bed from its garbage bag and set it in the cafeteria's recesses, far from the front window.

"Doesn't look like much," Gilda said. Imagine. Some doctor dealt out a load of cash for it. She poked her nose under the bed's canopy. "At least it doesn't smell like dog."

"It's been more than two hundred years since a dog lay there, you know." Mort lovingly traced the gilded carving on the bed's posts with his finger. "Nice work. Ruby's Chihuahuas would love one of these. She could keep it in the hair salon." He flipped the bed over to examine its bottom.

"Careful," Gilda said.

"Yep," Mort said. "I could make one of these for Ruby in no time. The sides would be balsa, but a thick balsa's tough enough to stand up to a Chihuahua."

"Unless the dog's a chewer," Father Vincent said.

"Enough of the chatter," Gilda said. "Now we've got the goods. What's next? We don't have a lot of time to waste."

"Where's Adele, anyway?" Father Vincent asked.

"Upstairs, painting. Warren was up there, too," Bobby said. He pulled a deck of cards from his shirt pocket.

Gilda exchanged glances with Father Vincent. Hopefully the visit wouldn't come to blows. Last night she'd managed to convince Warren that Adele hadn't meant the Villa any harm, and she'd stay in the Villa with no outside contact for as long as they said. He'd seemed mollified, especially when she reminded him Adele could die any time. Love and hate, Gilda thought. Two sides of a coin.

"Well, we need to get her on that operating table," Gilda said. "So, chop chop. Grady, are you already set up to send him a note through the computer?"

"No problem. We've got to have proof for him, though."

Father Vincent plunked the day's newspaper on the table. "Set the dog bed here, so the date shows, and we'll take a photo."

"Good idea," Gilda said. Being in charge suited her. Back in the day, she'd always been a little bossy with the girls at the club, but she'd found it didn't sit well with a lot of the guys she'd cultivated to make a living over the years. Except Hank, of course. Hank had liked her the way she was.

"How do we make sure he actually does the surgery?" Mort said. He flipped up the canopy's edge and examined a joint in the wood. "I mean, what if he says okay, then he botches it?"

"We discussed this already. We make it conditional. Adele comes out of it okay, or no dog bed. We'll have Doc Parisot watch by camera to make sure there's no hanky panky."

"No problem on my end," Grady said, adjusting his hearing aid. "Won't take me more than a couple of minutes to scrub the note and photo and send it. No matter how many police detectives they put on it, they'll never trace it. Should I send it now?"

"Let's give it until morning. We want him to work himself into a lather," Gilda said. "Let him sweat a bit. Then — boom! — we pop him with the note. All communications will be by computer. None of this face-to-face. Too risky. The day of the operation, we drop Adele off a few blocks from the hospital."

"I can fix up a laptop for her to take with her. She can set it up to connect with Doctor Parisot."

"I like it," Father Vincent said.

"Me, too," Mort said, still gazing at the dog bed.

"Great. Tomorrow morning we send the note."

Later that day, Gilda yawned and stepped into the hall. She was getting too old for this. There was a time when she was busy from first thing in the morning—okay, really about noon, when she rose—to two the next morning. Ever since she came to the Villa ten years ago, she'd subsisted on one activity a day. Two, tops. What had she been doing with her time, anyway? Talking about the old days, she guessed. While the rest of the Villa relived every moment of the dog bed heist, Gilda had gone upstairs for a nap.

Adele's door was ajar, and Gilda pushed it open with her walker. "You kids all right?"

Instead of the clenched fists and hot words she'd feared, Adele and Warren were actually smiling at each other. Warren was showing her one of his books, the romance about the mail order brides, if Gilda remembered right. A few other books lay toppled over the dresser.

When they saw her, they looked away from each other, Warren toward Adele's painting, and Adele toward the carpet.

"I was just lending Adele something to read." Gosh darn if Warren didn't look guilty.

"*First Class to Wyoming*, a mail order bride romance. Read it last week," Gilda said. "You like romances?" she added, looking toward Adele.

"I've never read one before," she said.

"Give it a try," Warren said. "It's about a lot more than romance. There's drama. You'd never believe what happens to the characters."

Poor girl. Probably was afraid she wouldn't be able to make it to the end before she died. "I'll save you the suspense and tell you it all works out."

"Is there something you need?" Warren asked, clearly irritated by her interruption.

If Gilda wasn't mistaken, romance was blooming here, and not just in the novels, either. For all the hundreds of thousands of pages Warren read, she'd never seen him so much as go to the movies with a girl. Strange, since he was a tempting blend of tough I'll-take-care-of-it and childlike vulnerability. Plus, he was handy. There was something in that boy's past making him gun shy.

She turned to Adele, whose face had pinkened. Realization dawned. Adele was dying. Just like the heroine in *Amish Heart*. Catnip to a romantic like Warren.

"No. Just checking in. You two carry on." She turned to leave, but Warren beat her to the door.

"I was going anyway," he said. Then, to Adele, "Will you be downstairs for dinner?"

She nodded.

Gilda didn't miss how Adele's gaze followed him. Gilda pushed the door shut and stayed behind. "He's a nice man, that Warren."

Adele held the novel against her chest. "I guess. Yes." Her gaze focused. "Warren told me about the surgeon's dog bed. Are you going through with it?"

"Already done. We're going to send him the ransom note in the morning."

Adele rose and hugged Gilda. "Thank you. But I don't see why you bother. Even if he operates and is successful, I still risk ending up in jail."

Gilda sat on the other side of the bed. "Is that all you have to say? 'Thank you, but'? We just stole a valuable artifact for you."

"I don't want to sound ungrateful—"

"Well, you do. If the operation is a success, you can take care of your forgeries yourself. That's what you wanted, right? As for return-ing to prison, well, first things first. For chrissakes." She folded her arms in front of her chest.

"It's not worth it. I'm sorry I ever bothered Uncle Larry about it. Now the Villa is at risk, and—"

"Hush up, girl. You can cut the 'poor me' business." Gilda silently counted to ten before continuing. She wanted Adele to think this over thoroughly. "Yes, we've put ourselves at risk, and, yes, we're going to a lot of work for you. And what do we get? Not gratitude, not joy, but regret." She raised her chin. "You should be ashamed of yourself."

Adele examined her fingers. Gilda thought she heard a sniffle. "I'm sorry," Adele whispered. "I guess—I guess I'm just overwhelmed."

"And acting like a scared kindergartner is going to help? Stop that boo-hooing. Honestly. Where's your moxie? Or did the professor take that, too?"

Adele brushed away a tear. "I'm sorry."

Gilda rolled her eyes. "Honey, I know you're in a tough spot. But we don't have the luxury of second-guessing things now. Now, we move ahead. All right?"

Adele didn't reply.

"I said, 'all right,' and I expect an answer."

She raised her head. "All right."

"Good." Beyond Adele, the easel faced the window so that she would have light from the barely opened blinds. Enough tough love for the moment. "Made any progress on that painting?"

Adele brightened. "A little. It's nothing, really. Do you want to sit for me?"

"I guess I have a few minutes. Let me see, first." Gilda made her way to the corner and stepped behind the canvas. A soft squeal escaped her lips. The last— the only— time she'd made that sound was when Mayor Bradley gave her an emerald parure in nineteen fifty-three. "Good lord, honey. This is gorgeous."

The painting's green outlines were filled in now, and Gilda had appeared in a mix of majesty and down-home appeal, like Queen Elizabeth dressed for a walk with her corgis. This was not how she appeared in the mirror, but she had to admit it was how she felt when she was explaining the intricacies of the mistress-wife relationship to Mary Rose after dinner in the cafeteria.

Adele smiled again and picked up her palette. She squirted blobs of red, blue, and yellow paint on it and started to mix with a paintbrush.

"I don't see why you bother with forgeries when you can paint like this. Honey, you could make a mint. Every rich lady in town would beg you to paint her. Heck, you could paint whatever you wanted."

"I'm not a real artist, just a craftsperson. I'm too commercial. Derivative." As Adele said the words, she didn't seem to listen. Her gaze was focused on Gilda and had taken on that faraway look she'd had in their earlier session when she'd painted the outline.

"Right. I remember."

Adele didn't respond. Her paintbrush moved with assurance between the blobs of color, making a handful of flesh tones.

"That art teacher who got in your pants."

She barely nodded.

"Good grief. We've been through this. Remember?"

Adele swallowed.

"Well, it's a load of hogwash. 'Derivative. Commercial.' I bet the loser never sold anything he made. Did he?"

At last, Adele looked up, and her eyes widened.

"He's a swindler, that's what he is. Taking advantage of young girls." Gilda had met a lot of men like that art professor. Boxcar loads of them. Usually it was someone with a little power. He used it to seduce girls and boost his ego. Like that second-rate boss she'd had when she waited tables, before her singing career. He thought that just because he owned a truck stop, he was entitled to nookie in the walk-in refrigerator. "We'll get you that operation, then you can sell a painting and hire yourself a shrink."

Silent, Adele stared at her.

"What? You don't have anything to say?"

"You told me to stop being a baby. I'm taking my medicine." She gave a small smile.

"Good girl." Gilda leaned back and tilted her head just a bit, to match her likeness on the canvas. "Keep painting."

CHAPTER SEVENTEEN

After dinner, Gilda pushed herself away from the dinner table and reached for her walker. "Padre, you ready?"

Father Vincent jangled a ring of keys from his finger. "You bet. I thought we'd take Claudine's Mercedes. She'll be happy to see it."

When they arrived, Claudine was waiting for them downstairs in the perfume boutique. She opened the side door, and this time Father Vincent came in, too, holding an umbrella over Gilda against the spring rain.

"Hey, Deanie," he said as he shook water off the umbrella. "I gapped your spark plugs. The Mercedes purrs like Eartha Kitt now."

"Thank you. What do I owe you?"

Father Vincent actually looked embarrassed. "I thought—well, I thought maybe you'd let me do a little sampling for a new cologne."

"Why don't you look around while Gilda and I talk?"

"You fixing to go out, Deanie? I like the lipstick." Hank's daughter never did wear much makeup. She always looked great, of course. Kept herself strong and limber for her old break-in work, and that moody look was a real turn-on for some men.

"I am, in fact. A late dinner."

"Not with the Oz?" Oswald was Deanie's ex-husband and a troublemaker. Catnip to the ladies, though.

"No, Gilda. I haven't seen him since the Cabrini heist. I probably won't see him again."

Gilda studied Claudine's expression for sadness or dissatisfaction, but all she found was the usual indifferent set of mouth. "We never had much of a chance to talk about that. Are you ever sorry you didn't go through with it?"

Hank had died on the heels of Claudine's decision to give up a gigantic jewel heist — the Cabrini jewels — to save the firehouse for a family shelter. It was the heist that would have set her up for life. Instead, she'd left it for her ex-husband to carry out.

"No." The word came without pause, but also without conviction.

"Truth, Deanie. Are you sorry?"

Claudine held her emotionless expression. "I told you the truth."

Maybe it was leftover anger simmering from her "grow up" lecture to Adele, or maybe it was the culmination of months of grief, but Gilda couldn't contain her feelings any longer. She nailed Claudine with her gaze, and using the force of years singing in a nightclub without a microphone, said, "I've had it."

Claudine's chair jolted back an inch, but she didn't respond.

"You planned that heist for months, and you gave it up. Your father died. You left your old life for some new gig as an insurance detective. And you are as cold as" — Gilda searched for the words as her anger gathered steam. Her gaze lit upon an oversized perfume flacon filled with amber water— "as that phony bottle of Shalimar."

Father Vincent didn't seem to notice the storm on their side of the room. He bent and sniffed over a bottle, his skirt whooshing against the glass display case.

Maybe it was Gilda's imagination, but she thought she noticed a softening around the girl's mouth. A moment passed, then two.

"I'm sorry I haven't been by to see you. It's been — hard." Claudine's words fell into the silence soft and soothing as feathers.

"Oh, honey." Gilda fell into Claudine's arms and erupted into tears. She didn't need Claudine to go into detail. For Claudine, this was detail. "I thought you didn't care about me anymore. I thought you'd found a new life, and we'd never see you." She pushed back into her chair.

Claudine smiled, a real smile. "I love you, Gilda. I really do."

Gilda sniffed and wiped her eyes. "You're avoiding us. I'm not the only one who notices."

"I still can't believe Dad died. If I stay away from the Villa, I can pretend he's still around."

"How do you think I feel?" Her words dropped to a whisper. "It's so hard."

"I know." Claudine's voice was just as soft. "I know."

Rain splatted through the gutter outside the window. Father Vincent tunelessly hummed at the other side of the boutique. A lump still clogged Gilda's throat, and she forced it out with an "ahem." "Tell me about this man you're having dinner with."

"He's a fellow I work with."

"Really?" This took a moment to sink home. Claudine, dating someone who wasn't on the make?

"You have anything with more of an automotive feel?" Father Vincent asked. He stood, seemingly stymied, in front of a row of bottles of pink perfume.

"Over there. Try the Bulgari Black," Claudine said. Then, to Gilda, "He's all right. I think you'd like him."

"Does he know about — ?"

"Nothing he can prove."

Gilda clipped and unclipped her purse. What would Hank say? He'd always liked the Oz, even though she'd pegged him for a player from day one. "Are you sure you want to get involved with someone who might, well, misunderstand our lifestyle?"

"He understands it, all right."

"But he doesn't approve."

Claudine sat upright. "He doesn't have to. I'm not part of that life anymore."

The room fell silent, except for Father Vincent's fumbling with bottles.

Not in the life anymore. That would explain her reluctance to drop by the Villa like she used to for Sunday suppers and the occasional card game. The hollow Hank's death had left deepened.

"All right." Gilda's voice was quiet. "I won't keep you, then. What's the progress on Adele's paintings?"

"Love this one, Deanie," Father Vincent said. "Nice whiff of rubber and smoke. I had a sixty-seven Mustang once that smelled just like it."

"Take the bottle," Claudine said. Bringing her attention back to Gilda, she said, "You were right. I got quite a bit of credit at the insurance company when I nailed eight forged paintings."

"They didn't ask you how you got the list?"

"Nothing I couldn't answer."

"What do you think, Gilda?" Father Vincent thrust a wrist under her nose.

She pushed his arm away. "Very nice. We're not through here yet. Why don't you check out Deanie's Toyota?"

"It has been running a little rough," Claudine said.

Father Vincent was out the side door before Gilda had time to reply.

"What happens now?" Gilda asked.

"I'm tracking down where they all are. Not all the insurance holders update their records when they move or sell something. A couple of her paintings actually ended up at the Holgate."

"That fancy museum?"

"The very one. Another painting is here in Carsonville. Besides the one at the golf club." She cast a sideways glance at Gilda.

"Carsonville. I'll be—" She stopped. Here in town. "Carsonville?"

"Some art professor owns it. I left him a message today."

Gilda turned this over in her mind. Adele's art professor. No. That would be too much of a coincidence, although Carsonville couldn't contain more than a handful of them. "I wonder if Adele knows him?"

"How is Adele, anyway?"

Claudine really did look lovely with lipstick, although the shade might be a bit orange on her. "She's all right. We're going to get her to a brain surgeon that Doc Parisot recommended."

"A brain surgeon? That's expensive, plus Adele's a hot commodity right now. How are you—oh, no. The dog bed."

Gilda felt her face warm. This straight life of Claudine's was too much. "I don't know what you're talking about."

"You don't know anything about an eighteenth-century *lit de chien* that was stolen from a prominent neurosurgeon's house this morning." She put it as a statement, not a question.

"Know anything about it? I can't even spell it."

Another of the awkward silences fell. This never used to happen. Not that Claudine was ever the talkative type, but they'd always had so much to catch up on. And not just about Hank, either. They were family.

Claudine rose and slipped her purse over her shoulder. "Good. Let's keep it that way. Now I have to go out."

"You're not mad?"

She slipped her arm through Gilda's and smiled. "Only if you're not still mad at me."

CHAPTER EIGHTEEN

Ellie had fallen onto the couch prepared for a sleepless night. Her afternoon and evening since the failed heist had been spent pacing the school's corridors trying to figure out where she'd gone wrong.

How had the dog bed disappeared? B. E. Lancaster always kept it in the shrine room. Mitzi had talked about it incessantly, about how he cared more about it than he did about her. Maybe the dog bed was on loan to a museum. Or maybe his wife had destroyed it.

No. Couldn't be. The shrine was set up exactly as it would be were the dog bed in place. Someone had stolen it.

Meanwhile, her plan to destroy the Booster Club was done for. By now, she should have been watching the police swarm the Villa and remove its residents in handcuffs. She should have been saying goodbye once and for all to this god-forsaken hellhole. She should have been heading off to a new life in Palm Beach — or wherever. She punched at the couch's lumps and turned over.

Despite the anger and disappointment that had needled her, she must have fallen asleep eventually, because she awoke Sunday morning with the boy mouth-breathing over her.

"Hi, princess," he said.

Ellie groaned and rolled away from him.

"It's morning now. Time to get up."

She sat and blinked at the sunlight. Last night's rain had given way to cold, clear sun.

"What's this?" The kid held up an empty whiskey bottle. Ellie didn't respond. "It's Mr. Iverson's," he added.

"Yeah, well, it was a tough night." She picked at the housekeeper's uniform she still wore. At least it was relatively clean. "What are you doing here?"

He drew a hand from behind his back and gave her a piece of folded paper. On the front he'd drawn a grayish disk and a pile of yellow spots. Inside, the card read, "Thank you for the food."

"Hamburgers and corn," he said, pointing at the drawing. "Can I have some more?"

"It's Sunday, um —"

"Josiah," he said. "What's your name?"

"Never mind that. It's Sunday, and I don't know what's in the kitchen." He stared at her, softly breathing through his mouth. Poor kid. Obviously didn't have breakfast. "Don't they feed you at home?"

No reply.

"Honestly. Tell me what you had for breakfast."

"When?"

She swiveled her legs around to face him. "Breakfast. This morning." Again, nothing.

She exhaled in exasperation. "What are you going to do when I'm not here?"

"Are you leaving?"

The concern in his eyes shot a javelin of warmth through her. "I can't stay in this filthy den forever. Where do you usually get breakfast?"

"They give it to me at school."

"And on the weekends?"

He continued to stare. The kid was skinny. She'd known dogs that were better cared for than he was. The thought reminded her of the Marie Antoinette dog bed, and she groaned again.

"All right," she said. "Go to the bathroom and wash your face. I'll meet you in the kitchen."

He darted toward the door and paused before opening it, giving her a broad smile that highlighted the missing tooth on his upper jaw. "Thank you, princess," he said.

Ellie rubbed the small of her back. What she'd give for a decent mattress. And a decent meal. No more odds and ends from the school kitchen. She took up the telescope. They were probably having a nice Sunday breakfast at the Villa. French toast and bacon, maybe. She'd given up carbs years ago, but now she'd kill for a stack of pancakes. She trained the telescope on the Villa cafeteria's window and gasped.

The dog bed. The telescope clattered to the floor and rolled away. The freaking dog bed was at the Villa, sitting right there on the table by the window that old redhead used for her floral arrangements. There was no missing its gilded posts and blue upholstery.

Then she remembered the Bombast Cable van she'd seen first at the Villa and then outside the Lancasters' house. They were so common that she'd hardly noticed. The Villa's residents had stolen the dog bed before she'd arrived. Why, she didn't know, but it also didn't matter.

She smiled, then flinched at the strain on facial muscles not often used. "Ha ha ha." The laugh sounded dry, but it was heartfelt. Providence had come through. She wouldn't even have to go to the trouble to plant the dog bed. The Villa's residents had taken care of it for her.

She'd call the police. Definitely. Right after she fed the kid.

CHAPTER NINETEEN

Breakfast over, the Villa's residents gathered in Adele's room. Gilda took up a commanding spot at the desk chair, once she'd pushed the easel closer to the wall. Grady and Mort borrowed chairs from Mary Rose's room across the hall. Father Vincent leaned in the doorway. Warren, not usually so interested in Booster Club matters, sat within protective reach of Adele.

"All right," Gilda said. Being a ringleader was really starting to agree with her. "Step one, steal painting at the Oak Hills golf club. Done."

"Thank you," Adele said.

"That was an easy one," Father Vincent added.

"Speak for yourself. Step two, the rest of the paintings. Claudine is working on it."

Adele lifted her head. "What's happened so far?"

"I talked with her last night." The memory of the awkwardness between them distracted Gilda a second, and she had to repeat herself. "I talked with her last night, and she says they've tracked down most of the paintings. A few have been sold since they were planted." Gilda turned to face Adele head-on. "One of them's in Carsonville."

"The Italian landscape. We got that one." Adele moved to the canvas. "Can I paint while you talk?"

"Fine. Mort, you move. I need that chair." Gilda situated herself and turned her head slightly to the side to pose. Once they were settled, she said, "Not the golf club painting. Another one. I can't quite remember the artist's name, but it's of a horse."

"George Stubbs," Adele said. "It was a job for the Cohen heist in New York. Some old heiress owned the original." She pushed at the blobs on her palette, seeming to wake them up.

"She died, and Christie's auctioned off her goods—what wasn't snatched up by her family, that is. The horse painting ended up in Carsonville. An art professor owns it." Gilda kept her gaze fastened on Adele's expression.

Adele's already pale face blanched as the realization sank in. The hand holding the paintbrush dropped. "He—"

"You think it might be him?"

"Who?" Warren asked.

Gilda sat back. This was Adele's deal to work out—or not—as she chose.

"I wouldn't be surprised if he was an art professor that I had in college." Adele's voice faltered. She set down the palette. "There aren't a lot of art professors in Carsonville. This one had the family money to buy a Stubbs."

"Speak up," Grady said.

"This is private," Gilda said.

"You're not happy about it. There's something else," Warren said. He looked so big compared to the girl. Gilda had seen a number of these Goliath-baby girl romances work out, though. Tiny little women with big, hairy guys. Often it was the women who ended up taking charge, too.

Adele tucked in her chin. "In college, I had a professor who worshipped eighteenth- and nineteenth-century artists. He called them the 'true' artists, and said they were some of the few who had mastered craft. He showed us so many slides simply of studies. You wouldn't believe how lifelike, yet spare, these drawings were. Not like anything these days."

"People learn to draw now," Mort said, undoubtedly thinking of his own mastery with his pocketknife.

"It's not valued the same way. Today, you can have a name for yourself as an artist and not be a competent draftsman."

It didn't escape Gilda that this era was Adele's specialty. The professor's ego couldn't take her skill. "And the professor's own work was contemporary, right?"

Adele nodded. "Can you find the name of the person who has the Stubbs?"

"Do you really want to know? I mean, given everything…."

She nodded again, this time with more urgency.

Gilda sighed. "I'll call Claudine right away, get a name."

"He took advantage of you, didn't he?" Warren asked. His tone held no menace. A big guy like him might have been threatening, but his voice was gentle. He didn't want to pummel the professor. He wanted to protect Adele.

"It was my fault, too," she said.

"It's never your fault when you're a child and he's someone with power, honey," Gilda said. "Don't you take the bait."

"I admit, I've heard enough of this in the confessional to back you up, Gilda," Father Vincent said.

"If nothing else, I must have that painting," Adele said, "I—"

The squawk of the P.A. system cut her off. "Mr. Copper on line one. Mr. Copper on line one."

The Villa's residents looked at each other. The announcement didn't have to do with a phone call. Oh, no. It meant something far worse. The residents scattered, Warren taking the lead.

"Get under the bed," Gilda yelled at Adele. "The police are here."

*
**

The Villa's residents sprang into action. With Adele hidden, Warren swapped out the room number outside with a plaque reading "Storage Closet" and locked the door from the outside.

Gilda only remembered having to do this once before, when a resident's nephew who was still in the business had decided to give the Villa a hot television set. That time, they played dumb, and the police were gone in twenty minutes. But that was a misdemeanor, and someone else's crime at that. Harboring a fugitive was serious business.

"Everyone!" Warren yelled. "Go to your places and get into your roles." He yanked an orderly's jacket from a closet and slipped it on as he raced down the stairs. Grady headed to his room to trace the police call.

"How did they find out about Adele?" Father Vincent asked. "I was sure no one followed us. The county's sedan was wiped. I don't get it."

"I don't know, but we'll walk through it later. For now, get to your room and get out that prayer book."

Gilda's job was to go to the cafeteria and play hard of hearing—but to listen intently and signal for reinforcements if needed. When she emerged from the elevator pushing her walker, two police officers stood in the entry hall, hands on their belts, talking to Warren.

"Sorry, officers," he said. "I was upstairs taking Mrs. Wilcox's blood pressure. How can I help you? Don't tell me one of our residents called you by mistake." He leaned forward in a conspiratorial way. "We see a bit of dementia from time to time, you know."

The officer on the right, the one nearly as big as Warren, wasn't having any of it. "We understand you have a rare dog bed on the premises."

Shoot. It wasn't Adele at all they were after. It was the dog bed.

Gilda saw Warren flinch. He recovered soon enough and pasted a surprised look on his face. "We don't allow animals in the Villa, officers, except for companion animals, and we don't have any in residence now. Could you be at the wrong address?"

Lord, that Warren was a smooth talker. They could have used someone with his talents back in the day. Now, if only he could keep them from searching out the dog bed—and finding Adele. Gilda knew that stealing the dog bed would probably cost them a few years in prison, but harboring a fugitive would shut the Villa down for good.

"We've got the right address, all right. Villa Saint Nicholas retirement home."

"If you don't mind, we'd like to have a look around," the smaller officer said. He had a dandy-ish way about him with his trimmed mustache and carefully manicured nails. In her younger years, Gilda would have had him eating out of her hand in five minutes. She shifted her gaze to Warren. He wouldn't insist on a search warrant. That would be too suspicious.

"Of course, by all means," Warren said.

One of the officers poked into Warren's office, right off the entry hall. He lifted a fat novel with a ballgown-clad woman and a bare-chested man on its cover and cast another glance at Warren, who kept a straight face.

"The residents' rooms?" the larger officer said.

"On the second and third floors," Warren said. "Down here we have the cafeteria, sick bay—that's the medical assistance room—and the TV room. Plus my office."

Gilda scooted to her place in the cafeteria. Bobby was already there, his deck of cards tucked in his shirt pocket. They both picked up magazines and did their best to affect a doddering look.

"Would you look at that," Bobby said. "A coupon for the casino bus." It was a well-known fact among younger people that seniors were obsessed with slot machines.

"I'll be darned," Gilda replied, keeping an eye on the police officers. If they were here for the dog bed, Grady knew by now. They'd take steps. Hopefully they had enough time.

"And here's the new TV schedule for the game shows. I just love game shows," Bobby said.

"All of us older folks do," Gilda said, then remembered she was supposed to be deaf. "Eh? I hope they have tuna noodle casserole for dinner." Dinner was, in fact, boeuf Bourguignon and a special Sunday dessert of lemon chiffon cake. Father Vincent was bringing out his homemade maraschino cherries for their Manhattans.

The policemen strode toward the table near the window. Gilda stiffened and looked back to Warren, who barely perceptibly nodded.

"What's this?" the larger policeman pointed to the dog bed.

"Eh?" Gilda added for good measure.

"Looks like a dog bed," the smaller policeman said.

Warren laughed nervously. "That thing?"

"You're a sharp one." She smiled and looked him in the eye. "It's a dog bed, all right."

"Wasn't the description of that Marie Antoinette bed that it was about this size, like a little canopy bed with blue cushions?" the dandy cop said, ignoring her.

"Yep, that's it," the larger policeman answered. "But something's not right."

They both stood, hands on hips, and studied the dog bed. Gilda glanced at Warren again, and this time he nodded more firmly.

"I don't see Marie Antoinette's dog bed having cushions made out of old towels," the larger cop said, finally. He pulled out the bed's cushion. "Says 'Lucky Casino' on it."

"We older folks enjoy our casinos," Bobby said from across the room.

"Kind of crude carving, too, on this post." The cop touched one, then drew back his hand. Gold paint stuck to his index finger.

"I see you found Mort's art project. He's making a bed for a friend's niece's Chihuahua." This part was true. Ruby would be delighted to have the bed for her rescues. "He saw something on the news about a queen's dog bed getting stolen, and he thought he'd make one himself."

"It matches the description from the tip line," the dandy said. "Ornate dog bed by the window."

"Busybodies." The larger policeman looked at his phone and pointed toward his partner, then the door. "Let's go. We're through here."

"Is that all, officer? Nothing else I can help you with?" Gilda raised an eyebrow, hoping her false eyelashes were still firmly secured. At the smaller cop's smile, she added, "Then I'll see you in my dreams."

The larger cop complained to his partner about "folks who call in anything they see" and "wasting our time."

As soon as the parking lot was clear, the Villa's residents crowded into the basement's furnace room. Everyone looked a few shades grayer under the room's single light bulb. The boiler kicked in, earning a yelp from Red, who stood next to it.

"You got it down here in time?" Warren said.

"Just barely. I told Father Vincent, and he hustled it into place."

Warren, pulling the orderly's jacket over his head as he crossed the room, adjusted a few knobs on the building's second water heater. Its front swung open. The Marie Antoinette dog bed rested safely inside. "Maybe we'd better keep it there for the moment."

"Good idea," Gilda said.

Warren closed the water heater and refastened its fake water lines. "I'll go up and let out Adele."

When the furnace room cleared, Gilda remained behind. Yes, they'd made it through this visit all right. They were prepared. But instead of being relieved, she was more wary than before.

Someone had called them in. Someone knew the dog bed was stolen and had seen Mort's model in the Villa's window. It could have been an innocent mistake. A passing pedestrian looked up, saw the dog bed, and called the cops. It happened sometimes. Some people didn't know how to keep their noses out of other people's business.

The old building's boiler kicked in, and its joists sighed in reply. Uneasiness stirred in her chest. Who would want to turn them in? Everyone at the Villa had run into trouble at some point in his career, but those chickens had come home to roost a long time ago. Gilda gripped her cane and made for the door. If it wasn't simply a nosy neighbor, they were in for a heap of trouble.

CHAPTER TWENTY

Gilda took the recliner in Grady's room, but perched on its edge to avoid the hassle of getting out of it later. After the police had left, the Villa began to quiet. Warren had extracted Adele from under the bed, where she'd said she had an idea for bringing more light to Gilda's eyes in the portrait. Father Vincent had brought out his high-end tools, in both American and metric measurements, and prepared to work in the carport until lunch. A few of the other residents had gathered in the cafeteria for a post-mortem of the drill.

Now, an hour later, Grady chuckled. "I wish I could have seen their faces when they found the one Mort started for Ruby."

"The carving was good," Gilda said. "It was the cushion that gave it away."

"Let's get down to business," Grady said. He swiveled his chair toward the computer monitor and woke up the screen.

With his bald top and cotton candy-like hair stuck out at all angles, Grady looked like the Wizard of Oz.

He clicked a few keys. "Okay, what do we write?"

"I'm worried," Gilda said.

"You want to tell him we're worried? How's that going to help things?"

"Ha ha. I mean I'm worried about the Villa. Someone tipped off the police about us. I think we're being watched."

"You don't think someone was walking down the street, happened to catch sight of Ruby's dog bed and said to himself, 'Say, that's the dog bed I saw on the news that belonged to that queen who got her head chopped off'?"

Gilda clasped her hands in her lap. "No, I don't. For one thing, you can't see the cafeteria window from the street. It's too far across the parking lot."

He leaned forward and lowered his voice. "Maybe we have a mole?"

She turned this over in her mind. All the Villa's residents except Adele had lived here for years. Warren was okay. Cook was okay. Their cleaning service was well vetted. Heck, they cleaned the manor for the head of the syndicate. The Villa was small potatoes for them. Hardly worth selling out for. As for the Villa's residents, everyone had a past to hide. For a resident to point a finger at another resident was mutually assured destruction.

"Nah. If someone here wanted to bring us down, it would have been done a long time ago. It's got to be someone on the outside," she said.

"Someone might have seen the dog bed come in," Grady pointed out.

"It was in a trash bag."

"Any visitors?"

"In the past day?" Gilda bit her lip. "Nope. Not even Mary Rose's niece."

"I hear she's moving to Omaha," Grady said.

"Hallelujah. I can't stand her griping. I see why Mary Rose plays deaf."

Gilda rose and pushed aside the curtains. Grady's room had a view of the street. No one would be able to spy on the Villa from this side, not with the trees in the way.

"Are we going to write this ransom note, or not?" Grady asked. "My show's on soon."

Gilda, still thinking, turned to Grady. "All right. Are you sure no one can trace it?"

"Absolutely. I use a dummy computer as a server, and send through that. The best experts won't be able to tell who or from where the message was sent. Now, hurry up."

Gilda returned to her chair. "I'm worried."

Grady pulled off his reading glasses. "I heard you the first time. I can't speak for the rest of it, but I can tell you that this note will be safe. It's fine." He patted her arm and swiveled again to his laptop. "I'm ready."

She unclenched her hands. "Okay. Take this down. 'Dear Dr. Lancaster. We have your Marie Antoinette dog bed. We will return it if you will perform surgery on a particular patient within three days."

"Slow down. I'm catching up." He clacked at the keyboard. "Three days. You think that's enough time?"

"We don't want to give him too much time. A week is too long."

"Fine. You got the photo, right?"

Minutes later, the note was sent.

Gilda returned to her room and raised the blinds. Her room was on the top floor, two floors above the cafeteria. If anyone watched them, she should be able to make out their vantage point from here.

Straight down, Father Vincent tinkered in the carport to the left. She caught flashes of his daisy-patterned work skirt. The parking lot's six spots were empty except for Warren's Jeep and Cook's bicycle. They didn't need cars with Father Vincent more than happy to chauffeur them wherever they needed to go.

To the right was the street. Soon the trees lining it would be fully leafed out, and she'd only be able to make out the occasional neighborhood resident walking his dog.

Across the parking lot, on the other side of a chain link fence, was the school. Its playground wrapped the school from the left in an "L" shape. The school was a floor shorter than the Villa and much bigger. Today was Sunday, so the playground was quiet, and the school's windows dark.

Gilda opened the door to the hall and yelled, "Red!"

Holding a magazine, the white-haired woman stepped into the hall. "What?"

"Can anyone see in on this side of the Villa?"

"I should say not. At least, I haven't noticed anyone."

"Can I borrow your binoculars?" Red kept a set of army-issue binoculars for watching the street. She'd especially chosen the room, despite having Grady and his TV below, for its access to the street. She'd even paid a tree trimming crew to prune away a few branches to widen her view. She knew everyone's business from the lawyer with the never-ending series of girlfriends in the blue foursquare to the bookstore owner in the bungalow.

"Not the night vision set?"

"No. The regular ones."

"All right. If you give them back. I'm expecting the Stephensons' mother-in-law to show up soon. That's usually a good show."

"I just want to borrow them for a few minutes." Gilda took the heavy binoculars to her window and trained them at the school. The improvement in the view was astonishing. She understood Red's attraction. Gilda could even make out the ratty sweater hanging behind a teacher's desk and the construction paper Humpty Dumpties on the wall.

Adjusting the binoculars slightly as she went, she swept the row of classrooms. If someone had seen the dog bed, it would have been just after they brought it in on Saturday or on Sunday morning, when Ruby's copy was finished. The school should have been closed.

Now this was curious. In a second floor classroom, a little boy sat in a beanbag chair and read a book. All by himself. Gilda scanned the classrooms again but saw no adults. How did he get in, and what was he doing there? The boy had a stack of books next to him with a dirty dinner plate and fork resting on it.

A boy wouldn't have turned them in. No, she couldn't see that. But there was no adult with him? None at all?

At a split-second glimmer, she raised the binoculars. It seemed to have come from the attic. Must have been her imagination. Dirt clouded the attic's windows. At best, it was used for storage. No one would be in there. Would they?

Gilda lowered the binoculars and took the elevator to Bobby's room, directly below hers.

"What?" came his voice from inside.

"It's Gilda. I need to look out your window."

"Can't it wait? I'm taking a nap."

"Let me in."

A moment later, the door opened, and Gilda marched to the window past Bobby's stack of *Popular Mechanics* magazines and memorabilia from his honeymoon in Honolulu fifty years earlier. She raised the blinds here, too, and trained her binoculars at the attic, hoping the new angle would reveal something. Nope. The attic was just as dark, its windows just as blackened by dirt.

It must have been her imagination. She lowered the binoculars.

"You finished?" Bobby's comb-over flopped to the side. "I need my beauty rest."

"Yeah. Thanks." Gilda took the elevator upstairs again. She wanted Red's back-up binoculars.

CHAPTER TWENTY-ONE

Ellie lounged in the school's attic and read the Sunday newspaper, thoughtfully delivered to the school's front door and brought in by Josiah. A plate recently divested of trail mix and a stale ham sandwich sat next to her, along with two Hiya-Toots candy bars, a thermos of tea, and enough assorted liquor bottles to create a serviceable bar—all pilfered from teachers' desks.

A few shots of rum after lunch had helped her overcome her anger at watching the police go into the Villa and return to their cars ten minutes later, empty-handed. She'd given them as clean a tip as they needed: the Marie Antoinette dog bed was in the Villa's cafeteria. She'd watched as they'd examined it. And she saw them point and laugh. And leave.

Beneath the rum's haze, her blood simmered. All those months of planning down the toilet, then this. Why? She'd given the police a hot lead. Either they'd blown it, or the dog bed was bogus.

She gripped the newspaper so tightly that a fistful ripped away. Sucking in a deep breath, she turned the page and ran her gaze over the local news. A headline drew her attention. Someone had escaped from the Carsonville Women's Correctional Facility. Ellie remembered John the orderly mentioning it. He'd actually been concerned for her, the chump. She drew the paper nearer the lamp she'd taken from the faculty lounge. The mugshot showed a fine-boned woman with long, wispy hair and huge eyes. She looked scared witless. Yet she somehow had the moxie to escape. Go figure.

Facing the article about the escapee was a story on the Marie Antoinette dog bed. Its accompanying photo matched Mitzi's description exactly, except that it didn't appear to be dampened with bitter tears. B. E. Lancaster was offering a fifty thousand dollar reward for information leading to its discovery.

"I don't care," she said aloud. "Why should I give a damn?"

"What?" Josiah said.

She'd almost forgotten he was there. He was an easy kid to hang around. "Nothing."

She shook the paper between her hands to straighten it and turned the page to international news. War, unemployment, environmental crisis, famine. Famine. The article about families going hungry showed ridiculously thin children. Not even the Blaylock sisters at the Women's League wanted to be that thin. Ellie glanced at Josiah. He still had fat on his bones, but shouldn't a kid his age have a little extra padding on the cheeks? He was awfully pale, too. And his pants were practically capris at this point. Well, he wasn't her problem.

"Food insecurity," the paper said, and went on for half a page peppered with words including "malnutrition," "dysentery," "anemia," and "bone loss." Someone should do something about that. She was no bleeding heart liberal, but dang it, kids needed to eat.

She tossed aside the paper's front section and picked up the society pages. The Carsonville Women's League was holding one of its infernal fundraisers tomorrow night. Betsy would be swanning around like a pasha, so proud to be president of the club now. That loser.

Ellie stretched her arms and let them flop to her side. What was she going to do now? She couldn't live here forever eating elementary school gruel and sleeping on a couch. It crossed her mind that she could return to the Bedlamton Arms. She could go back and say that she'd learned her lesson, and she knew she was better off with them. They'd take her back in a heartbeat, what with the hefty fees they charged. Plus, they wouldn't have to admit that she'd escaped. The mattresses were comfortable. She sighed at the memory of her featherbed. The food wasn't bad, either. She could wait out her time.

But the Booster Club would have won. It would have had the last word. Her resolve steeled. She shoved the society section aside and picked up the telescope. Down in the Villa, the regulars doddered around in the cafeteria. The skirted man polished a vintage Mercedes's hood. The old redhead was doing something in her room. She had the shades up, too. That was unusual.

Ellie moved away from the window. She couldn't have caught on to her, could she? No. Impossible. She took the telescope to the window again and trained it on the redhead's window. The old woman had moved back now, but there was no mistaking the binoculars on the nearby vanity, right next to a giant bottle of cologne.

Now the woman — Gilda, Ellie reminded herself — was back, but she was facing the room, not the window. She had someone with her, a smaller, younger woman with short hair. The smaller woman went to the window and looked out, her wide-eyed gaze sweeping the parking lot, the street, and up to the school, before the old redhead yanked her back and closed the blinds.

The girl looked very familiar.

"Josiah, bring me that paper."

"This one?" The boy had folded the front section into a hat.

"Give it here." Ellie hastily unfolded the paper and smoothed it on the couch. She held up the photo of the prison escapee and gasped. It was her, no doubt about it. She now had shorter hair, but the woman she had just seen at the Villa was the woman in the newspaper. There was no mistaking those eyes and the shape of her chin. Plus, Gilda had tried to hide her.

The Villa was harboring a fugitive.

Adrenaline streaked through Ellie's body, exploding into joyous fireworks. She leapt to her feet. She'd call the police right this minute.

"Princess, are you okay?" Josiah asked.

"I'm better than okay." Laughter sputtered from some unknown internal fount and poured out. At once, she frowned at the strange eruption.

"Are you sure?" The boy, a book about dinosaurs in one hand, stared at her.

"Yes, you're right," she replied to her own thoughts, not the boy's words. "You must be careful."

"Careful about what?" Josiah said.

Ellie sat on the couch. "Hush. I'm thinking."

She could call the police again. They'd be suspicious about another tip about the Villa, especially when the first one had been a dud. She snatched up the paper. Adele Waterson, the escapee's name was. It was possible that Adele was simply passing through. Merely dropping by to visit the redhead or pick up supplies to leave town. But Ellie thought this was unlikely. As she herself well knew, you didn't run off from a lockdown facility and publicly take the air afterward. Once you went to ground, you stayed there until it was safe. It was not yet safe.

Ellie leaned back. She wadded her shawl and stuffed it under her derriere to soften the jab of a sofa spring. She needed to be sure

Adele was hiding out at the Villa, and she needed details. Then and only then would she call the police.

The plan started to fall into place. School would be in session tomorrow, but she had the rest of the day and all night tonight to work. Ellie relaxed, a feeling more mellow and satisfying than Miss Morris's bottle of rum had provided. Luck favors the prepared, they always said. No one was more prepared than Eleanor Whiteby.

"I'm hungry," Josiah said.

"You just ate."

"I'm still hungry."

With purpose and direction, Ellie rose. "Come on, kid. I'll fix you an extra large bowl of chili and a hamburger."

"Can I have another chocolate milk?"

"Sure. But then you're going home. Princess has work to do."

CHAPTER TWENTY-TWO

The weekend had been a big one for breakups, Gilda noted. She tucked a branch of teasel into an especially elaborate bouquet ordered by a woman who'd told her, "Spare no expense. The uglier and deader the better." She was sending a messenger to pick it up in a few minutes. Gilda carefully glued a dead fly, harvested legs up from the cafeteria's windowsill, to the teasel's spiky globe. She didn't like to brag, but she had a knack for this.

"Gilda," Grady said, coming in the door, "we got back a reply from the brain surgeon."

"And?" Her old blackmail sangfroid was back. She was the conductor of this orchestra, and Grady was letting her know the violins were tuning up.

"He says no can do."

"What?" She pricked herself with the teasel and dropped it on the table. "That can't be."

"Here, let me read it." Grady slipped on a pair of thick-lensed glasses. "No salutation."

She nodded. "Go on."

"'You cannot expect me to operate on a patient without knowing his medical background and without the proper tests and scans, particularly a CT scan.'"

"What's a CT scan?"

"That picture we showed Doc Parisot. I'm not finished. 'I want the Marie Antoinette *lit de chien* returned.'" Grady looked up. "That's got to mean 'dog bed.'"

"What else?"

"'However, I cannot violate the Hippocratic oath by taking my scalpel to an innocent's skull.'"

"Good grief," Gilda said.

"What do we do? He's right, you know." He swiveled toward her. "I could send him her medical file."

"You could. Then, on top of everything else, they could bag us for stealing private info. Plus, we don't know exactly what the surgeon needs." Giving herself a moment to think, Gilda returned to her floral arrangement. They hadn't worked this all the way through. She fluffed a branch of dead oak leaves. "I'm sure Dr. Lancaster has to get records from other doctors all the time. He can get these." As the words came out of her mouth, she realized what they meant.

So did Grady. "He'll know who she is. He'll know he's operating on an escaped prisoner."

"Will that matter to him?"

A minivan pulled into the parking lot outside the cafeteria window, and Warren went out to greet it. Gilda tensed. She was still on edge from the police's visit that morning. She still wondered if they were being watched.

Warren appeared in the cafeteria with a man chewing gum. "I'm here for the floral arrangement," the man said.

"Here's a Bad Seed original for you."

The man's jaw froze for a second before resuming chewing. "Got it." A dead leaf fell off the bouquet and skittered in his wake as he left.

Warren frowned. Whether it was because of Adele's presence and risk to the Villa, or anxiety left over from the police's earlier visit, Gilda didn't know. "Don't be upset," she told him. The aroma of coq au vin wafted from the kitchen. Cook would want to set the tables soon. "It won't be for long. We'll have the business with Adele wrapped up soon, and Larry will get our relicensing taken care of. We'll be clean again."

"I know." He turned toward his office, but Gilda grabbed his sleeve.

"How are things with Adele?" she asked.

His expression softened. "Fine. I'm giving her a tour of the Villa after dinner."

"Enough of this romantic nonsense," Grady said. "What are we going to tell the surgeon? I need a reply."

They didn't have much time. They needed to get Adele to the surgeon the sooner the better—for a lot of reasons. If Adele were captured after the operation, at least she'd have the possibility of living. Larry the Fence would certainly rather she be alive in prison than dead on the streets. They'd have to gamble that the surgeon cared more about his fancy dog bed than he did about the law. They had no choice.

"Tell him Adele's name and the prison's. Then say the rest is his problem."

✳︎
✳︎✳︎

"Adele? Are you ready?"

Dinner was over, and most of the Villa's residents were playing cards in the cafeteria or watching *The French Connection*—again—in the TV room.

She'd eagerly said yes. She'd had a good day painting and still felt the exhilarating combination of exhaustion and amped-up energy she remembered from her days in the studio. The portrait was really coming along. As tired as she was, she wasn't ready for bed. And she'd been looking forward to Warren's company. The Villa's residents were great—caring, funny, sweet—but with Warren she felt she was with a real friend.

Warren, ever the gentleman, waited in the hall while she exchanged the too-large slippers Red had lent her for her own prison-issue sneakers.

"Ready," she said.

"Follow me. We'll start in the basement." Warren led her down the stairway at the far end of the hall.

Even after the police's visit that morning and hiding under the bed, she felt safe at the Villa. Warren would protect her. "How did the Villa get started?" she asked once they were in the stairwell's quiet.

"After World War II, a few members of the community—"

"The criminal community," Adele ventured.

"Right. Well, they started pitching in one percent of their earnings into a kitty for their retirement. Not everyone would be using the Villa, but it was a way they could look after each other. Art Mandenheim, an embezzlement consultant—he's passed now—did the investing and bought the Villa. Hank Dupin, also passed, managed it."

"Was it a house before?" The Villa didn't quite feel like an old mansion, but it didn't feel like an institution, either.

"An old hospital, actually. Abandoned during the Great Depression."

"It doesn't seem like a hospital." The Villa's walls smelled of old wood, not antiseptic. Plus, it was so small.

"They used to be like this, I guess. Some were smaller, more like homes."

They reached the heavy basement door. Warren selected a key from his crowded key ring and unlocked a deadbolt. "Here's the building's heart and soul."

"You keep it locked?"

"You'll see why."

Adele might have called the cafeteria the Villa's center, not the basement. At the sight of the pride radiating from Warren's face, she didn't contradict him. She shifted her gaze to the basement. "It looks so tidy."

They stood in a large, open room with the usual machinery Adele expected in a basement—water heaters, boiler, a workbench—but it might have been a salon for its cleanliness and faint scent of roses. The cement floor and the pipes running along its ceiling were white-washed and scrubbed.

"Thank you." He gestured toward a bulky machine connected to pipes and vents. His pit bull tattoo rippled over a bicep. "Here we have the furnace. I'm a licensed boiler operator, you know."

"This is yours?" She touched a framed certificate. "That's terrific."

"It's not an easy boiler, either. Original to the building. But I bet you haven't heard a single clank in the radiators."

"I barely even knew they were there," Adele said truthfully. "I see you have a reading spot. Looks cozy." In the corner was an armchair and reading light with a stack of paperback novels next to it.

"During the day, I stick to my office to keep an eye on comings and goings. I like some time to myself, though. It's quiet down here."

She understood why he might find the dim light and occasional hum of the furnace comforting. If she half-shuttered her eyes, she could pretend she was in a gentleman's den with the curtains drawn.

"How did you come to the Villa?"

He looked at the ceiling and touched a valve before replying. "I used to be a prison guard."

"Oh."

"I, well…."

She waited.

"It's kind of embarrassing." He crouched to straighten the stack of novels. "I accidentally helped someone smuggle in plans to escape."

"By accident," Adele said.

"I thought they were love letters."

For a moment, their gazes met. For such a tough-looking guy, he had the soft brown eyes of a Labrador puppy. He looked away first.

"Love letters," Adele said softly.

"That's what they told me. They didn't want the guards reading their, um, sentiments, so I said I'd deliver them, bypass the other guards. I guess I was a sucker."

"Or a romantic," she said.

Seeming embarrassed, he gestured toward a door. "Let me show you the laundry facilities. I installed energy efficient front-loading washers last fall."

For the next hour, they roamed the building. Warren pointed out the heavy safe built into a closet's wall. He spun its dial. "It was here when the residents moved in. It gets cracked at least once a month for practice." He opened the linen closet to stacks of white towels and the scent of lavender. He pointed out the old morgue, now Grady's air-conditioned server room.

Warren showed her the basement storage units he'd carefully labeled and the laundry chutes on both sides of the building. She noted a rack of sequined and feathered gowns labeled with Gilda's name. He walked her through the cook's larder, complete with a ham airing in the cooler and a shelf full of cookbooks. A chalkboard carefully laid out the month's menus and the residents' dietary restrictions.

They ended the tour in Warren's office. He unlocked a closet, revealing a computer with two screens. "Here's the Villa's security center."

"For what?"

"We have alarms set up at the entrances and a few special systems depending on the situation. Remember when the police arrived?"

She nodded. "I didn't hear an alarm."

"Remember an announcement on the P.A. system about a call from Mr. Copper on line one?"

She smiled. "Clever." They really had thought of everything. Even how to hide an escaped criminal, she reminded herself. She pointed at the grocery sack of novels on the floor. "Those your books?"

He folded his arms. "Yes, I like romance novels. So what?"

"I didn't say anything. I think it's sweet."

"They're going to the cafeteria for the others to read. Then I'll take them down to Twice-Told Tales to trade for new ones." He picked up a book featuring a voluptuous woman in an empire-waisted gown and a man in a kilt holding a sword. "Do you believe in love at first sight?" He partially turned away. "I don't know why I asked that. You don't have to answer."

"Warren," she said and waited until he faced her again. "You don't have to be embarrassed. It's a good question."

When she'd first seen Oliver Degraff, her professor, he'd stridden into the classroom late. The students already sat at their easels in a circle. From the first moment, she couldn't tear her gaze away from him. He was so sure of himself, so confident in how he snatched a stick of charcoal from one student's hand to demonstrate the proper line and turned another student's easel toward the rest of the class and drew a fat "X" through his drawing.

He mesmerized all the students, but he chose her. Almost immediately he singled her out, asking her to stop by his office after class. Her stomach had roiled with nerves, and she'd jealously watched his interactions with other women. She'd been desperate for him to feel the same overwhelming need for her that she'd felt for him.

It had happened at first sight, all right. But was that love?

"I don't know," Adele said. "What do you think?"

Warren had been watching her turn it over in her mind. He dropped his gaze and busied himself straightening the books. "I don't know, either. Just a question."

To change the subject, Adele picked up a framed photo on his desk of a pit bull lounging on a bed next to a tabby kitten. "That's the dog in your tattoo, isn't it?"

"Goldie. My old dog and my ex's cat." He took the photograph and smiled. "She was a tough-looking dog, but had a heart of gold."

She raised her eyes to him. His ex. Interesting. He had a lot in common with his dog, too, at least heart-wise. "What happened to her?" Adele asked.

"She was chasing a squirrel and got hit by a car. I still can't bear to remember it."

"I'm sorry. I meant your girlfriend."

"Oh. Her." He dropped his arms and nudged the bag of books with a foot. "Didn't work out."

"I see."

"You" — he swallowed, and his cheeks pinked — "uh, would you like a cup of tea?"

A flowered teapot sat on the credenza behind his desk. Instead of the matching teacups she'd expected, he had a John Deere mug.

This was the tipping point. She felt it all the way through. If she accepted his mug of tea, she was committing to knowing him better. They might talk about death, and life, and maybe even the future. They would cross a line, whether they explicitly recognized it or not.

Had it been another day, she might have taken him up on his offer. She would have wanted to get to know that romantic part of him as well as the part that was so handy with boilers. She might ask him about the hook-shaped scar on his thumb or what tricks he'd trained Goldie to do. She hadn't learned anything yet about his family, where he went to school, what he planned for the future. If anything.

But she'd only be at the Villa for a little while longer. As soon as she knew her paintings were taken care of, she'd leave. As for the surgery the Villa's residents were so keen on her getting, she wasn't counting on it. Convincing a famous brain surgeon to operate on an escaped felon was a tall order. But she was strangely calm about the fact.

She touched Warren's hand. Her finger rested on the callused edge of a thumb. "Thank you, but no. I'd better get to bed."

Warren dropped his gaze. She couldn't miss his disappointment. "Good night," he whispered.

She slept fitfully. Her thoughts, full of "what if?" kept her from dropping into the rest she needed. Occasional noises—steps in the hall? The stairwell door opening?—nudged her from the shallow rest she managed.

In her head, the dull ache began to grow.

CHAPTER TWENTY-THREE

Finally, the last lights flicked off in the Villa. Ellie lowered her telescope. She'd give the geezers another hour to settle down, then she'd investigate in person.

She mixed herself a Manhattan as she waited out the time in the dark. Too bad the school's food offerings weren't as good as its liquor. She'd already tidied the school kitchen so that no one would suspect her having been there when classes started in the morning. Naturally, she'd packaged up some food to go for Josiah, the poor little brat. What kind of parent left her kid to wander the neighborhood like a stray dog? Honestly.

By two in the morning, according to the digital watch she'd pilfered from the lost and found box, Ellie was ready to go. She wasn't going to muff it this time. Before she called the police, she'd have rock-solid evidence that the art forger was there.

She slipped out the school's side door, carefully sticking a strip of duct tape over the lock to keep it open. The spring night was cool, and a fine mist permeated the air. In the distance, a car engine rumbled, then passed. Not a single light was on in the row of houses facing the Villa.

Keeping to the school's wall, Ellie hurried to the street, then up to the Villa's side entrance. Oh, she knew better than to simply pick the lock and enter. She examined the door with the pen light she'd taken from the nurse's station. There it was. A tiny wire, barely perceptible, ran down the doorframe to the door's latch. She snipped it and bit off a laugh. They thought they were so smart. Working with her body over the latch to muffle noise, Ellie easily picked the lock. She was in.

She was on the first floor corridor running the Villa's length. She knew from floor plans that on her right beyond the wall was an office, then, moving down the building's length was the hall to the front entrance, then the kitchen and cafeteria. On her left were two public rooms, a hospital room, and the elevator. Immediately to her left was the staircase to the second and third floors, where the bedrooms were. And where the art forger—if she were here—most likely slept.

Breathing through her mouth to keep from making the slightest noise, Ellie turned the door handle to the stairwell. The door opened without a creak. She mentally tipped her hat to whoever maintained the place. On the second floor, the door opened just as soundlessly.

Carpet lined the second floor's corridor. A single ceiling light shone by the elevator, but otherwise the floor might not have been inhabited, for all she could tell. But she knew each room held some old person dreaming of denture cleaner or President Eisenhower or whatever old folks dreamed about. Seniors were supposed to be light sleepers. It didn't matter. She wouldn't make a sound.

Each door had a nameplate beside it. She raised her penlight. "Red," this one said. Then "Grady," "Mary Rose," and others. At the end of the hall, the side opposite the school and furthest from the street, the room's nameplate was empty.

Ellie's nostrils quivered. Turpentine. That's what she smelled. Turpentine and oil paints. A shot of joy more potent than Miss Morris's rum hit her bloodstream. The art forger was here all right.

Just then, on the opposite side of the building, a door creaked, followed by a shuffle across the carpet. Someone was coming. Ellie swallowed a curse and flattened herself against the wall. Her heart beat so loudly she was sure it would awaken everyone along the corridor. The person—it looked like a man—hitched slowly to the elevator and pressed the call button. The elevator hummed to the second floor and opened. Ellie wanted to close her eyes to shut out the inevitable, but she couldn't. She stared toward the man.

Just as he went into the elevator, he turned his head toward her end of the hall. She didn't know if she was deep enough into the hall to be lost in the dark. She could only hope in her black outfit, her hands pressed behind her, she melted into the shadow.

He didn't flinch. He showed no signs of having seen her.

The elevator door closed. Ellie fled down the hall, down the stairs, and out to the street.

CHAPTER TWENTY-FOUR

Gilda dreamed she was on a battleship, far at sea. The ship's alarm whoop-whoop-whooped through the dark. It was especially annoying since she'd just made a date with Gary Cooper for a trek around the ship's deck — the long way.

As consciousness surfaced, she realized she wasn't dreaming at all. It was the Villa's alarm system, code two. A break-in. She looked at the clock. Good Lord. Not even dawn. She stumbled for her robe and pushed her walker into the hall.

The elevator was already filling with the Villa's residents. Someone had roused Grady, who shut off his hearing aid at night and wouldn't have been able to hear the alarm. Bobby put in his dentures as the elevator clacked to the ground floor. They filed into the cafeteria.

Warren was already there, the television's remote control in hand. His pit bull tattoo was a jarring counterpoint to the teddy bear-covered pajamas. Despite the dark and early hour, he'd closed the blinds. Blessedly, he'd also started coffee brewing.

"Is everyone here?" he asked. Gilda saw him scan the crowd, counting heads.

Bobby's comb-over dangled in strands over his left ear. He patted the chest of his bathrobe, then dropped his hand as if realizing he didn't have on his usual work shirt with its handy deck of cards.

Father Vincent also had on a bathrobe, but a long flannel nightgown peeked from its bottom. In her pink peignoir, Mary Rose dressed better than she did during the day. Grady sat behind her. Mort had somehow managed to grab his pocketknife on the way down and was finessing the ears on a carving of a basset hound.

"Where's Red?"

"Here I am." Red found a seat and unstrapped off her night vision goggles.

"What's going on?" Adele stood in the cafeteria's doorway, tiny in her oversized flannel nightgown.

"Break-in, eh?" Bobby said. "Or a false alarm?"

"Nope. Someone clipped the alarm at the north entry, but they didn't know about the security cameras."

Chills ran down Gilda's back and arms. Just as she'd expected. Someone was after them. Who? They had two liabilities on hand now, the dog bed and Adele. They'd taken measures to hide both of them. Could someone have found out?

"Father Vincent, will you dim the lights? Thank you." Warren pointed the remote at the TV.

The black and white film showed a small shape, likely a woman, coming down the first floor hall in jerky motion. She wore a long, black dress. The time stamp said three a.m., less than half an hour ago. Warren paused the video.

"No bag, no tools," Bobby said. "A thief would come prepared."

"But she's in all black," Red pointed out.

"And she picked the side door locks and disabled the alarm," Warren said. "Signs of a professional."

And yet, not. A professional would have anticipated the cameras. "Was anything stolen?" Gilda asked.

"Not that I can find," Warren said.

"Or planted?" Father Vincent asked.

A good question. Gilda's pulse quickened. Someone was after them. They might have set up a bug—or planted something worse, like stolen goods.

"I'll do a sweep. But watch the film. She didn't pause long enough to plant anything, at least, nothing carefully." Warren resumed the video.

The film showed the woman's shape disappear into the stairwell. Warren clicked the remote, and the feed shifted. "Third floor," he said. The shape hesitated a moment outside the staircase door, then moved past the elevator and down the hall.

Gilda held her breath. "Adele," she whispered.

"That's my room," Adele said. "I didn't hear anything."

The shape hovered outside Adele's door. For a few seconds, the fish eye's view showed she didn't move. Then, so fast that the camera caught it in only two frames, the woman flattened herself into Adele's doorway. The Villa's residents jumped.

Warren clicked the remote again, and the camera shifted to show Grady, oblivious, getting into the elevator.

"I'll be a son of a sea biscuit," Grady said. "I went to get a liverwurst sandwich. Had no idea at all. My hearing aid, you know."

"She's after Adele," Warren said. "Right there, in her doorway. If Grady hadn't shown up…."

The shape on the security camera shot down the hall and disappeared into the stairwell. Warren clicked off the television.

"Who knows you're here?" Father Vincent said.

Adele looked genuinely bewildered. "No one. No one knows I'm here. Except Uncle Larry, I guess."

"What about the art supply person?" Mary Rose said.

"He didn't have a name, just instructions on where to leave the box."

"None of you—" Warren started.

"No, no," a chorus of voices and shaking heads replied.

Gilda's uneasiness deepened. "The police came yesterday. Someone called them about the dog bed. So it might not just be Adele they're after." She gratefully took the cup of coffee Father Vincent handed her, but she left it on the table untouched.

"You mean someone's watching us?" Red said.

"Someone wants to bring down the Villa," Gilda said. "Somehow, he saw Adele and put two and two together. I've looked out all our windows, and I can't figure out where he's watching from."

"The bigger question is, who is it?" Warren said.

Mort shook his head. "Someone willing to break in, and someone crafty enough to snip off the alarm."

"But not notice the camera," Bobby added.

"If this is true, he knows Adele is here. We can expect another visit from the police," Warren said.

"At any time. Probably sooner than later," Red said.

Adele shrank against the wall. "I'm sorry, everyone. I've put you all at risk."

It was time. No more monkeying around or relying on their wits, like they did the last time the police came. Whoever was spying on them wasn't content with watching from the outside. This time, the intruder had only spent a few minutes in the Villa. But next time?

CHAPTER TWENTY-FIVE

When the police arrived just after dawn, they were all in their places. Most of the Villa was down in the cafeteria, talking about their fictional Bingo outing that night. Everyone knew that seniors liked Bingo. The fact that they were up with the birds wasn't a problem—people expected seniors to be early risers. A few of the residents would be in the TV room loudly discussing the finer points of liquid meals.

Adele was in her place. At least, she should be by now, Gilda thought. And Gilda was in hers. In Adele's room.

"Mr. Copper on line one," the P.A. system announced. It was happening. Two minutes later Gilda heard the policemen's steps in the hall, creaking the floorboards under the carpet. Of course, they'd come here first. She wasn't surprised.

The door burst open. Gilda leapt back, rattling her walker. "Gentlemen."

Two policemen, the same officers as before, filled the door, each with a hand on his gun. "Stay still," one of them said.

Gilda lowered her paintbrush. She felt a thrill standing behind the easel, and she'd added a few dabs of paint to brighten the portrait's diamond bracelet. She even liked the painter's smock she borrowed from Red, who used it for gardening. Maybe when this was all over, she'd take up painting, too.

The vacuum cleaner roared in the hall.

"What's the idea here? Julia," Gilda yelled. "What do they want?"

Adele clicked off the vacuum and ducked her head into the room. "I don't know, ma'am. They came right in and insisted on coming to your room." Her wig and glasses, combined with the housekeeper's dress, made her look like a nerdy maid on her way to chess club. This was Bobby's idea. He'd suggested that the best way to hide Adele would be to put her in plain sight.

Gilda stepped from behind the canvas and put her hands on her hips. "You've heard about me? Take a look at my work. Not bad, eh?"

The policemen exchanged glances. "We're going to need to search the room," the skinny one said.

"You painted yourself?" the other one said, looking at the canvas. "Why shouldn't I?"

"You take the bathroom," the dandy cop said. "I'll search in here." Keeping an eye on Gilda, he crouched to look under the bed.

"What exactly are you looking for, gentlemen?" Gilda asked. "Maybe I can help you."

"A woman named Adele Waterson."

Gilda shrieked in laughter. Deciding she'd overdone it, she cut it off mid-cackle. "You're joking. You think I've hidden someone in here?"

"We got a citizen's report. We need to follow up."

"What did this Irene—?"

"Adele. Adele Waterson," the policeman said.

"Yes, well, why are you looking for her?"

"She escaped from prison."

Gilda fumbled with the paintbrush. "And someone saw her run in here? I don't suppose this citizen has a name?"

"Anonymous tip line," the smaller cop said.

"This Ir — I mean, Adele. She's a murderer, then."

The bigger cop lifted the curtains behind Gilda and, finding them empty, let them go. "An art forger."

"Is there money in that?" Gilda squinted at the canvas. "I'm asking for a friend."

"If you have what you need, I'd better get back to making up the rooms," Adele-alias-Julia said.

"Sure, go on." Gilda waved her paintbrush toward the hall. "Wait. You. Policeman. Any dust bunnies under there?"

The dandy policeman rose from the floor. "That's not my business. There's no woman under there."

"Never mind," Gilda said. "You can go." This part she directed at Adele, who disappeared down the hall.

The larger policeman went to the bathroom and emerged with a bra dangling from one hand. "No one. But I found this."

The policemen looked at the bra's tiny cups, then shifted their gaze to Gilda's ample chest.

She lifted her chin. "And?"

"That's yours?" the skinny cop said.

Gilda raised an eyebrow as if daring him to question her.

The dandy cop let out a long breath. "Anything else in there?"

"Toothbrush, hairbrush, the usual."

"All right. It could be that crank again who called about the dog bed. I suppose we'd better have a look around the rest of the place, though." On his way out the door, he stopped and turned. "You people have any enemies? You've been called in twice in three days."

For the first time, Gilda let her voice drop to its normal register. "Not that I know of."

He shook his head. "Usually it's the other way around. The older folks call in the high school kids next door."

"You're sure you can't tell me who called? We should know. If people are harassing us, like you say—"

"Nothing I can tell you. Anonymous tip." He touched his hat. "Have a nice day, ma'am."

In the distance, doors opened and shut as the policemen went room to room.

Gilda settled on the bed's edge. Who was after them? Who wanted to bring them down? Each of the Villa's residents had left a disgruntled person or two in his or her past. One of Ricardo's exes used to come by regularly and curse him out for bigamy, but Ricardo had died at least five years ago. Every once in a while someone from the diocese would stop by to try to convince Father Vincent to return to the ministry, but he told them he had his own ministry now. For the most part, the Villa's residents had quit their careers years ago. They hadn't received as much as a threatening letter since.

The only recent business the Villa was involved in had been the Booster Club. Last fall, they'd brought down a real estate developer who'd wanted to thwart their plans to turn an old firehouse into a family shelter. Gilda stifled a chuckle. Eleanor Whiteby Millhouse. That goody two shoes that Claudine had always had it in for. She was in an institution somewhere now, though.

Or was she?

*
**

Telescope pressed to the attic window, Ellie watched the police drive away. Alone. They had spent longer in the Villa this time, searching door to door. She'd seen them pop up in bedrooms here and there and then again in the cafeteria, where they'd even pointed at the dog bed and laughed. Half a dozen of the residents had waved goodbye to the police as they drove off an hour later holding what looked like homemade muffins.

How did the Villa's residents do it? The fugitive had to be there. Had to. She'd smelled the paints. But somehow those criminals had hidden her. She pulled away from the window. Then again, she'd only glanced at what looked like the escaped art forger. Maybe she was mistaken. Maybe the police had searched, thoroughly, and found no one. In her desperation to nail the Villa, she'd been too hasty.

Ellie tossed the telescope on the sofa and paced the attic. The bell rang for the start of school, and sounds of children laughing and yelling rose from the playground. Josiah would be there. She wondered if he'd had breakfast. She'd half expected him to come up to visit her. It was probably best that he hadn't. Maybe he'd stop by after school.

By then, she needed to have a plan to deal with the Villa. Maybe she was foolish to try to get the police to do her work. Maybe she needed to do it herself. *Think, Ellie. Think.* What tools did she have at hand?

She idly picked up the telescope and examined the Villa once again. The homeless guy she'd seen the other day pushed his shopping cart full of dying flowers to the Villa's front entrance. The old redhead, clothed in some kind of ridiculous paint-stained smock, came out to greet him.

Ellie set down the telescope, this time carefully. She laughed once, a shotgun "ha." She had an idea.

CHAPTER TWENTY-SIX

At this hour, the school was lousy with children. Ellie could have screamed with frustration. But, no. Calm was what she needed.

When she ran the real estate development company, she'd been known for her ability to make a quick, clean decision without getting emotional. People needed to be let go? No problem. Five minutes in Ellie's office, and they'd leave with a wad of moist tissue. Ellie's eyes were dry. A few houses needed plowing under for an office building? Ellie wrote a check for the bare minimum the law allowed and washed her hands of the matter. The families would find housing somewhere else. Or not. It wasn't her problem.

Since leaving the Bedlamton Arms, she'd felt curiously subject to having—she coughed out the word—*feelings*. Loathing, for instance. She'd never cared enough to detest anyone or anything before last autumn. Now she loathed the Booster Club. Another feeling was joy. She couldn't say her days had been larded with it, but she'd definitely felt exhilaration on escaping the Bedlamton Arms. The memory of Josiah's face popped unbidden into her mind. Caring. Maybe—she wasn't sure, but possibly—she'd experienced caring. Her marriage had never inspired this kind of tenderness. She'd never cooked as much as a piece of dry toast for Roger, let alone reheated hamburger patties.

With emotion would have to come a certain foolhardiness. She grabbed her jacket and black scarf and plunged into the school's halls. Class was in session, and the classrooms vibrated with young voices. But the halls were empty. A woman emerged from one classroom, and Ellie, striding toward the exit, nodded at her. If she wasn't mistaken, it was Miss Morris. Ellie wondered if she'd replenish her rum soon.

And Ellie was out.

The homeless man slowly pushed his shopping cart, now empty of dead flowers, half a block up the street. Ellie caught up with him and laid a hand on the cart. "Excuse me, what's your name?" she asked.

"What's yours?" he replied.

"Marie Antoinette," she said, blurting out the first name that came to mind.

"Lady, I might push a shopping cart, but I'm not an idiot."

"Okay, it's Mitzi Lancaster."

"I'm Fred. What do you want? I got this cart fair and square. Lady who used to be married to the Granzer's Market guy gave it to me."

"Oh, no," Ellie said. They were safely out of sight of the Villa. She took a roll of hundreds from her jacket and flipped through them. "I need information."

Fred's eyes followed the cash as Ellie folded it and returned it to her pocket. He swallowed. "Like what?"

"Just a little something about the Villa's residents."

Suspicion tightened his mouth. "They're good people."

"I didn't say they weren't." A purple minivan trawled the street looking for a parking spot near the school. She needed to make this quick. "I just want to know if you've seen anything—or anyone—new there."

"Like what?"

"You tell me."

Fred pondered this. For a street guy, he smelled faintly of lime, and his clothes were pressed. He was freshly shaved, too. The Villa's work, probably. Thought they could sucker him with the occasional shower. Money talked a lot more loudly than hot water.

"Grady says there are new developments on *Practical Hospital*," Fred said.

"That's not what I mean," Ellie snapped. Fred stepped back. She lowered her voice. "That's not what I mean. I mean, something significant. Maybe a new resident. One who's not a senior."

"How much will you give me if I tell you something? Not that I'd say anything to hurt them. They're fine folks." His eyes darted up and down the street.

Ellie removed a hundred dollar bill from her pocket. She held it flat between her hands, then shoved it back into her pocket as a station wagon crept by. "That. If it's worth it."

"Well. I suppose it wouldn't hurt to tell you there's been a younger gal staying there."

Ellie's pulse leapt. "You saw her?"

"Nope."

"Then how—"

"I saw her underwear in the laundry room. They let me wash my clothes."

Ellie stood back, hands on hips. "Underwear."

"It was small. Not like the other stuff I've seen."

Small. Unusual. "And?"

Fred shrugged. "Other than the prison's laundry mark, it looked like any underwear a young woman might wear."

⁑

Adele was still wary. She wore her maid outfit and kept away from the cafeteria windows. She was playing hearts with Bobby when the insurance detective—the one Gilda called Claudine—arrived.

Adele had caught from passing conversations that Claudine had once been a high-end burglar, but she wasn't prepared for the model of cool elegance who entered. Some people might not have noticed her at all, the way she moved so quietly. It was as if she made a point of not drawing attention to herself. But if you did notice her, you'd see the cheekbones and wide-set brown eyes of a nineteen-forties film star—soft, like a pre-Raphaelite model, but more sculpted. And tougher.

The Villa's residents dropped whatever they were doing to call out "Deanie" and ask her how she was. Even Cook came out of the kitchen and, wiping her hands on her apron, asked if she wanted some cherry pie.

Claudine smiled vaguely—a Mona Lisa smile if there ever was one.

"Deanie, honey, come say hello," Gilda said. After Claudine's kiss on the cheek, Gilda rose and gestured toward Adele. "Julia, you come with us. We'll go up to my room."

Claudine's gaze took her in and Adele thought she caught a raised eyebrow. They took the elevator to the third floor. Gilda's step had extra bounce, and she barely leaned on her cane. Real happiness radiated from her.

"You two wait here," Gilda said. "I want to shut the blinds and draw the curtains before you come in."

Claudine didn't seem to be paying attention to either of them. Instead, she looked lost in thought as she examined the room's layout, the tiny kitchenette. "Besides the vanity table and this armchair, you haven't changed much in here since Dad died."

Adele looked first at Claudine, then Gilda. It was starting to come together. Gilda and Claudine's father had been a couple. Then the father had died. The muscles at the base of Adele's skull tightened, and she clamped a hand to them.

With cat-like grace, Claudine moved to a chintz-covered armchair. Gilda clicked on the side lamp next to the bed, and Claudine pulled the chain on the lamp nearest her. Now the scene had become a Vuillard domestic tableau.

"Someone's watching the Villa," Gilda said. "At least I think so."

"That would explain the binoculars on the dresser."

Gilda told Claudine about both police visits, about how they first searched for the Marie Antoinette dog bed, then came to look for Adele.

"Also known as Julia," Claudine said. Both women stared at Adele.

"It was the first name that came to mind," Gilda said. "Grady had been talking about Nurse Julia on *Practical Hospital*."

"This is serious," Claudine said. She went to the window and pushed aside the curtains. The muffled cries of children on the playground next door reached the room. Adele had the sense that in the few seconds she'd taken to scan the view, Claudine had taken in details most people would never notice.

"I know," Gilda said. "The woman was inside. In the Villa."

"Armed?"

"Warren says no, but the film was dark." Gilda scooted forward. "We could lay on more security—get a dog, hire Mo's team—"

"Too risky. Too much of a flag to the police. Retirement homes don't need to be guarded like banks."

Adele ventured her first words since they'd come upstairs. "I'll go to Uncle Larry's."

Claudine and Gilda turned to her as if they'd forgotten she was there. "Honey?" Gilda said.

"I said I'll go to Uncle Larry's. I should have done it in the first place."

"It's too late for that now," Gilda said. "You need to be here to recover from your surgery. Larry isn't set up for that."

"Besides," Claudine said, "you're being watched. Leaving is risky."

"She has to leave for the surgery."

"And come back. But that's it until we know who's watching and where they're hiding," Claudine said.

Too late, Gilda had said. Adele was beginning to feel like the illustration in her childhood Winnie-the-Pooh book with Pooh stuck halfway into the beehive. She'd never finish her mission. "Any news on my paintings?"

"I just can't figure out who'd rat us out," Gilda said.

"Your paintings," Claudine said. She reached into a briefcase. "That's why I stopped by."

Gilda held up a hand. "That can wait just a minute. She's not going to keel over this second."

"I could," Adele said.

Gilda ignored her. "After the incident at the firehouse, Ellie Whiteby was locked up somewhere, wasn't she?"

"Indefinite treatment at a psychiatric hospital. The Bedlamton Arms, I believe. You don't think she's after you? If anything, she'd come after me."

"We all played a role in bringing her down. She might think the best way to get at you is to go after us. This is the Booster Club's unofficial headquarters, after all."

Gilda must suspect Eleanor Whiteby of watching them. The clenching at Adele's skull tightened.

"She couldn't have escaped, could she?"

Claudine clasped her hands in her lap. "The Bedlamton Arms is locked up tighter than the Tower of London. They made their reputation on the Ritz's hospitality and San Quentin's security. No way she's getting out of there."

"I got out of Carsonville Women's."

Both women turned to Adele as if they'd once again forgotten her existence.

"The girl has a point," Gilda said. "How do we figure out if she's still there?"

"They won't tell you if you call." Claudine drew a finger up the arm of her chair. "They might not even tell if she'd escaped. You really think she's the one calling in the police?"

"What about my paintings?" Adele ventured again. Once the paintings were found, she could leave, and the Villa would no longer be at risk.

"Honey, this concerns you, too," Gilda said. "We wouldn't be at risk if you weren't here, and if we hadn't heisted the dog bed for you."

Adele felt her face warm. Gilda was right, of course. If this Ellie had spotted her or the dog bed—and she clearly had good reason to think both of them were at the Villa—she could bring the whole place down, turning every one of them out into the street. And Adele back to jail. Where she'd die. With all her forgeries still out in the world.

"I'm not sure who'd know what Ellie's up to," Claudine said. "Her husband left her, and I don't recall her having many friends. At least, not outside the Carsonville Women's League."

"I don't know anyone there to ask," Gilda said. "They don't run in our circles."

"The Women's League. They're having an event tonight," Adele said. "I saw it in the newspaper." After the police had left, she'd read through the paper as Mort had handed it to her by section. He'd skimmed over the society pages quickly, and Adele had had to make do with them until he'd finished his long perusal of the front section.

"What event?" Gilda asked.

"Some kind of springtime membership celebration. They give out awards or elect officers or something." With both women watching her, she suddenly became nervous. "At least, I think so."

"I could go," Gilda said.

"How are you going to pull that off?" Claudine crossed her legs with a dancer's grace.

"When you're old, you can get away with a lot." Gilda rose and went to the closet. After rummaging in its depths, she pulled out a pink shantung silk dinner suit that Jackie Onassis might have chosen if she were considerably bustier. "I might wear this."

"That won't work." Adele was surprised the words she'd thought came out aloud.

"Why not?" Gilda lowered the suit.

"It's too old-fashioned. They're label conscious at the Women's League. You need something modern."

"This suit was good enough to get the governor's attention when I needed it." Gilda held the suit to her body. "I might have gained a few pounds since then."

"Gilda, Adele has a point."

Adele pulled off her maid's hat and itchy wig and scratched at her scalp. Her headache seemed to be easing. "I think you'd love some of the dresses of a few of the contemporary Japanese and German designers. I have one in particular you'd look great in."

Gilda returned to her chair. "That's sweet, and I know I hide my size well, but we'd never fit into the same dress."

"That's the beauty of these dresses. They're loose, but have interesting structure." This was actually a good idea. She could do something to help the Booster Club for a change. "Uncle Larry has my wardrobe. I could give you a note, and he'd get the dress you need. Do you have any black ankle boots?"

"No boots, but more pumps and sandals than you can shake a stick at."

In the Rundholz dress with her hair styled right, Gilda could easily pass as a stylish society matron. Maybe they'd buy her attitude as "eccentricity." Even better, Uncle Larry might liberate a few other outfits from her closet for her, too, and Adele wouldn't have to wear the Villa's cast-offs.

"You could send Father Vincent," Claudine said. "Tell him he can take my Mercedes."

"My clothes aren't good enough?"

"Times change," Claudine said. Adele nodded.

Gilda sighed. "Fine. I'll do it." She reached for the house phone.

"Why don't we wait a minute, and I'll give you an update on Adele's paintings?"

Finally. Adele sat back on the vanity's stool.

Claudine opened her file folder. "Of the eight paintings, four have already been reclaimed or will be as soon as we can get an agent to pick them up. Another one mysteriously disappeared from the Oak Hills golf club." Claudine raised an eyebrow at Gilda.

"What about the other three?" Adele asked.

"It's a strange thing."

The playground outside fell silent. A breeze rattled the window.

"Yeah?" Gilda said.

"A museum—the Holgate—has two of the forgeries, and they won't give them up."

Adele's brain seemed to stop functioning for a moment. It took that long for her to speak. "They won't give them up," she repeated.

"Yes. We told them that they're fakes and reminded them of the insured value. At first they were grateful and said we could send someone for them any time. But this morning they called back and said they want to keep the paintings."

"Which ones are they?"

Claudine looked at her paper. "A Boucher and a Jean-Louis David. The trustees bought the David and had the Boucher willed to them."

The David was pretty good, especially given her lack of interest in Greek themes, but she never did think the Boucher was her best work. She liked painting with precision, and Boucher's stylized figures with their plump arms and rosy cheeks never grabbed her. "Did they say why? They're such different works."

"The curator apparently refuses to let them go. He plans to make a big stink with the museum's board if they give them up. He says they're works of art on their own."

"The fakes?" Gilda said.

"Something about 'art and message.' He was talking so fast that I didn't catch it all, but he wanted to know if we could get him more of the forgeries."

"You didn't tell him where to find them, did you?" Adele let go of the wig. She'd been twisting it in her hands and had crushed its wave. "Art and message." He must have seen what she'd done to them. Somehow.

Claudine looked away. "I'm not sure what will happen. If the insurance company can arrange sales between the owners and the museum, they might do it to avoid a payout. I'll let you know." Her voice softened. "I saw the photos, Adele. Good work, especially the David. Must have been quite a job for the break-in team, with a canvas that size."

It was true. The canvas had been nearly as tall as she. But painting it was wonderful. She'd played Mahler and rarely had felt so completely enveloped by her work. The swells of the orchestra, the tang of turpentine, those hours that vanished like seconds as she painted.

"She knows her stuff," Gilda told Adele. "She's heisted some of the best."

"I can't believe it." She looked up, wide-eyed. "Not that Claudine doesn't know art, but that they want my paintings. They're forgeries." The Boucher contained an especially pointed message, Adele remembered. She shivered. "I can't let them have them."

"You may not have a choice," Claudine said.

"What about the other one? The one in Carsonville. You ever get a name?" Gilda asked.

Claudine looked at the list again. "The George Stubbs? Belongs to an art professor, if I remember right. Let's see."

Adele sat, her breath frozen.

"Yes. Art professor named Oliver Degraff. We've left messages, but he hasn't replied. You don't happen to know him, do you?"

CHAPTER TWENTY-SEVEN

Gilda slipped the dress over her head and turned to the mirror for a three-quarter's view assessment. Odd, but not bad. She plucked at an unusual seam curving in to give the hem a tulip shape.

"That's supposed to be there," Adele said. She'd changed out of her maid costume and now wore a pair of drapey capris and a loose-cut sweater Father Vincent had brought back with the dress for Gilda.

"I don't get it. What about my waist? And ta-tas? They're my best features."

"This kind of dress hints at your figure. The wide neck is flattering. As you move, the seams give people an idea of your curves without being too obvious. German designers are genius at it."

All afternoon, Adele had seemed distracted. Even Warren had had trouble getting her attention. Gilda was glad to see the girl focused for a change.

Humming, "Hey Good Lookin'," Gilda stepped forward, then back, to test Adele's assertion. The dress flowed around her torso. Not bad. "I don't have to hold in my stomach. I could get used to that." Not getting a reply, she added, "Adele?"

"Hmm?"

The girl had seemed out of sorts since their earlier meeting with Claudine. She'd barely picked at dinner. "Honey, is it the operation that bothers you?"

As if she'd been waiting for Gilda to ask, she said, "The paintings. The Holgate can't keep them. I need to get them back."

"First things first." Gilda had never had children, but she'd mastered the motherly tone of voice. "You get the surgery, recover, and you'll have all the time in the world to get your paintings." She brought down the volume. "Why is this so important? It's that professor's painting, isn't it?"

"I explained all this. Please. I don't want to talk about it right now."

"Fine. Don't worry. Let Claudine deal with it. Now for earrings. Try the box on the vanity," Gilda said. "People really dress like this nowadays?"

"The chic ones do." Her voice started slowly, as if she were willing herself to leave old thoughts behind. "It's more of an artist's look, but it suits you." Adele drew a pair of orange daisy earrings from the box. "What about these?"

"Oh, honey, those are cheap things."

"I like them."

"Shouldn't I be wearing diamonds? I have some, you know." And emeralds and rubies. The rubies went surprisingly well with her hair, despite the old saw about red on redheads.

"The daisy earrings give the dress an offhand look. More nonchalant, not too self-conscious. We should rough up your hair a bit, too, make it look more European."

At a double rap on the door, Gilda said, "Come in."

Grady entered, a sheet of paper in hand. "Why's it so dark in here?"

"We're keeping Adele out of sight, remember?" Gilda posed, one leg slightly in front, hand on hip. "What do you think?"

"About what?"

Grady never did have much of an eye for fashion. "My dress. The look."

He squinted. "Kind of like the heiress in *Practical Hospital*. She was off the show for a while, then just came back this week from Europe with a new husband."

"Never mind." Gilda sat on the bed's edge. "What's that you've got?"

"Answer from the surgeon." He glanced at Adele.

"It's about time," Gilda said. "What does he say?"

"He got the CT scans from the prison, and he's cleared up a spot on his schedule for tomorrow at two."

"He's going to do it, and right on schedule." Despite their plans, despite her confidence, the relief loosened muscles in Gilda's neck and shoulders that she didn't even know were tense. "Good."

"Got a few things he wants, though."

"Go on."

"The patient can't eat past eight p.m.," Grady read. "That's tonight. You got a couple more hours to chow."

"Okay," Adele said. Her voice, so sure and firm as they'd talked about fashion, now sounded faint.

"And he wants proof that the dog bed is still in good shape."

"Take another photo with the newspaper. That should do it."

"He says he won't operate unless the dog bed comes with the patient."

Gilda's hands dropped to the mattress. "How are we going to do that? I mean, once he has the bed...."

"I know. But he says it's a no-go, otherwise."

She was already worried that Dr. Lancaster would involve the police. Without the dog bed, they didn't have any leverage. What would stop him from refusing to operate and having Adele arrested?

"Did he say anything about Adele escaping Carsonville Women's?"

"Nope," Grady said.

They'd already taken all the risks they could bear. Dr. Parisot said he'd watch the operation remotely, but they couldn't risk having him in the room. With so many nurses and anesthesiologists and so on present, the police could easily sneak in. Dress an officer in scrubs, and he'd be incognito until it was too late. Losing Adele was a risk already factored into the equation, but losing Dr. Parisot, too, couldn't happen. There would go the Villa's medical care.

But, if Doc saw something awry, he couldn't reach through the laptop's screen and stop it. He could say something, though, and Gilda could step in. Gilda needed to be there. With the dog bed.

"That's it, then. I'll go with her."

"Oh, Gilda, you don't have to do that," Adele said.

"I don't have much of a stomach for blood, but I don't see the alternative. Besides, if I'm arrested, they won't give an old lady much time."

"He might have the police waiting in the operating room," Grady said. "You two go in, and it's finished."

"Father Vincent would give me a nice hammer, I'm sure," Gilda said.

"Hammer?" Adele raised an eyebrow.

"I'll sit next to the dog bed," Gilda said. "If there's any funny business, smash goes the dog bed. It's the only way." Lord, she hadn't been so busy since the Nixon administration. This Booster Club business was keeping her on her toes.

"Then you're busted for aiding and abetting a fugitive plus ruining a priceless antique," Grady pointed out.

"I'm helping a poor girl get the brain operation she desperately needs. What would a jury say to that? Plus" —she put a hand on her hip— "we'll do the cat in a bag."

Grady pursed his lips. "Cat in a bag. Could work. Does Mort know?"

"He'll be okay."

"What do you mean?" Adele said.

"You'll see," Gilda said. "No cats involved."

"That's how it's going to be, then," Grady said. "I'll send along the photo of the bed, and we'll get you ready for tomorrow afternoon. Father Vincent will drive getaway. We'll get Doc Parisot to double-check that the sick bay is set up for post-op care."

"Honey, what's wrong?" Gilda said.

Adele was grasping her head between both hands. "It hurts."

Gilda took Adele's chilled hands and folded them between hers. "You're just nervous." Poor girl. "Now you take it easy. In twenty-four hours, it will all be over. Cook will give you a nice dinner, then you'll lie down for a while. Can you do that?"

Adele closed her eyes and nodded.

"You'll be okay. Leave it to us. All right?"

The girl didn't respond, but she stood and, with tentative steps, made her way to the door. Yes, she was anxious about the operation, but something else was going on, too. What was it?

Gilda leaned back and sighed. Everything would be fine, all right. As long as the aneurysm was operable and Adele didn't die first. And as long as their spy didn't have any plans for another police raid.

But first, she had a party to go to.

CHAPTER TWENTY-EIGHT

Father Vincent dropped Gilda at the Women's League's front door. The League Lodge, as it was known, was in a Moorish-style mansion in the old-money part of town. A lantern that might have been lifted from the set of *Morocco* glowed coral over the arched doorway.

Gilda pulled her purse up her arm and set forth. Tonight she'd traded her walker for a rhinestone-encrusted cane.

"May I help you?" the young man at the door said.

"I'm here for the membership meeting."

"Your name, please? I'll check you off the list."

"I'm on the rolls."

The man took a step closer. "May I have your name?"

"Gilda." Damn, this boy was annoying. Beyond him, past the tawny-tiled floor and waxed woodwork, tinkled a piano.

"Your last name, please." When she didn't reply, he said, "This is a members-only club."

"I am a member." Enough of this kid. She pushed her way past him to the party.

"Ma'am," the boy called out. "Your last name, please. I need to check you in."

"Go check yourself in." Gilda crossed the hall, descended a few steps, and got her bearings. It had been a while since she'd been here, and when she had, it hadn't been for long.

In the lodge's main room, women milled around a central buffet with not too groaning a board, Gilda noted. A miasma of perfume mixed with the odor of Sterno and meatballs. A woman a bit into her cups was playing "Send In the Clowns" on the baby grand to the side. For a so-called membership meeting, this had the feel of a full-on bacchanal.

A woman sporting a bob so perfect that it might have been a wig approached her. "Ma'am? I don't believe we've met. You're here for the membership meeting, am I right?"

"Sure am," Gilda said.

"I'm Betsy Dobber."

"Gilda." She scanned the crowd. No Ellie Whiteby here. If the nuthouse released her, she wasn't up to being in public yet.

"I don't believe I heard your last name." Betsy's smile was insistent.

"Gilda. I don't know what last name I'm registered under. It's been a while since I've been here." When she was last here, drinking was limited to sherry—unless you knew the valet parker, who usually had a bottle for special members—and the women wore hats with peonies on them. Today, it was a bunch of bleached-teeth, too-skinny broads who were overly concerned about a gal's last name. "Look, have a gander at the rolls. You'll find me."

She didn't have a lot of time to waste. Father Vincent was parked below the lodge, waiting for her signal to come around. His hot rod magazine wouldn't get him through the night.

"An Old Fashioned," Gilda told a passing waiter. "And none of that fruit and soda nonsense, either."

"Classic Old Fashioned, coming up," he said. Here was a sensible boy. Not haranguing her like the others.

As she moved toward the buffet table, the crowds of women parted, tossing fake smiles her way, then looking away again as quickly as was decent. No one would talk to her here. She picked up a napkin with League Lodge printed on it in gold and surveyed the buffet's offerings. One bowl, barely large enough to hold Warren's breakfast cereal, held grayish meatballs. Slices of orange cheese were fanned over a platter. Some kind of chunky white dip filled another bowl next to a plate of crackers. And that was it. Cook would have been ashamed to put out a spread like that for the garbage man, let alone a pack of Carsonville's finest. Not that it mattered. As long as the pinot grigio flowed, no one seemed to bother with food. Gilda set down her napkin in disgust.

"Say." She pulled aside one of the older members, a woman whose facelift had been ratcheted two twists too tight. "What's the agenda tonight?"

The woman first scowled, but it melted into a smile. She glanced to her right and left, and a few women materialized to flank her. "Why, we're voting on this year's officers, of course." Her smile sweetened. "I don't recall seeing you around town."

Gilda wanted to tell her that she had a short memory. Not only had they met forty years ago or so, her husband had been responsible for Gilda's ruby brooch.

"Just back from Europe," Gilda said. "With my lover. That's why I need the cane. Before I left, I walked normally, if you get my drift." She winked.

The woman backed up. "I see."

"Now, about these elections, isn't Eleanor" —she struggled for a moment before remembering her married name— "Millhouse on the ticket?"

The women all looked at each other. "I believe she's out of town," one of them said.

"So to speak," another said and giggled.

"Get to the point," Gilda said. "She's in the club, or not?"

"I'm afraid we've had to revoke her membership," the older woman said. "Legal matters."

"Although she was awfully organized," a tall woman in a plain black dress, much less artful than Gilda's, said.

"But the lodge is warmer now," another woman chimed in.

"You're saying she's in the joint. Not on parole," Gilda said. She moved her cane a few inches closer to the older woman.

"That's one way to put it, I suppose," the older woman said.

Gilda stepped forward, placing her cane and her weight on the woman's foot. The older woman yelped and leapt back.

"Sorry," Gilda said mildly.

"Are you a member here?" the older woman said.

"Yeah, sure."

"I'm going to have to insist you prove it," the woman said.

There was a time when Gilda could enter a room, and all heads turned. Certainly, the men's did. When she took the stage at the nightclub, she'd looked out at tables of friends with smiles on their faces — as well as enough secrets to make *Peyton Place* look like *Romper Room*. Gilda calculated that she hadn't bought herself a drink for a good thirty years.

But time had passed. When you hit a certain age, you began to melt out of the public's eye. Even with her hennaed hair and flamboyant manner — oh, she knew how she came off — she wasn't worth a second look. First, it was the men. But after a while, even the younger women, some of them, began to turn on her. Well, she wasn't entirely helpless.

"Go ask the gal in the bob." Good lord. They all had bobs. "Betsy. Betsy Dobber, I think her name was."

When the woman left and people around her dispersed, Gilda put her hand on the arm of a brunette, empty glass in hand, on her way to a refill. "Excuse me."

The brunette turned, clearly curious. "Yes?"

"I'm looking for Eleanor Whiteby Millhouse. She's about yea tall, wears pearls, kind of—"

"I know who you're talking about." The brunette's face was as soft and powdered as a loaf of risen dough. Not a wrinkle to be seen. Gilda's gaze dropped to the woman's liver-spotted hands. They always told.

"You haven't seen her, have you?"

A bare smile spread over the brunette's lips. "No. Doubt I will."

Gilda let her go. It was time to leave, anyway. Ellie clearly wasn't here, and these women, who probably had a hotline to the town's gossip, sounded convinced she was still locked away.

The older woman hotfooted her way back with Betsy Dobber in tow. "Her," she said, nodding at Gilda. "Is she a member?"

"I went through almost five decades of membership records—"

"Is she a member or not?" The older woman's face, despite its frozen state thanks to the plastic surgeon's knife, was at maximum smug.

"Some of those records are so dusty I could barely read them. How come we don't have them put on the computer?"

"Get to the point, Betsy. Yes or no?"

Beyond the two women, the waiter had returned, an amber cock-tail with a lemon twist floating among the ice cubes. Too bad she wouldn't be able to enjoy it.

"Well," Betsy said. "Let go of my arm, please." After the older woman released the arm, Betsy said, "Yes."

"Yes, what?"

"Yes, she's a member."

For goodness sake, Gilda thought. She thought she'd been made a member, even though she'd only come in that one night because she had to use the restroom. When the doorman had refused to let her in, she'd dropped a hint of what she knew to the mayor's wife, and, presto, she had a lifetime membership. Not that she'd ever been back. Until tonight.

"Your Old Fashioned, ma'am," the waiter said. "I hope you like it."

"Thank you." She took a quick sip and nodded. Dry with a hint of clove and citrus. Mort would have added a cherry, but this was a fine cocktail. "Very nice."

"It's my first event here," the waiter said. "I don't have a lot of experience with cocktails. I used to work in the mental health field until, well…. I'm glad you like your drink."

"Then I guess it's no use asking if you know Ellie Whiteby Millhouse."

The boy's smile froze, and shock registered in his eyes. "Eleanor?" he whispered.

"Yes" — Gilda's eyes lowered to his name badge — "John."

CHAPTER TWENTY-NINE

Ellie gripped the child's telescope. She felt like the man in the crow's nest at the top of a ship's mast. All she did was stare into the horizon. Tonight, the old redhead had left for a few hours, driven by the priest. She'd looked better than usual, Ellie had to admit. More stylish. Odd. Ellie's experience owning the Shangri-La spa had taught her that getting a woman to change her look usually took nothing short of a divorce.

She set down the telescope. Why? She almost heard Josiah's little voice asking her, *Why?* Why did the Villa have a replica of the Marie Antoinette dog bed? If they stole it, was it to copy it and sell the copies? Or was it another reason? And what about the art forger? That paint Ellie had smelled, the girl she'd spotted, and the prison-issue underwear the homeless guy had seen in the laundry. She was sure the art forger was hiding there. *Why?* If she could answer these questions, she might find the key to bringing down the Villa.

She sipped from the tumbler she'd filched from the principal's desk drawer. A little too much honey in this daiquiri, and it really needed lime. The triple sec was a lame stand-in.

She couldn't live in the school's attic the rest of her life. Something had to give. She had to drop the idea of revenge against the Booster Club, or she needed information. Ha. As if she'd give up on the

Villa now. Ellie downed the cloying daiquiri in a gulp and marched toward the attic's door. Time for answers.

She'd grown used to moving around the school in the dark, and her housemaid's dress—her black dress was drying over a stall in the faculty washroom—was surprisingly comfortable. She flipped her black dress over and plopped onto the couch in the teachers' lounge, setting her feet on the coffee table. She glanced toward the small refrigerator that held the teachers' lunches, but she wasn't hungry. The fourth grade teacher was apparently on a low-carb diet, and Ellie had cleared out her jerky and almonds a few hours earlier.

She picked up the school phone and dialed information. After getting the number she wanted, she pressed *31 to block her number from showing up on caller ID, and she dialed again. She let the phone ring.

"Hello," a woman's groggy voice answered.

"Mitzi? This is Eleanor Whiteby."

The phone clattered, as if it had been dropped. A second later, the woman said, "Eleanor? I thought your last name was Millhouse." She sounded a lot more alert now.

"I'm getting a divorce."

"And—" Whatever it was she was going to say, she must have changed her mind. "It's so late."

"Oh." Ellie had got so used to prowling at night that she'd forgotten that the rest of the world wouldn't necessarily be up, too. "Sorry. It's the time difference. I'm in—Aruba."

"For three months? But I thought—"

"Yep. Thought I'd get some sun, some relaxation. Work has been so stressful. This vacation has done me a world of good." She barely suppressed a hiccup.

"Oh," Mitzi said. "It does sound like you've had a few drinks on the beach."

"Of course I have. I'm on vacation, aren't I?"

"I didn't mean anything by it. I mean, is it a nice resort?"

Ellie looked around the teachers' lounge at the ratty microwave and the months-old magazines. "It's okay. To tell the truth, I feel bad living in luxury. So many hungry kids out there. Did you know some school districts are cutting free lunches?"

She heard a swallow. "You really have relaxed."

Ellie snapped to. "Well, that's not why I called. I heard about your husband's dog bed, and I just wanted to say I'm sorry." She didn't worry that the husband would be in Mitzi's bed. She'd seen the separate bedrooms herself during her failed attempt to steal the dog bed. Not that she was judging. She and Roger had had separate bedrooms, too. He'd stay up all hours doing acrostics, and when he slept, he snored.

"Oh, Eleanor, it's awful. He can't focus, he can't sleep—he even let a tub of hydroponic tomatoes dry up. His temper is out of control. I've never seen him like this. It's really getting to him." Her voice dropped. "I'm thinking about divorce."

So, the dog bed hadn't come back. It had to be at the Villa. "I suppose there's some antique dog bed collector out there who would pay a lot for it. Unless, of course…."

"Unless what?"

"Unless…."

Mitzi took the pause as a sign to resume her complaining. "I don't know what to do about him." Her voice picked up urgency. "Eleanor, I'm so glad you're not in an institution. I need a friend. We had the spring elections tonight at the Women's League, and I'm just about through with them. Joan passed out in the broom closet again." She droned on about a strange member from fifty years ago returning, staying for a drink, then leaving.

Ellie only half-listened. She mumbled something about passing along the number of a good attorney, but her mind was still on the problem of the dog bed. If the Villa's residents wanted to turn a quick buck, they'd hardly steal an antique dog bed. But what other reason would they have? She sat up and gripped the phone. Ransom. They were holding the dog bed as ransom. They planned to demand money to return it — or to collect the reward Lancaster offered. Why hadn't that thought occurred to her before?

"How are things financially?" Ellie relaxed into the chair and sweet-ened her attitude. "I mean, if you split up, will money be all right for you? Any recent large cash outlays?"

"We're doing all right, and B. E. hasn't said anything about having to cash out our securities. In fact, he's offering a huge reward to anyone who finds his dog bed. No one's claimed it yet. I should do well enough to buy a cute condo downtown."

So, if it wasn't money, the Booster Club wanted something else from him. "You said he's been edgy. Could he be hiding something about the theft?"

"Could be." From the tone of her voice, Ellie concluded it wouldn't be the first time her husband had hid something from her. The phone rustled. "I think he's even up right now," she whispered. "He's worried about something tomorrow."

"Maybe he has a tough surgery."

"No. He never frets about those." She sniffed. "Do you think he's having an affair?"

"Why? What else has he been doing out of the ordinary?"

"The morning after the dog bed was stolen, he kept pacing the house and checking his phone for messages. Then" — Mitzi sobbed, then reined in her voice— "the next day I heard him mutter a woman's name."

Ellie nearly held her breath. "What name?"

"It sounded like…. It sounded like…."

"Spit it out, Mitzi."

"Adele."

Eleanor gasped. "Are you sure?"

Mitzi sniffed again and blew her nose. "Yes."

So, that was it! The art forger needed surgery, and the Villa stole the dog bed to make sure she got it. Good grief. Something was happening right under Mitzi's nose, and the woman was absolutely clueless.

Ellie's pause must have lasted too long, because Mitzi said, "Hey, are you really in Aruba?"

"Of course I am," she snapped. "I was just concerned about you. That's why I called. I have a facial and mani-pedi in a minute, so I'd better go. Good luck with your husband." She slammed down the phone.

From the sound of things, there would be action tomorrow. She headed for the attic. She needed to be rested and ready.

CHAPTER THIRTY

Head throbbing, Adele lay in bed. The bedside lamp cast a dim circle on the ceiling. Among the cracks, she made out the shape of Iowa and thought she even saw the letter A.

After dinner, Warren had wanted her to stick around for a game of cards and was openly disappointed when she excused herself to go to her room. But she needed time to herself. To think.

The Holgate museum had kept a few of her forgeries. She didn't like it, but she didn't know what she could do. Maybe, if tomorrow's operation went well, she'd eventually be able to paint forgeries of her forgeries and replace them. These forgeries would be clean. How and when she could pull it off, she didn't know.

But the Stubbs. Oliver's painting. He couldn't keep it. He couldn't discover her secret. The vise-like grip on her skull tightened, and she closed her eyes.

Her dilemma was clear. She could sneak out the side door and find Oliver and get her painting back to destroy it. If she were caught, the Booster Club would never forgive her. She risked putting the Villa and all its residents in peril.

And Warren? He'd be infuriated. He'd take her outing personally. His words during dinner drifted back to her. "There's no one like you," he'd said. "You bring out the good things in me." And the way he looked at her portrait of Gilda, as if Adele were a magician and could spin paint into soul.

She rolled toward the wall and pulled her pillow closer. It was those romance novels. If she weren't dying, he'd never have looked at her twice. She shouldn't fool herself.

The alternative was that she stay put. They'd drag her in for an operation tomorrow, an operation that put the Villa at risk anyway. At some point, the Booster Club would be done with her. If she survived the operation, she'd be a fugitive the rest of her life. And Oliver might discover her secret.

Adele rose and wrapped herself in a bathrobe. Maybe Cook wouldn't mind if she made some tea. The surgeon had said she couldn't eat after eight p.m., but he hadn't said anything about liquids. The Villa's halls were quiet and cool now that the furnace was ratcheted down for the night. She padded down the steps, turned into the cafeteria, and stopped. Seated at a corner table was Father Vincent, blindfolded. He held something in his hands the size of a shot put. The overhead lights were off, and the glow of his table lamp gave the scene the feeling of a Holbein tableau.

"Father?"

The priest ripped off his blindfold and relaxed when he saw it was her. "Adele. Why are you up? You need to rest before your surgery."

"I thought I'd make some tea. What are you doing?" Closer, she saw that the object he held was some sort of mechanical device. A screwdriver and pliers lay next to it.

"I was rebuilding a carburetor. I like to test myself by doing it blindfolded. Most cars are fuel injection these days, but it keeps my mind sharp to stay on top of the old skills."

"You couldn't sleep, either? You took Gilda out tonight."

"It wasn't that. I'll be fine soon."

She suspected she was what worried him. Until she was home from the operation, the Villa's residents weren't safe. "I'm sorry for the risk I'm putting all of you through. All to relicense the home."

"Maybe it started that way, but we're attached to you, child. We all want to see you safe and healthy."

She lowered her eyes. If only he'd known what she was considering. "When you were a priest. I mean, not that you aren't a priest now, but—"

"I know what you mean." He pushed the carburetor aside and swiveled to face her, hands in his lap. Likely the position he'd taken in the confessional for all those years.

"Did people ever talk to you about revenge?"

If Adele had surprised him, he didn't show it. "Frequently. Why do you ask?"

"I took revenge on someone once. Actually, eight times."

"Yes?" He would surely remember she had forged eight paintings.

"It felt good. It felt really good." Adele leaned forward. "My anger had been burning away inside me for years."

Father Vincent's hands, still settled on his plaid bathrobe, didn't move. "And then?"

She remembered lying on her prison bed thinking about what she'd done and feeling none of the satisfaction. "I was ashamed. The revenge—it was against someone I really care about, and I don't want to hurt him." But he would know sometime. Unless she got those paintings back.

The priest tilted his head. "The situation is complicated. You were angry about someone who means a lot to you."

She nodded. "Heartbroken."

"Sadness is not the same as anger."

She sat back. Did she feel sad that Oliver had ended their affair? With surprise, she realized she didn't. Not really. He'd dropped her for another student, but after the initial shock it didn't bother her much that he was with someone else. But, thinking of him, she had been angry. Really angry, and it had grown over time. It had deepened as she'd honed her forgeries and festered as she passed days in prison. The anger had to be heartbreak. What else could it be?

"All that anger, then my revenge—I was the only one hurt," she said.

The priest nodded. "Forgiveness is a bitter pill, but it's also a medicine."

"I know that now. I want to make amends."

"There are many ways to make amends, my child. One of them is to live with a pure heart and let go of the past."

"But if you have the chance to do something about the revenge, maybe even before it takes effect, shouldn't you do it?"

Father Vincent tilted his head. "I suppose, in theory, yes. However, it's not always that simple."

"What do you mean?"

"Being wronged stirs up strong feelings. Sometimes forgiving and letting go of the past is the best way to heal."

Adele drew her brows together. "I still don't understand. The only reason I wanted out of prison so badly was to make things right."

"You took your revenge through your paintings. Am I right?"

She nodded.

"Whatever wrong was done—and I'm not asking you to tell me—stirred up tremendous passion in you. You still feel that passion after all these years. Perhaps you haven't truly forgiven this person."

Adele shifted in her seat. "You don't understand, I—" She bit her lip and started again, this time more slowly. "I need to do the right thing. I have the opportunity now."

"I'm sorry to upset you, Adele. Let me caution you, though. Before you act, be sure you are certain what the right thing is."

*
**

Near midnight, Adele stuck her head out the bedroom door. The hum of a television came from down the hall, but all the doors were shut and the elevator was silent. Grateful for the cache of clothing from Uncle Larry's, she pulled on an asymmetrical dark sweater over her T-shirt and swapped her jeans for loose black cargo pants. A black stocking cap made it less likely she'd be recognized. A glance in the mirror showed what might have been an avant-garde dockworker.

Tomorrow was her surgery. It was now or never. She crept to the end of the hall and out the side door.

Her breath steamed the brisk air. She stayed close to the building to evade Red's night vision goggles and darted to the cover of street trees up the block. Carsonville wasn't a huge city, but large enough that walking to Oliver's place was out. She didn't have a cent to her name, so a bus or taxi weren't options, either. Besides, she didn't want to be recognized.

A tricycle on the porch of a nearby house told her that children lived there. The house's first floor was still and quiet, but the upstairs windows showed moving figures behind the backlit curtains. Someday she'd like to paint something like that. This reflexive thought tightened her headache further. If she lived to do it, she amended. Some people didn't survive brain surgery. Or, if they did, they were changed. Couldn't remember things. Didn't have full use of their bodies. She flexed her fingers.

Up the driveway, a child's bike leaned against the house. It would have to do. In a minute, Adele was cycling up the street. Half an hour later, traveling through dark residential streets, eventually turning to the warehouse district near the river, Adele arrived at Oliver's studio.

"Forgiveness is a bitter pill," Father Vincent had said. If she destroyed the painting, Oliver wouldn't be hurt by its secret. She was protecting him, and in that way showing her forgiveness. Or was that what it was about?

With family money and the salary of a tenured professor, Oliver could afford to have a house and even a home studio, but he preferred hanging out with other artists in the converted floors of an old storage warehouse. The difference was that while the other artists kept cheap beer and beans and rice in their dorm-sized refrigerators, his full-sized Sub Zero was stocked with Dom Perignon and leftover New York strip from the steakhouse downtown.

She left the bicycle near the loading dock and pushed the up button for the huge freight elevator. Inside, she watched the wall slip by the car's slats. She could almost imagine that the elevator stood still, and the building descended around it. At last, it clunked to a stop on Oliver's floor.

The usual late night sounds of artists at work—a violin concerto from one unit, the Rolling Stones from another—drifted into the corridor. Someone down the hall was hammering something metal. The familiar smells of turpentine and incense mixed with that of warmed-over Indian food.

Oliver's unit was in the corner with the view, of course. Adele stood in front of his door, wanting, and yet not wanting, to knock.

Her heart tightened. So did the muscles cradling her skull. Maybe he wasn't even home. Maybe her artery would burst and she'd drop dead, here, in front of his door, and he'd find her.

If that happened, it would be because he was coming back from fooling around with some student, probably, Adele reminded herself. As Oliver's artfully unshaven face appeared in her imagination, Warren's sturdy face, its neck tattoo creeping to his jaw, replaced it. If she did collapse, Oliver would look around, shocked, worried about his own guilt or how he would explain her body to the neighbors. Not Warren. Warren would carry her inside and call an ambulance and whisper that she'd be all right.

Adele steeled herself, then knocked. No one answered.

She pressed her ear to the door to hear Miles Davis on trumpet, and she made out a faint rustling. She knocked again. This time, the door opened. And there stood Oliver.

The shield she'd put up dropped instantly. She'd remembered him as taller, with a force field of nearly palpable charisma, but he was just a man, no different than Bobby or Mort. Her anxiety dissolved.

They stared at each other a full three seconds, before a woman's voice beyond Oliver said, "Oliver? Who is it?"

Adele pushed her way inside and stood, hands on hips, in the middle of the studio.

"What are you doing? You can't be in here," Oliver said, but made no move to close the gap between them.

Downtown Carsonville's lights twinkled through the special weather-resistant windows Oliver had paid to have installed. A young woman—Adele recognized herself in her—sat on the couch arranging her shirt. Two half-empty glasses stood on the coffee table in front of her.

Adele took in the room. There were the stainless steel appliances the other artists could only dream of having. There was the corner with the king-sized bed. Adele let her eyes sweep quickly past that. There was the drafting table with a partially drawn concept for an installation. Likely the same project he'd been working on five years ago.

And there was her Stubbs. It hung on the wall adjacent to the door, where its shady depths would mirror a winter storm through the windows across from it. She didn't often get to see her work out in the world. It had been five years since she'd painted this one. Not bad, really, and the horse's eyes had an especially keen, vivid look.

"Um," said the girl on the couch. "Should I go?"

"Stay," Oliver said.

Adele raised an eyebrow. "You don't mind her knowing — everything?"

"Like what?" He glanced back at the couch.

"Like when — "

"Okay, go," he amended.

The girl downed the rest of her wine in a gulp — she was smart, it was probably a nice Bordeaux — then stopped. A look of recognition came over her, and she set down the glass. "Wait."

"What?" Oliver said.

"You." She swallowed. "Aren't you the prison escapee I saw on the news?"

Adele froze her with a stare. "I don't know what you're talking about."

"You told me she'd been your student, that — "

"I didn't," he said.

The girl opened her mouth, and Oliver shook his head. "But I, she's — "

"No, she's not."

The girl would believe whatever Oliver told her. Adele had, too. He could tell her she'd been born in Persia, and she'd start studying Farsi. Or that he'd never felt love like this for anyone before her. Or, he could tell her she had no talent.

With barely a backward glance, the girl shrugged on her coat and slipped out the door.

Oliver folded his arms over his chest and stood, legs wide. Again, Adele thought of Warren. When Warren stood like that, he wasn't messing around. Oliver only played the tough guy.

"She's right. You're supposed to be in prison."

"And yet I'm not."

"I could call the police right now, and you'd be put away."

She stepped forward. "You could. But you won't. I'd tell them about your—your habits with students. Besides, you want to know why I'm here."

A look of uncertainty cracked his facade. His gaze traveled from Adele to the empty wine glass and back to Adele. "What do you want?"

"The Stubbs."

"What?" Oliver's hands and jaw dropped in unison. "You're joking."

"I want the Stubbs," Adele repeated.

"What is it about that painting? An insurance detective called twice this week and said it was a fake." He adopted the "wise professor" look Adele remembered so well. "She was wrong, of course. Any numskull can see it's an original. She was probably on the make. Has a market lined up for it."

At one time, she'd glowed when he'd deigned to share his nuggets of insight with her. Now, her stomach turned. "I painted it."

"What?"

"I painted it. If you know I broke out of prison, you know I'm an art forger. I forged the Stubbs." She hadn't wanted to tell him, because she hadn't wanted him to discover her secret. Now here she was, telling it all.

"I'm an expert in eighteenth-century British art, Adele. I know an original when I see it. Plus, it came certified."

"You always said my drafting skills were good."

"Technically proficient, yes." He wandered to the couch and sat.

Now that he was on old ground — putting her down — he was at ease. She waited for the familiar pang of hurt, but it didn't come. Amazing. On some level, she must no longer believe him. "You think that painting lacks soul?"

"Of course not. It's a Stubbs. I told you, I have the paperwork. I'm not sure what kind of scam the insurance company was running, but no" —here he let out an irritating chuckle— "it's genuine, all right."

Marty was awfully good with the forged certificates of authenticity, she had to admit. She shrugged. "I'll prove I painted it."

"Delly—" he began, using a nickname no one else called her.

"My name's Adele."

"Well, whatever. You're delusional. You don't have the talent for this kind of work."

Again she marveled. At one time, these words would have devastated her. They had devastated her. He'd kept her so securely in his harem of girls he could denigrate to boost his ego that she'd given up her own work. Her time in jail to think, her few days at the Villa with her paints, just those few hours talking with Warren — they'd changed her. Instead of cringing, fearing another blow, she was curiously unharmed.

"I'm not delusional anymore. Take that painting off the wall," she said.

"Why?"

"I said to take it down. I'll prove I painted it."

"No, I'll prove you didn't. You'll see his signature and the character-istic marks on the back from his studio." His voice became patronizing.

He lifted the heavy canvas from the wall. She remembered painting it so well. She'd driven to the racetrack's stables and run her hands over a stallion's firm jaw and shoulders, letting her fingers dip into the creases his muscles formed. She'd listened to Yo-Yo Ma on the cello as she'd worked and felt she'd understood the artist in a way that no class or textbook or slides of his paintings could impart.

"Now turn it on its side."

"What?"

"I said to turn the painting on its side." As he complied, she said, "Do you have a flashlight? Get it. And turn off the lights." She mar-veled at the words that came out of her own mouth. For years, she'd feared he'd see what she was now willingly showing him.

"I won't do it." He leaned the painting against the wall. "You want to steal my Stubbs, don't you? You need the cash to skip town."

"It's not real, Oliver. It's a fake."

"There you go again."

"All I ask is that you do as I say. Get a flashlight and look at it. You'll have your proof."

"Fine." He went to the kitchen for a flashlight and turned off the overhead light, leaving the lamp on the end table on.

Adele faced the painting. She knew that behind her Carsonville's skyline glittered over the river, a sight she loved. Oliver could call the police, and she might never see that skyline again. But she didn't turn around. She clicked on the flashlight and held it at an angle so it caught the delicate relief of the painting's surface.

"Look. Do you see what it says?" she asked.

"I see something in the painting's texture, but I'm not sure."

"Keep looking. Tilt the painting a bit more."

"It's words." Oliver sounded genuinely excited. Well, that would change. "Stubbs is a master. No one has uncovered his messages before. I wonder if his other paintings carry messages? I could make my career on this discovery."

Adele was unmoved. "Read it."

"Give me the flashlight." He snatched it from her hand. "I can't believe this. This will turn the art establishment upside down."

"Read."

"Oliver Degraff…." His voice dropped off.

"Keep going."

"Oliver Degraff's weenie is the size of a…"

"…fingerling potato," she finished. "Convinced now that I painted it?"

He slumped to the couch. "I don't believe it."

At last Adele turned toward the skyline. The lights twinkling from office buildings and the cell phone towers on the ridge all seemed to sparkle for her. What was it Father Vincent had said? Something about the calm of forgiveness. She felt it. Now she was truly free.

"I guess I'll be going," she said. "You can keep the Stubbs after all."

CHAPTER THIRTY-ONE

Adele left the borrowed bicycle where she'd found it and slipped through the Villa's side entrance. She wanted to sing or dance, but she kept her movements contained, knowing she'd smile as she slept.

She skipped up the stairs. All the rooms were dark. And as far as she could tell, no one knew she had been outside the Villa. She wished she could tell Warren about it, but it was too soon. Someday, if she survived the surgery, she'd talk about it with him.

Funny, until now she'd gone through the motions of preparing for the surgery because Gilda and the others wanted her to. Not because she wanted to. Now, she did. Even if she had to wait out her prison sentence — plus whatever they'd stick her with for escaping — it would be worth it. Eventually she would be free and able to paint. In prison, she could teach drawing. She'd help other women feel confident about what they could do.

The Villa's faded wallpaper and worn carpet welcomed her. Home. People who cared about her. She had the feeling of having turned a corner in her life.

She opened her bedroom door and stopped cold. There, seated on the bed with an expression that could freeze lava, was Warren.

"Where have you been?" he asked.

"What?" was all she could think of to reply.

"You tripped the camera on your way out. You didn't remember it was there?"

She hadn't. It had been too easy. She should have known. For the first time, Adele had a sense for what Warren would have been like as a correctional officer.

"I had to take care of something," she said.

"And put the entire Villa at risk."

"I was careful."

"You're a fine artist, not an escape artist. Someone is watching us, you know. All they need is to catch a glimpse of you coming and going, and we're sunk." Fire leapt into his voice. "You think everyone is helping you here because they have nothing better to do?"

"I—"

"You think they want to end their days in prison?" He stood. "That's what you're doing to them."

Adele refused to be cowed. "It doesn't matter. It's over now, and no one saw me. You need to leave. I'm going to bed."

"So, your business didn't involve another person. Someone, for instance, who knows you're an escapee."

She turned her head away.

"See?" He didn't even wait for her to reply. "He calls the police, they remember the tip they got yesterday, and they're back here and won't fall for our ploy this time."

Her lip started to tremble. "He won't call. I know he won't." In the thrill of finding her painting, she hadn't even thought he might press charges. He'd seemed so—so broken when she'd left him. He might change his mind. He did have a temper. "I told you, it's fine." She wanted to believe it.

"You're coming with me." Warren grabbed her by the waistband of her pants and pulled her out the door.

"You will not manhandle me." She flopped to a dead weight. Sure, it would be easy enough for Warren to pick her up, but if he did, he'd know it was against her will.

Instead, he let her go. "You care about the Villa, right?"

She kept her eyes on the carpet, but nodded.

"Then you understand that staying in your bedroom is asking for trouble. It's the first place the police would look."

She didn't reply.

"You're coming to the basement."

This got her attention. "The basement?"

"Down by the boiler. I'll bring a mattress."

"I refuse to be locked up in the basement."

He held her firmly but gently by the upper arm. "It's the only place that's safe. For you, and for everyone else here. You're coming downstairs."

She could scream, but for what? No one in the Villa would trust her. Not now. She released her breath slowly. "All right."

Warren led her down the quiet hall to the stairs. With a hand firmly under her arm, he walked her down the three flights to the basement. He unlocked the basement's back room and pulled the chain to turn on the single lightbulb suspended from the ceiling.

"Stay here. I'll be back."

She looked at his armchair with his shape molded into it, and the framed photo of Goldie the pit bull he kept on the bookshelf crammed with thick paperbacks. She doubted this was what the doctor would have recommended for the night before brain surgery.

A few minutes later, Warren returned with a rolled-up pad under one arm and blankets over the other.

"You can sleep in your clothes. Take your shower in the morning before you go to the hospital." He laid the mattress on the floor and tossed the blankets, except for one, on it. The last blanket he kept over his arm.

What had happened to sweet, goofy Warren? Where was the Warren who talked about adventure and read romance novels and loved animals? She didn't know this man. She might as well have been talking to a tree stump for all the emotion he showed.

The thing is, he was right. Father Vincent had tried to warn her, but she didn't understand. "I'm sorry," she said. "I was selfish. It was one of my paintings. I thought I had to destroy it."

"Why? Why was it more important than all of us?"

"My surgery is tomorrow. I might not have another chance."

Warren appeared to struggle to keep in his anger — or was it another emotion? "Claudine and Gilda are taking care of that. I don't understand. Why does getting the paintings back matter so much to you? I mean, for real. It's not just about respect for the artist, is it?"

She looked at her feet, then back at him. "No, you're right. That's not all. It's embarrassing."

"I don't understand."

"I, well, I hid messages in the paintings." At Warren's puzzled look, she added, "I had a grudge, and I used the paintings to get revenge. Oil paints leave a texture on the canvas, and I figured out how to manipulate it to write words."

"What kind of words?"

The boiler fired up with a whoosh, and the pipes groaned with the fresh surge of warm water. Adele stood straighter. Either he would understand, or he wouldn't. "They were insults about an art professor I had an affair with."

"He broke your heart," Warren nearly whispered.

"Yes, but that wasn't it. I thought it was, but I was wrong. He told me I could never be a real artist. And I believed him."

"You believed him? How—?"

Adele held up a hand. "Let me finish. I didn't understand what was going on until tonight, actually. I thought" —she shook her head— "I thought I was ashamed of the messages, and I didn't want to hurt him. That's why I had to destroy the paintings before I died. Now I know that, yes, I was ashamed, but I was still really angry with him. Some part of me thought I had no talent, but another part refused to believe it." She caught his gaze. "Do you understand?"

"Go on."

"So, tonight, at his apartment, I realized that he didn't have power over me anymore. I finally believed in myself. Once I knew that, my anger vanished" —she snapped her fingers— "just like that. I was done with him."

He didn't respond, and she couldn't read his expression.

"You see?" she prompted.

He dropped his arms. "All right."

She waited for more, but he kept silent. If he'd said something, anything, she might have told him that he was part of her new strength. But he didn't say a word. Finally, she laid out the blankets. "Do I get a pillow?"

"No."

She untied her shoes and sat on the mattress, pulling up her knees. "Okay."

"Turn off the light?"

"I guess."

He pulled the light's chain once again, and absolute darkness choked the room, except for the minuscule flicker of the boiler's pilot light. She didn't hear him move for the door.

"Aren't you going?"

"No." His voice was as icy as ever. The armchair squeaked. "I'm staying here to make sure you don't leave again. Once you're out of surgery, you'll be too out of it to slip away. Until then, I'm not leaving your side."

"You don't have to stay down here. I won't leave. I promise."

Again, silence.

After a few minutes, she stretched out on the mattress and pulled up a blanket. At least it was warm down here with the Villa's mechanical system ticking efficiently around her. After a few muffled creaks as Warren shifted in his armchair, he was quiet. But she didn't hear the deep, even breathing of sleep.

She hated this coldness between them. But she understood it, too. She turned away so she didn't face the armchair barely an arm's length away.

"I should have known better," he said. His voice was still cool, but quiet.

She waited to see if he'd elaborate, but he didn't. What the hell. She risked it. She rolled onto her back so her voice would reach him loud and clear. "If I wasn't going to die, you wouldn't have looked at me twice."

It was the truth, and he had to know it. Warren liked reading about adventure and living romance through a novel. He could never handle it in real life.

"Tonight you proved what a bad idea it would have been. I'm lucky you'll be gone soon. We're all lucky."

If she wasn't mistaken, his voice cracked.

CHAPTER THIRTY-TWO

Gilda set down her coffee cup. "Grady, turn off that television."

This was the day they took Adele in for surgery. Gilda had been up all night turning it over in her mind. The plan had been risky enough — taking a prison escapee to a hospital under an assumed name for surgery by a doctor who was only doing it to get back something that was rightfully his. She counted three felonies right there.

Certain things were taken care of. Adele's fake ID was in the bag, and Doc Parisot had moved all the medical equipment he'd need after the surgery into the Villa. Gilda would accompany Adele to guard the dog bed and be ready to destroy it should the surgeon welch on his part of the deal.

What she worried about was Ellie. Ellie was smart and cold-blooded. John, the bartender from the Women's League, had told her all about how Ellie had suckered him into helping her escape. That hadn't been enough for her, because two days later, the Bedlamton Arms had fired him, citing an anonymous note. Cold hearted, she was.

Now Ellie was gunning for the Villa as a way to get at the Booster Club. The Booster Club had to outsmart her first.

"I need some of you here," Gilda said. "Father Vincent, you sit there. Grady, Bobby, Mort, and Red. I need you, too."

They gathered at the cafeteria's far wall, away from the windows.

Gilda knew Ellie was watching them. Exactly where and how, Gilda couldn't say. They'd been lucky so far. The police hadn't made a third visit.

"You're worried about Ellie, aren't you?" Father Vincent said.

"She won't rest until she's taken us down," Gilda said. "This morning, we're going to be vulnerable. If she's paying attention—"

"How could she know what we're up to?" Bobby asked.

"How did she know about Adele and about the dog bed?" Gilda said. "We have to seal up this hospital visit tight, and I'm going to need all of your help to do it."

They all looked at her. Grady even held his speared piece of grapefruit mid-air.

"Adele went out last night," Red said. "I saw her with my night vision goggles."

"Ah, jeez. What was she doing that for?" Bobby said.

Warren had told Gilda about Adele's midnight adventure, and Gilda didn't look forward to calming down the others, too. "That's over, and she's safe. Now, let's move on." Shoot. She hadn't wanted them to find out about Adele. If they were going to pull this off, she needed their cooperation.

"She put us all at risk," Mort said. "She didn't care enough to stay in just one more night."

"It wasn't about us. We'll talk about it later."

With priestly authority, Father Vincent clasped his hands in his lap. "The girl is ill. We must forgive her. God is calling on us to help her heal. Now, Gilda, you were saying?"

Father Vincent's words shut them up. Mort sat back in his chair, and Bobby took his ever-present deck of cards from his shirt pocket and began to shuffle. She cast the priest a grateful glance. "Before we go any further, tell me. Are you up to it? If not, say so now. It's been a while since any of us have pulled off this complicated a maneuver. This is more complex than boosting the painting or the dog bed."

Even in the old days, they'd rarely worked together. Gilda remembered an early morning in the nightclub's back room back in the early 1960s when they — less Red, she was a secretary at the Dictaphone shop at the time, and Father Vincent, who was in seminary — had huddled to plan a poker room sting. Bobby with his mop of black hair and no arthritis in his hips, Mort moving with the elegance of Fred Astaire. Gilda had helped organize the heist as a way to make her friends some money, plus please the police commissioner, who was keeping her in a comfortable hotel suite at the time. She flashed to seeing him in the golf club's locker room. Times had changed for all of them.

"I'm in," Bobby said. She thought she caught an edge of excitement to his voice.

"Me, too," Father Vincent added.

"Why not?" Red said.

"Then listen up."

It was going down this morning. After her conversation with Mitzi, Ellie was certain. She'd tidied up the attic, preparing to leave for good, and dressed herself in the housekeeper's uniform. While school bells sounded recess and children laughed and yelled in the halls, she kept the telescope trained on the Villa's front entrance.

At last, action. The priest — their driver, she'd figured that out already — strolled toward the street and unlocked a white minivan.

Ellie darted for the attic door and flew down the stairs, scattering grade schoolers around her. As she burst out the side entrance, she caught sight of Josiah.

"Princess!" he yelled.

She couldn't stop, but she smiled and waved. One last smile. She wouldn't be returning to the school. Her ticket was waiting at the airport.

The priest pulled the minivan up to the Villa's entrance and kept the engine idling while he walked inside. Ellie looked up and down the street. In her studies at the Bedlamton Arms, she hadn't learned how to hotwire a car, so she was going to have to do this the old-fashioned way. But what car? Later on, parents would be idling in the streets to pick up their kids, but now?

Around a corner, an ice cream truck trundled into view, playing "Pop Goes the Weasel." Not ideal, but it would have to do. Now, if she could get the timing just right....

The priest led a small woman wrapped in a large scarf to the minivan. The escapee. Another woman — looked like the old redhead — followed, pushing a walker. She carried a boxy object covered with a blanket. The corner blew back, and Ellie glimpsed gilding. The dog bed.

Ellie almost laughed. As if it were the real dog bed. The Booster Club wasn't stupid enough to risk that.

The ice cream truck, crawling at a speed easy enough for an eight-year-old to overtake, was twenty yards from the Villa's parking lot. Now fifteen. Kids in the playground ran to the fence and yelled at it.

The priest hoisted himself into the driver's seat. The smaller woman and the redhead were now in the minivan's backseat.

Ten yards.

The minivan pulled back.

Now! Ellie ran for the ice cream truck. Using strength that had simmered for days, she yanked the driver, a skinny guy in a Snoopy T-shirt, from his seat. She pulled herself up to the driver's seat and stepped on the gas.

"Hey!" he yelled from the pavement. "That maid just stole my truck!"

The minivan was a block ahead. The ice cream truck bounced at a decent pace, given that it was probably used to a consistent diet of second gear. She shifted up and swatted at a switch. "Pop Goes the Weasel" switched to a Joplin rag. Shoot. She flipped the switch again, and the music slowed to a stop.

The minivan drove steadily on, and, as far as she could tell, was unaware of being followed. A couple of kids waved at a street corner, and, frowning, dropped their arms as she raced past.

Now the minivan was turning on to the artery that led to the highway. Could the ice cream truck take highway speeds? She wasn't sure. It wasn't exactly her BMW at home.

Then another thought crossed her mind. Why was the Booster Club headed for the highway at all? The hospital where Lancaster was a neurosurgeon wasn't out that side of town. It was south. Up on the hill. The minivan was going in the opposite direction.

Ellie slammed on the brakes, unleashing the sound of a dozen sidewalk sundaes hitting the freezer wall. The Booster Club was on to her. They knew she was after them, and they were leading her on a wild goose chase. At this very moment, the real art forger—and the real dog bed—was on her way to the real hospital.

Ellie yanked the wheel, whipping the ice cream truck into a

parking lot and spinning it to the opposite direction. Gas pedal to the floor, she merged into traffic, bringing a cavalcade of honks behind her. For the first time in her life, she flipped the bird.

They thought they could fool her. Well, that wasn't going to happen. A cocktail of excitement and anxiety flooded her veins.

Her hunch had been right. The dog bed was ransom. This was the moment she'd been waiting for, planning for. She'd had a few false starts, but at last it was coming together.

CHAPTER THIRTY-THREE

Adele bumped and swayed with the sedan as they barreled toward the hospital. Beside her was the Marie Antoinette dog bed. It was supposed to be some kind of relic, but Gilda hadn't even bothered to toss a blanket over it. Adele pressed her hands to her temples and rubbed. You'd think that the fact she was on her way to get her head sawed open would at least inspire an anxious hum. But, no. Nothing but the tom-tom in her skull that had kept her from sleep last night.

After her fiasco, she'd handed herself over to the Booster Club. Whatever they wanted was fine. If things went well, her aneurysm would be gone, and she would leave the Villa to find a new life undercover.

But she didn't have to think about that now. She didn't have to think about anything.

"For chrissakes, Bobby, can't you go a little easier on the corners?" Gilda clutched the dashboard.

"You said to hurry. I'm hurrying." Despite his Indy 500 foot on the gas pedal, Bobby drove with one hand on the wheel and one stretched out on the seat behind Gilda.

Gilda glanced behind her, as she had every few seconds during their ride. "It's okay. She took the bait. She even heisted the ice cream truck as planned. No one's following us." Gilda shifted her gaze to

Adele. "What's eating you, honey? Feeling bad about last night, or just nervous about the surgery?"

She didn't want to respond. She didn't want to do anything but ease the throbbing in her head and the ache in her chest. If she felt anything at all, it was the desire to be put under. Bliss.

"I'm okay." The flat words didn't even sound like her own.

Gilda turned toward the windshield. "You haven't eaten. Lack of protein. You'll be better once the operation is over." She hummed a few bars of "Bad Case of Lovin' You" as the sedan traveled up the hill.

At last, Bobby slowed the car and pulled into the hospital's cement parking structure. He eased the sedan into a handicapped parking spot and hung the tag over the rearview mirror.

"Hang on a minute," Gilda said. Once again she scoured the road behind them. An ambulance, lights flashing but siren muted, was pulling into the emergency area, but otherwise all was clear. "We're good."

Bobby retrieved Gilda's walker from the trunk, snapped it into position, and wheeled it toward her. He opened the car's rear door and slid out the dog bed.

"What do you want me to do with this?" he asked Gilda.

"Set it on top of the walker. I put a cloth in the trunk to cover it — yeah, that's it."

Bobby wafted a card-table-sized cloth over the dog bed. Underneath was eighteenth-century workmanship. On top was a dance party of apples holding knives and forks. "Are you sure you want to do this? It's not too late to take her home. We might be walking straight into a trap."

He was whispering, but Adele heard every word. She closed her eyes and leaned her head back against the seat.

"It's the only option to save her life. Besides, I'm the one at risk. If anyone asks, the whole thing was my deal."

Bobby patted her on the back and set the dog bed on Gilda's walker before opening the sedan's rear door.

"Come on, darling," Gilda said. "It's time."

Adele lifted her head. "Okay." Whatever. She just wanted it to be over with.

"I'll wait in the car, unless you need help with the dog bed," Bobby said.

"No. I've got it." Then, to Adele, "Come on, honey."

As they moved closer to the hospital's entrance, reality began to set in. Soon, she'd be lying on the operating table. At some point, she'd wake up. If all went well, she wouldn't have to worry about dying. At least, not immediately. Yet, the struggle would continue. She'd turned Warren against her for good. She'd have to find a way to survive financially. But—and this was a tiny flicker of hope—she could continue to paint. Even if she had to live in the back of Uncle Larry's TV repair shop, she could paint. That was something to live for.

"That's the spirit, darling. You hang in there."

They crossed the hospital lobby and took the elevator to the third floor. Gilda, Adele at her side, pushed her laden walker to the admissions desk.

"We're here for surgery with Dr. Lancaster," Gilda said. She pushed Adele's fake papers across the counter.

"Your name, please?" the nurse asked.

"It's not for me, it's for Gloria, here. Gloria Curtis."

Adele only half heard her. The waiting area was painted in a yellow that had probably been intended to lighten the mood, but instead gave the room the air of a downmarket laundromat. A gray-faced woman knitted while a kid squirmed over the chair next to her. The scene might have been a painting in the California realist tradition named "Dusk at the Sanitarium."

"I have Miss Curtis seeing Dr. Lancaster in his office, but no surgery scheduled for today."

Adele's sluggishness dissolved that instant. What was going on?

Gilda pushed the walker up against the counter. "That can't be right. Check again."

"It's right here." The nurse pointed to the computer screen. "Gloria Curtis, 2 p.m., Dr. Lancaster's office. A half hour meeting. Nothing about surgery prep."

Adele had never seen Gilda so alert. Gilda's eyes widened and mouth pursed into a mauve-tinted O. This couldn't be good. In the space of a second, she took in Adele, then the lobby, then her head swung toward the elevator.

The elevator's doors opened, and a disheveled brunette in a housekeeper's outfit emerged. She locked eyes with Gilda, then Adele, and a smile widened across her face. It was not a friendly smile.

Sucking in her breath, Adele turned to Gilda. "What—?"

Hands planted on her walker, Gilda said, "Run!"

CHAPTER THIRTY-FOUR

Gilda gave Adele a shove. Eyes wide, the girl stumbled, then took off down the hall.

Gilda froze in place. Ellie advanced in slow, determined steps, hands hovering over her hips like a gunslinger in a spaghetti western.

"They force you to work as a maid in the institution, eh?" Gilda said. What a change that woman had been through. She'd always been so well groomed. Now her eyes were sunken and dark. And if Gilda weren't mistaken, she'd been into the rum.

"I've got you this time. You're not slipping out of this one," Ellie said.

Really? She couldn't come up with anything better than that? Gilda kept her expression placid but adrenaline burbled in her veins. She glanced right and left. The halls were busy with patients in wheelchairs. A gurney wheeled by.

"Heads up!" Gilda yelled, and in a deft motion, lifted the dog bed while kicking her walker toward Ellie.

Ellie oomphed as the walker hit her belly.

Gilda leapt toward a thin woman on a motorized scooter. "Sorry," she whispered and elbowed the woman to the floor with one arm and slung the dog bed on top with the other. She cranked the scooter's speed dial from turtle to rabbit and rocketed down the corridor.

Man, this unit had pep. Imagine what Father Vincent could do with it. The only problem was that the dog bed blocked her view. She steered the wheelchair around a corner, scattering a doctor and two nurses.

"Hey," said a man wheeling a stacked cart of lunch trays as Gilda nicked him.

She heard a crash and the sound of shattered crockery and looked over her shoulder to a landslide of beige food—turkey and gravy, maybe, and, judging from the smell, some kind of custard. And here came Ellie. Gilda turned ahead and stepped on the gas. The scooter was jetting at full throttle.

"Watch out, lady!" came a voice behind her. The man with the lunches. Ellie had slipped and fallen. Good.

An elevator just ahead opened, and Gilda yanked the scooter to a hard right to steer it in. She slammed on the brakes, slicing between a rabbi and a gent hooked to a portable oxygen tank. "Sorry, fellas. I'm kind of in a hurry."

The door shut behind her just as a custard-smeared Ellie neared.

"And I thought I had it bad," the man on oxygen said.

"What floor?" the rabbi asked.

Gilda faced the elevator's rear and couldn't remember how many floors the hospital had. "Um, fifth, please."

"What have you got there?" The man with the tank pointed at the dog bed.

"Don't ask."

The elevator opened and Gilda backed out the scooter. To her left was the staircase. Ellie could be running up it right now, looking out every floor for her. Gilda zipped the scooter past a long window, then pointed it toward an opening door.

"You can't go in there," a nurse said as the scooter buzzed by. "You're not authorized. The nursery needs to be kept germ free."

She halted the scooter just before ramming into a shelf of diapers. The dog bed rocked from side to side but didn't topple. She was in the maternity ward. To her right were rows of babies in bassinets. "All right. Hold that door."

She backed out, mastering a tidy three-point turn, and buzzed through the open door and down the corridor, throwing a glance back every few seconds. She rounded a corner.

"I know you're here somewhere," came Ellie's voice behind her.

Gilda zipped into the first open door she saw and pulled it shut behind her. Dang it. She set down the dog bed and regained her breath. Dang dang dang. How was she going to get out of this?

A low moan, gathering steam, came from across the room. Gilda raised her head. She was in a patient's room, and the patient was clearly in labor.

"Breathe, honey," Gilda said. Shoot.

The patient's moaning subsided, and she began to pant.

The door opened, and Gilda started, hands on the scooter's controls. But it was only a candy striper with a pitcher of water.

"Lock the door behind you," Gilda said.

Without asking why, the candy striper locked it. She set the pitcher by the patient's bed, then turned to Gilda, arms crossed. "What do you want?"

"Can't you do anything for her?" Gilda nodded toward the bed.

"I'm a candy striper, not a gynecologist. Besides, she's only at three centimeters and she wants to go natural. Isn't that right?" she shouted toward the bed.

"Arghhh," the woman moaned.

"The nurse will check in on her."

Gilda examined the candy striper. She was a bit overdeveloped for her age and clearly had the attitude to match. Gilda would bet her red lipstick and gum smacking weren't regulation. In short, Gilda knew her type well.

"Here's the deal. I'm on the lam. I'm being pursued by an escapee from a mental institution, and one of your surgeons has the police after me."

The candy striper didn't flinch. "What's that?" She jerked a thumb to the tablecloth-swathed shape next to Gilda's scooter.

"Marie Antoinette's dog bed."

She nodded once, took a wad of gum from her mouth, and stuck it on the bedside table. "Gotcha. Wait here."

As soon as the door closed behind her, the woman in labor began to moan again. "Another one's coming." She broke into pants.

"Oh, honey. Where's the kid's father?"

"At the basketball game." The poor woman was drenched in sweat.

"Doesn't he know you're here?"

The woman nodded and grimaced. "Playoffs."

"Get a lawyer," Gilda said. "It's not going to get any better. While you're at it, look up Bad Seed floral arrangements. I'll do you up one for free."

A moment later the door burst open again, jolting Gilda. The candy striper was pushing a gurney and had acquired a fresh wad of gum.

"Get on."

"I need to take the dog bed—"

"I know. Get on."

Gilda complied. Truth be told, she was through with the scooter. The saddle could use more padding. With the candy striper's help, she sat on the gurney's edge and swung up her legs. The candy striper placed the dog bed on her belly, then covered her up to her neck with a sheet.

"Where are we going?"

"To the candy striper's lounge."

The woman on the bed started moaning again.

"A good lawyer, I tell you," Gilda shouted as they left. "You deserve better."

The candy striper pushed her into the hall. "Look pregnant."

Gilda glanced down at her boxy middle and closed her eyes. No professional would fall for it, regardless of how much Oil of Olay she used. "Give me a break, hon." And hurry, she wanted to add. Ellie could be around any corner.

"Helen," a woman's voice said. Gilda opened an eye to a middle-aged woman with a clipboard. "Where are you taking her?"

"Delivery. Dr. Grigson's orders." She sounded remarkably convincing. Gilda suspected the Villa might welcome her someday.

"Her?"

The candy striper lowered her voice. "Probably not her own eggs."

"Fine. Just hurry up. We're on lockdown. The police are searching the building."

The candy striper rolled Gilda down the hall and into an elevator. "Can you go any faster?" Gilda asked.

"We don't want to attract attention."

They got off the elevator and rolled down another hall, and, after a pause for the candy striper to unlock a door, into a dim room. A supply closet. The door clicked shut after them.

Gilda sat up and caught her breath. "Get this thing off me, will you?" Once the dog bed was set to the side, she grunted off the gurney to a surprised trio of candy stripers eating potato chips. One of them was looking at her phone. They'd cleared out the rear of the storage closet and kitted it out with lounge chairs and a mini-fridge.

"Who's she?" A candy striper waved a chocolate bar at Gilda.

"Fugitive from justice."

Gilda took a chair while the first candy striper pushed the gurney to a corner. Gilda rubbed her backside as she sat down. "That scooter has nice power, but the seat's not too comfortable."

"Are you the one the police are looking for?" The candy striper with the phone put it away and stared at her.

"Probably." That double-crossing surgeon hadn't scheduled an operating room. He wanted to get his dog bed and send her up the river. And now Ellie was after her, too. She'd no doubt drag Gilda to the police and convince them of all sorts of things. The Villa would be forced to shut down. With luck, Adele had escaped. And, even more desperately, Gilda hoped the stress hadn't been too much for Adele's brain.

Gilda let out a sigh. At least she appeared safe here. She noted a row of well-thumbed romance novels on the floor. Warren had the one with the yacht on the front. The candy stripers had something good going. "You know where I can get a walker?"

"I'll say." The candy striper on the end, the one with the straight black hair and name tag that read Maria, pointed to three collapsed walkers leaning on a supply shelf. She moved the dog bed to the front of the shelf to pull one out. The rest of the shelf was full of neatly stacked boxes of disposable gloves, bottles of rubbing alcohol, and a pack of cigarettes. Cigarettes? Come to think of it, the air did carry a hint of menthol.

"You know a way to get out of the hospital without being seen?"

Gilda hoped Adele had made it back to the car.

"I suppose we could put you in a box and smuggle you to the loading dock."

"Or take her through the morgue."

Behind Gilda, the doorknob rattled. "Gilda?" It was Ellie. It rattled again.

"Hush," Gilda whispered to the candy stripers. They stared at the knob.

Gilda held her finger to her lips to signal silence. At last, the rattling stopped. They waited one minute, then two. Ellie must have moved on. How and when Gilda was going to get out of the supply closet, she didn't know, but at least she had somewhere to hide out for a few hours.

"I think we're safe," Gilda said finally.

Now metal-on-metal scraping came from the door handle.

"What's that noise?" the candy striper with the chocolate bar asked.

Gilda knew the sound of a picklock all too well. With horror, she watched the doorknob's lock pop out. They were in a storage room with no other exit.

The door burst open, and Ellie flew in, smashing into the shelf and sending bottles of rubbing alcohol bouncing to the ground.

"Surprise!" Ellie said.

CHAPTER THIRTY-FIVE

When Gilda had shoved her and hightailed it in the opposite direction, Adele had run, no questions asked.

Now she found herself in the hospital's bowels, wandering through darkened corridors, every once in a while passing an orderly or what looked to be maintenance workers.

Finally, a nun stopped her. "Are you looking for the cafeteria, dear? You just passed it."

The cafeteria. Her stomach gurgled. She hadn't eaten since last night, and it didn't sound like the operation was going to happen. But she didn't have anything with her. No money, nothing. Just an ID for someone named Gloria.

"Thank you." Adele tried to smile, but she knew she sounded disappointed.

"You follow me," the nun said. "Lack of a few dollars shouldn't stand between a hungry woman and a square meal."

Adele obeyed. The nun led her to a room bright with fluorescent lights.

"Jimmy." The nun's habit waved a bit as she pointed toward Adele. "You fix this girl up with whatever she wants. Put it on my account."

Even in the harsh light, the nun's face radiated pink. Her eyes were the milky blue of a Van Gogh iris. Adele's gratitude blended with the intense urge to beg the nun to come to the Villa and sit for a portrait.

"Thank you," Adele said. "Thank you so much."

"Never you mind about thanking me. We thank the Lord."

When the nun left, her skirts whisking about her ankles, Adele turned toward the steam table. Flaccid hotdogs, pale macaroni and cheese, and a sorry imitation of spaghetti filled its stainless steel tubs. Further on was a salad bar under a grimy sneeze shield. The hospital appeared to share a recipe book with the Carsonville Women's Correctional Facility.

"The milkshakes are good," the man the nun called Jimmy said.

Yes. A milkshake. She smiled. "I'll have a chocolate milkshake and a tuna salad sandwich, then."

"With fries?"

"Please."

She carried her tray to the corner where she could watch the room. An anonymous mix of hospital staff and visitors came and went. She was reminded that her aneurysm was one of thousands of serious health problems in the county. The woman in a wheelchair asking for coffee was clearly bald under her stocking cap. Chemotherapy, likely. Another woman struggled to quiet two playful toddlers, but her mind was somewhere else. Maybe upstairs with an ailing parent. A man with a fat ankle cast limped by on crutches. All Adele had cared about was herself. The truth was, all these people — and more — were burdened.

Last night's trip to Oliver's apartment had been selfish, too. She'd let her anger overcome her good sense, and the Villa's residents might still pay the price for it.

Where was Gilda, and why had she run? Gilda was hardly in shape to sustain a high-speed chase. Warmth and worry suffused her as she considered the risks Gilda and the other Villa residents had taken for her, first by breaking her out of jail, then stealing the Italian landscape and the dog bed, and setting up this operation. Adele lowered a french fry before it reached her mouth. But the doctor hadn't scheduled surgery. He wanted them to meet him in his office. Now she understood why Gilda had run. The police were waiting to take Adele back to prison, and Gilda had known it.

Adele absently hoovered up the last drops of milkshake with her straw. Except for risking the Villa by getting art supplies and sneaking out to destroy the fake Stubbs—she winced remembering Warren's cold greeting on her return—she'd been passive this whole time. She'd let them do all the work, relying on the excuse of her brain aneurysm.

She pushed away her tray and stood. The old folks at the Villa had put their future on the line for her. That wasn't right. It was her life at stake, not theirs. She wouldn't make them pay for her own stupid mistakes.

She was going to see Dr. Lancaster and turn herself in.

Ellie shut the storage room door behind her and twisted its lock. Victory was so close she could taste it, and it tasted delicious. "Didn't think I'd find you, did you?"

The redhead, Gilda, sat in a chair holding a collapsed walker. Up close, she looked even older than through the telescope, with vivid hennaed hair and powder-white skin. Her mauve lipstick had worn away, leaving purple stains feathering around her lips. Beyond her hovered three candy stripers, one of them holding a half-eaten chocolate bar and another holding a bag of chips.

"Are you from the housekeeping staff?" one of the candy stripers asked.

"No."

"Then why are you wearing—?"

"I said, shut up." Ellie took a step closer to the redhead.

"You've been watching us," Gilda said.

"What if I have?"

"You want to take down the Villa. To get at the Booster Club."

"You deserve it." The boxy object next to the shelf had to be the Marie Antoinette *lit de chien.* She yanked off its cover. Yes, the dog bed. Bottles of rubbing alcohol had toppled onto it. One bottle's cap had popped, and alcohol seeped over the bed's velvet canopy.

"What's going on? You two know each other?" the busty candy striper asked, cool as a flagpole in January. She patted her apron and came up with a pack of cigarettes.

"Shut up," Ellie said. Then, to the redhead, "You. You screwed up my life. I had money. People paid attention to me. My marriage was a model. Then you sent me to the Bedlamton Arms."

"What's that?" the candy striper with the chocolate asked.

"Funny farm," the busty one whispered.

"You did it to yourself," Gilda said. "It was your greed, pure and simple, that got you in trouble. You were making sweetheart deals with the county. You wanted to stop the family shelter from being built—"

"I was fine with the shelter. Remember?"

"Only because the Booster Club tricked you into thinking it was sitting on money. You're responsible for your failure. Don't you put that on us."

The whole bottle of rubbing alcohol had now emptied on the dog bed's cover, and other bottles toppled around it. If the bed were gone, so was the Booster Club's ransom for the surgery. Not only would the surgery not take place, Dr. Lancaster wouldn't hesitate to jail them all. The Villa would shut down. Claudine and the rest of the Booster Club would be crushed. As they should be.

"You're nothing but a criminal," Ellie said. "All of you. Criminals. You shouldn't be allowed to see daylight."

"I think she's been drinking," a candy striper said, waving the unlit cigarette. "I smell it."

"Maybe we've broken a few laws over the years," Gilda, now standing, said. Even on her feet, she was a head shorter than Ellie. "But we've done a lot of good. We take care of each other, and we look out for people who need it. That's more than I can say for you. All you care about is yourself—your bank account, who'll kiss your keister, who you can screw over to make your next buck. You don't obey the law—you use it to hurt people." The disgust on the older woman's face was palpable.

Ellie did care. Maybe it had taken her a while to get there, but at last there was one thing she cared about. Right now, though, her anger overshadowed it. "Give me a cigarette," she said to the candy striper.

The girl bit her lip and shook one from the pack. With a trembling hand, she passed it to her.

"Matches."

The girl reached into her apron and handed Ellie a matchbook.

Ellie peeled a match from the book and examined its red tip a second before pressing it to the flint. None of these idiots seemed to realize what was going to happen. The girls watched, slack jawed, but the redhead's eyes suddenly widened.

"No!" Gilda yelled. "Run, girls, she's going to blow the place up." She grabbed the folded walker and shoved it at Ellie, but it was too late.

Ellie had lit the match and used it to flame the entire matchbook. It whooshed to life. She tossed it toward the dog bed. The candy stripers, their fear of Ellie transformed into fear for their lives, pushed past both women and burst out into the corridor.

A tiny flame rippled over the dog bed, then, fed by rubbing alcohol, spread until it encompassed it. Ellie stood, transfixed. The Marie Antoinette *lit de chien* was now truly history. Orange flames devoured the centuries-old blue velvet as if it were dry straw.

"Get out of there!" Gilda yelled from the hall. "You'll be roasted alive!"

Ellie's head jerked up. She ran into the corridor and turned toward the emergency exit. A shrill whoop-whoop-whoop sounded through the halls, and a muffled explosion in the closet told her the oxygen tanks were going fast.

The last thing she saw as she turned to run was the elderly redhead, flanked by candy stripers, hustling in the opposite direction. Running wouldn't make the dog bed come back. The Booster Club's plans were finished.

Victory.

CHAPTER THIRTY-SIX

Adele retraced her steps to the hospital's front desk. The receptionist gave her Dr. Lancaster's office number without a second glance.

She crossed the hospital's courtyard. It was turning into a glorious spring afternoon, and a flowering plum tree dropped petals into a fountain. She breathed deeply. She might not taste warm fresh air for a long time.

Consulting the number the receptionist had written on a slip of paper, she made her way to his suite. She opened the door and went to the counter.

"May I help you?" The receptionist didn't even look away from his computer monitor.

"Yes. I'm" — she paused a moment to gather courage — "I'm Gloria Curtis." She steeled herself. "My real name is Adele Waterson."

The receptionist didn't even flinch. "You're late. The doctor's been expecting you." He picked up the phone and pressed an intercom button. "Ms. Curtis has arrived."

So, the police were in the back. That's the way it was. They would do it the civilized way, then. She pulled at the hem of her shirt and followed the receptionist to the rear.

"In here," he said and opened the door.

Despite her determination to turn herself in, her heart hammered against her ribs. Maybe she'd have her aneurysm right here and die. Wouldn't that be rich? She stepped through the door.

"Ah, Adele." A short, middle-aged man with a neatly trimmed beard sat behind a wide oak desk. He didn't bother to rise. The disgust on his face made it clear why.

The doctor. The massive desk. A filing cabinet. A few framed prints of tomatoes. And that was it. No police.

"Where are they?" Adele asked.

"Who?"

"The police."

For a second, he looked flummoxed. "And how would I get my dog bed?" He pointed to a small chair across from him. "Sit."

"I'd rather stand, if you don't mind."

"You make me nervous. Sit."

She sat.

"Yes, I cancelled the operation."

"I know. You see—"

"But not to arrest you. I was tempted to call them, of course. Who wouldn't be?"

Adele waited without speaking.

"You stole a valuable artifact. Marie Antoinette's dog bed." He examined a fingernail. "Well, her country dog bed, anyway."

"I know." Adele's voice was barely audible.

"A national treasure."

"I thought it was French."

Dr. Lancaster fastened her with a clear, cold gaze. "I didn't say which country's treasure, did I?"

Adele relaxed a bit. Art was not the only loot trafficked illegally. "Where did you get the dog bed, anyway?"

He dropped his voice and turned away. "That's not your concern."

"I get it. You have legitimate papers for it, I assume."

His skin colored under his beard. "We're not here to talk about the *lit de chien*. We're here because of your surgery. I cancelled it because you don't need it."

"What?" Adele halfway rose, but the doctor motioned for her to sit again. "I saw the scan. I have an aneurysm at the base of my skull. The doctor explained it all."

"That doctor got his degree in a box of cereal. His license should be revoked."

Adele stared at him. "It was very clear."

"You don't need an operation. Not from me, not from anyone."

"But my aneurysm —"

"It's not an aneurysm."

She leaned back and crossed her arms. "I don't believe you. You're just trying to get out of this."

"Why would I? To me, operating on someone's brain is like you faking a quickie Picasso sketch. Not that it's easy, but it's routine. I've done it a thousand times." He turned to his computer screen. "Come over here. Let me show you why your brain is fine."

Adele moved to his side of the desk.

"When your associates demanded I operate on you, I needed your CT scan. I can't just cut willy-nilly into your skull, you know."

Adele nodded. "Go on."

"I had to get your scans from the prison" — he spat out the word like it was grit in his spinach — "but obviously couldn't reveal your identity. I told the chief medical officer I was conducting a study of brain health and requested all their CT scans from the past three years. Clever, if I do say so myself. Among them was yours."

Gilda hadn't seemed all that concerned about Dr. Lancaster getting the records he needed. She must have known he'd figure out something. "Good thinking."

"Yes. Well, here they are." He clicked the keyboard. "All twelve CT scans." A cloudy film filled the screen with a brain's topography laid out in white. "See that?" He tapped a pen at the base of one scan. "Looks like an aneurysm, doesn't it?"

It did. "Is that one mine?"

Without responding, he clicked to the next screen. "There's another." He tapped its base then advanced another screen. "And another."

"We all have aneurysms?"

"In short, if we layer the films, we see the exact" —he tapped his pen on the screen— "same" —tap, tap— "abnormality." With a final tap, the pen's cap flew off and landed behind her.

Now she understood. "It's the machine, isn't it?"

"This doctor has diagnosed twelve aneurysms in three years." Dr. Lancaster swung his chair to face her. "I've reported it, naturally."

"But…." Everything she'd done over the past few weeks had been because an artery in her brain could explode. The trouble she'd dragged the Booster Club into, the relationship she'd started and destroyed with Warren, the schemes to get back her forgeries—it was all based on a lie. "Why didn't the doctor catch it? Twelve aneurysms in the exact same place seems like a real coincidence."

"Dr. Bradley." Dr. Lancaster shook his head. "Not very bright, but thorough."

She remembered Dr. Parisot saying almost the exact words. "You mean, I'm not going to die?" Her numbness had to be shock. The truth—that the aneurysm was a computer glitch—she couldn't quite absorb yet.

"Of course you're going to die. Just not right this minute," he said, in another echo of Dr. Parisot.

"But my headaches." She looked up. Yes, the headaches.

"Where do you feel them?"

She clapped her hands to her temples. "Here."

"And the world seems a bit fuzzy right before one comes on?"

"Yes."

"And you're intensely sensitive to light and sound when you have one."

"Yes." She was still in a daze. "So I'm going to die, right?"

"Migraines. I can write you a prescription for something that will help."

Adele slumped into a nearby chair. She wasn't going to die. A mix of elation and fear filled her. Now what? What would she tell the Booster Club?

"Now that we have that settled, I'd like my *lit de chien* back. Please."

An alarm shrieked through the office, and both Adele and the surgeon jumped. "Code 9, code 9. Please evacuate the building. There's been a fire."

CHAPTER THIRTY-SEVEN

Adele got off the bus and walked the few blocks to the Villa. After the hubbub at the hospital—fire engines racing in, lights ablaze, more alarms and recorded messages to evacuate than she'd ever heard—Adele had huddled with Dr. Lancaster in the parking lot. At last they'd negotiated that as long as Adele returned the dog bed to the doctor's house by that evening, he wouldn't report her. The doctor had even given her a few bucks for bus fare.

Warren didn't look up when she came in the Villa's front door. He mumbled a greeting but didn't stop reading. She might have been just another of Gilda's Bad Seed delivery boys.

"Did Gilda make it back?" she asked.

"In the cafeteria."

A handful of Villa residents were watching news of the fire on TV. They turned when she came in, and Red ran over to hug her.

"Adele, honey. We were so worried," Gilda said. "You're all right? Father Vincent thought we should call the county detention center, but I knew you'd make it out okay."

The warmth of their greeting was more reassurance that she'd done the right thing by trying to protect them, even if it hadn't been necessary. She glanced through the cafeteria.

"Where's the dog bed?"

The Villa's residents looked at each other. "Dog bed?" Grady asked.

"Yes," Adele said. "The Marie Antoinette dog bed." Something was up.

"We've got some bad news." Bobby stole a glance at Mort.

"You left the dog bed back there?" Mort jerked a thumb at the television behind him, still showing fire hoses pointed at the hospital. "When were you going to tell me?"

"After dinner," Gilda said. "I thought you'd be more mellow after the cassoulet."

"You've got to be joking. The dog bed?" Mort said.

"Gone, I'm afraid," Bobby said.

"Worse than that," Gilda said. "It was the cause of the fire."

Mort groaned. "All that work."

"I know. I'm sorry, Mort. You see, we were trapped in a supply closet with some candy stripers, and Ellie knocked over some rubbing alcohol, and one of the candy stripers was smoking, and—"

"You're saying the dog bed is burned up. Gone," Adele said. "Are you sure?" She held her breath and prayed Gilda was mistaken.

"I'm afraid so," Gilda said. "I saw it with my own eyes. Spectacular, too. Once the flame hit it, it—"

"No." Mort flattened his hands over his ears. "I can't bear it."

So that was it, then. Without the dog bed, Dr. Lancaster would make sure they paid the price. The best she could do was to find him and turn herself in. Beg for mercy. She'd never rat out the Villa or the Booster Club. Maybe he'd be satisfied with returning her to prison.

"Why so glum, darling?" Gilda said.

Adele collapsed against the wall. Red steered her to a chair. "We needed that dog bed. For Dr. Lancaster."

"But the—" Father Vincent started.

Gilda held up a hand. "Let her finish."

"After you left, I went to find the doctor—"

"Why?" Gilda said, her chair rattling with her indignation. "He was set to turn us in. You heard the admissions clerk. No operation."

"Now look who's interrupting," Father Vincent said.

The Villa's residents were rapt. Adele even noticed Warren lurking at the group's edge.

"You were trying to save us, weren't you, honey?" Red said.

Adele tilted her chin and said, "That's not why the doctor cancelled the operation. He looked at my CT scan. I don't have a brain aneurysm."

It took a moment for this to sink in. From the corner of her eye, she caught Warren stepping back and disappearing into the hall.

"Don't be so hasty about that," Bobby said. "Didn't Dr. Parisot look at your records? He said it looked like an aneurysm to him."

"It did look like that. Thing is, Dr. Lancaster got all the prison's CT scans for the past three years, and they all had that exact same mark. It's a problem with the scanner."

"Well, I'll be darned," Mary Rose said from the back of the room. Adele didn't even know she'd been listening. "Cook!" Mary Rose yelled. "Break out the champagne."

"He didn't want to tell us, because he wanted to make sure we showed up with his dog bed." Adele's voice quieted. "I don't know what he's going to do now. You stole it for nothing. Now that it's destroyed—" She didn't finish her thought. "I'd better go pack."

"She's worried about the dog bed, bless her heart," Gilda said.

"Well, it was a damned fine piece of work," Mort said.

"Not yours. The real one," Gilda said.

Adele wasn't sure she understood. "The copy went on the decoy ride with Father Vincent, right? And you brought the real one to the hospital."

"Why would we do that? We wouldn't have any leverage," Gilda said.

"But…." Adele's voice drifted off.

"Get the good coupes, too," Mary Rose yelled toward the kitchen.

"We sent the prototype with Father Vincent. That's the one the police saw when they raided us," Gilda said gently. "It's an old con. A swap. The cat in a bag. You promise a pig, and you show him something like a pig, but in the bag is a cat."

"Cats don't have as much meat," Mary Rose said.

"As if we'd eat a cat," Mort added.

"Anyway, we took the copy with us," Gilda finished.

"You don't think I work up a copy just like that, do you?" Mort snapped his fingers. "I wanted Ruby to have a real nice bed for her rescues, so I did a prototype first. Prototype, then the copy."

"So there were three dog beds," Adele whispered.

"It really is a shame it burned up. That was some topnotch craftsmanship," Father Vincent said.

"I suppose I could build Ruby another one, although the carving really cramped my fingers."

The day had brought almost too much for her to absorb. She didn't have a brain aneurysm. And now she didn't have to go back to prison, as long as they returned the real dog bed. She glanced toward the door for Warren, but he was gone. "So, let me be clear. The Marie Antoinette dog bed is okay."

"Sure," Gilda said.

"Of course," Bobby said at the same time. "Locked up in the fake water heater where it's been the whole time."

Adele's mouth moved, but nothing came out.

"Look at that. She can't believe it. I told you that bed was good work," Mort said. "Think you could set me up with a forgery job, Adele?"

"Hush, Mort. We'd better get the real dog bed to Dr. Lancaster."

CHAPTER THIRTY-EIGHT

Dinner at the Villa was over, and Gilda was clearing the last bite of cherry pie from her plate, but she didn't really taste it. Adele was safe and healthy, Claudine was working on rounding up the paintings — less the one that had been destroyed — and the dog bed was with Dr. Lancaster.

Bobby and Gilda had returned it. Adele had wanted to come along, but Gilda thought it was too risky. There was still the chance they were being set up. B. E. Lancaster had practically cried when they carried the bed to the door. He'd put on white cotton gloves and gently set the bed on the hall carpet, telling his wife to stay way back.

And that had been that. Once he was sure the bed was safe, he hadn't even bothered to say goodbye. The door clicked shut in their faces, and they returned.

All in all, a satisfying conclusion. But it wasn't over yet. Ellie was still out there. They wouldn't be safe until she'd dropped her vendetta against the Booster Club, and, so, the Villa.

"Gilda, what's wrong?"

She'd been so absorbed in her thoughts — and, truth be told, tuning out Bobby's arguments over their post-dinner card game a few tables down, that she hadn't heard Claudine come in.

"Hi, Deanie. Honey, it's great to see you." Gilda rose and wrapped her arms around Claudine's neck. She smelled cool and damp and slightly green, like spring. "Want to check if Cook has any more pie?"

"No. I just stopped by after work to give you an update on Adele's forgeries."

"Wonderful," Gilda said, but she thought, *that's all?*

"And to say hello, see how you're doing. I hope you don't mind if I drop by from time to time."

Gilda's smile widened. "That's sweet of you."

Claudine looked so professional in her plain black suit. On Gilda, the suit would have looked like someone stuck a bunch of sweet peas in a tin can. Claudine's austere — but still somehow romantic — features elevated even wool gabardine.

"I like your hair that way," Claudine said. "It's modern but suits you."

Gilda ruffled her new hairstyle, a variation on the one she'd worn to the League Lodge. "Thanks. Adele helped me with it."

"Should we get her?" Claudine asked.

"She's had one heck of a day. We all have, actually." Gilda led Claudine to a table and motioned for her to sit. "I'll fill her in later."

Claudine moved to the chair across from her. "What happened?"

"What hasn't happened, is more like it. Adele was supposed to have surgery today, but it turns out she doesn't have an aneurysm after all. Just migraines. Then we accidentally started a fire at the hospital — "

"Don't tell me." Claudine almost smiled. "Maybe I'd better not know."

Red stopped by to pat Claudine's back. "Deanie, great to see you. Don't be a stranger, you hear?" Red winked at Gilda and settled with Mary Rose in front of the television.

"It's probably for the best that Adele's not here. I'm not sure she's going to be happy." Claudine drew a list from her leather case.

"Basically, the museum still refuses to give up their forgeries, and they're making noise about buying up the rest. The insurance company will happily broker the deal so they don't have to pay out."

"You're right. Adele won't be happy. She insists her forgeries are disrespectful to the masters."

"That's just it. The museum says they're not forgeries at all. They're works of art in their own right."

"Can't be." Gilda pushed the dessert plate to the table's edge. "I've seen her paintings. They're copies all right."

"Apparently the curator has found messages in them. It was by accident at first. He had one painting on its side, and the light was right. He examined both paintings and found insults about some man named Oliver."

Gilda's laugh burst out so loudly that across the room Bobby dropped his deck of cards.

"What's so funny?" he asked.

"Oh, my." Gilda wiped a tear from one eye. "Adele—hee hee hee." She snorted. "You tell him. I can't."

"Adele apparently has something against someone named Oliver, and you can read her thoughts in her canvases, if you know where to look."

"No joke. Like what?"

"I only remember one," Claudine said. "It was something about 'Oliver grows too much hair for his nostrils.'"

Gilda's laughter spiked again. "That's my girl." She blew her nose. "I heard a little about this fellow. He was her art professor. Took advantage of her, and, worse, told her she was no good as an artist. It really did a number on her self-esteem."

Claudine leaned back. "Go tell it to the Holgate. They've already settled on a date for an exhibition."

"She wouldn't be able to go to any museum openings," Gilda said. Adele was on the lam. The last thing she needed was her face in an art catalog.

"I know. Too bad, though. She could make a bundle of money. Straight, too."

"Yeah," Bobby said. "A straight ticket back to prison."

Claudine rose. "That's all I have."

"You coming for Sunday dinner, Deanie?" Red asked.

Gilda didn't speak. She wanted to look at Claudine, but kept her gaze on her clasped hands instead.

"Definitely. You mind if I bring a date?"

Gilda let her breath out with a smile. "Please do. If you think it's safe. I mean, yes, please come."

The Villa's residents, except Grady, who had his hearing aid turned off, exchanged glances.

"It'll be all right." Claudine picked up her notepad. "Say, we got notice this afternoon that the Marie Antoinette dog bed turned up. Apparently its owner sent it out for cleaning and forgot. You don't know anything about that, do you?"

A chorus of "no"s came from throughout the cafeteria.

Claudine glanced toward the bed prototype back in its place on the table near the cafeteria window. "I didn't think so. I'd better be going." She turned toward the door.

"Wait, Deanie," Gilda said. "Remember how I was telling you about Ellie?"

Claudine set down her notebook again. "Yes."

"It's time for us to pay her a visit."

CHAPTER THIRTY-NINE

"She's in the school attic," Gilda said. "I'm almost positive. I need you to come with me."

"Why me?" Claudine asked. She didn't look afraid—or charged up to see Ellie, for that matter. Merely curious.

"Because you understand her," Gilda said. "If anyone can make her see the futility of trying to get revenge, you can. She failed against you and the Booster Club last time. Maybe talking with you will get her off this idea."

Claudine rested a hand on her hip. "It might fire her up more."

"By now, she has to be feeling defeated. She thinks the dog bed burned up at the hospital, but when she finds out it was a fake, she'll lose it."

"All right. Say we talk with her. Say she agrees it's best for everyone to give it up. Then what? You can't expect she'll voluntarily go back to the Bedlamton Arms."

"You think I care where she goes?" Gilda said. She pushed herself to standing and grabbed her cane. "Come on."

Claudine fidgeted with the catch on her purse. "All right. I guess so. Where to?"

"The school. The kids are gone. I'm pretty sure she's been watching us from the attic. It's the only possible vantage point. You've got your tools, right?"

Gilda knew she did. Hank had given Claudine a set of picklocks when she was a teenager. They rolled up into a packet the size of a manicure kit. They were likely in her purse right now.

She sighed. "Of course I do."

"Then let's go."

The day's sun was waning, and crisp spring air chilled their short walk to the school's side entrance.

"You wait here," Claudine said. "I'll open up and make sure the place is empty."

"All right, but be snappy about it. I'm cold." Gilda leaned her cane against the school's brick wall and rubbed her shoulders.

It took seconds for Claudine to break into the school. She disappeared down the dim hall, and the door, on a pneumatic hinge, shut slowly behind her.

Gilda looked over at the Villa. The cafeteria lights came on. Bobby moved toward the television. Red was probably shaking up a post-dinner cocktail.

Gilda had tried to make a confrontation with Ellie sound easy, but it was likely to be a lot more difficult — maybe even dangerous. She'd hidden a knife up her sleeve, and Claudine carried a concealed handgun for her job.

After a few minutes, Claudine was back at the door. "All clear."

"Here are the stairs," Gilda said, looking at the stairwell to the right of the door.

"That one doesn't go all the way up to the attic. We'll have to take the far stairwell. Are you up to the walk?" she whispered.

"I'm fine, as long as we're not making it the Daytona 500."

They made their way down the waxed floors past open classrooms with impossibly tiny chairs and the alphabet pinned to the walls. The water fountains hung low.

"Were we ever that small?" Claudine said.

"You were. I remember."

"Come on. The staircase is here. When we get to the second floor, I'll go up to the attic first and break in, if we need to. I should be able to do it without her knowing, even if she's there. Then, when you arrive, we'll be ready to go in. Sound good?"

Gilda nodded. The stairs took a lot out of her. She was already breathless, and they were barely halfway up the first flight.

At the second floor, Claudine nodded and, light as a panther, moved ahead. She had been a world-class thief, on par with the cat burglars who raided summer homes on the Riviera and stole jewels from the safe at the Paris Ritz. After Hank's health started declining, she'd stayed in Carsonville. And now she was straight. Well, kind of. Hank had been so proud of her skills. Gilda thought he would have been proud of her now, too.

At last, she arrived at the attic. Claudine already stood just to the door's side.

"Unlocked," Claudine mouthed. "Ready?"

Gilda nodded.

Claudine drew a gun from her jacket and gestured for Gilda to move out of the doorway. In one swift motion, Claudine pushed the attic door open and swung to face the room, her gun leading the way. From where Gilda stood, she couldn't see in the attic. She saw only Claudine. And what she saw was first focus, then surprise.

Claudine dropped her arms. "She's not here."

"What? She has to be. Where else could she be watching from?"

The women stepped inside the attic and examined it first from the doorway. It was barely light enough now to see.

Claudine nodded toward the furniture grouping in the middle of the room. "Looks like she used to be here."

"Or she's out and is coming back."

"Possibly." Claudine closed the door behind them. "Why don't you look around? I'll stay by the door just in case."

Gilda leaned on her cane as she walked to the couch. A lamp on a side table appeared to be plugged in, so she clicked it on, casting a warm pool of light. Ellie had been here, all right. She'd even done a little housework, from the look of the swept floor. Gilda picked up a rum bottle with half an inch of amber liquid sloshing at its bottom.

She waved the bottle at Claudine. "Ten to one it belongs to one of the teachers."

Then she saw it. Right there on the couch, leaning on a pile of folded children's coats, was an envelope with "To Whom It May Concern" written on its front.

"Deanie. She left us a letter."

Claudine hurried to Gilda's side and examined the sealed envelope. "You think it's to us?"

"Who else could it be to? You read it. I don't have my glasses."

Claudine pried the flap open as if it had never been sealed. A woman with her talents would never do anything as crass as rip open an envelope. She slipped out a sheet of wide, brown-tinted paper with pale blue lines meant to teach kids cursive.

"To whom it may concern," Claudine read in her low tones. "By now you know that I was here. If I've done my work right today, I destroyed the Marie Antoinette dog bed and unmasked the Villa Saint Nicholas's residents as criminals. By the time you read this letter,

I'll be on my way to Africa to work for an international children's hunger relief program."

"Africa? Hunger relief?" Gilda said. "This doesn't sound like Ellie. Could someone else have been up here?"

"There's more," Claudine said and continued to read. "In exchange for merely destroying the dog bed and not turning in the art forger, I request that you locate Josiah Townsend, a student at this school experiencing food insecurity, and connect him with services at the firehouse's family shelter. Respectfully, Eleanor Whiteby."

"I'll be danged." Gilda sat on the couch, then rose to cram some of the children's coats folded nearby under her posterior. She picked up a child's telescope, examined it, then set it down on the end table.

"I can't figure it out, either. This is Ellie Whiteby?" Claudine went to the attic window and looked out. "There's the Villa."

"Ellie Whiteby. Hunger relief activist." Gilda rose and wiped her hands together. "So I guess that's that."

CHAPTER FORTY

Adele rose the next morning at dawn. She wanted to leave the Villa before anyone was awake. Grady might be up, but he'd probably be in some chat room debating the merits of *Practical Hospital* soap opera with a hacker in Kosovo. Or trying to, at least.

Last night, Uncle Larry had given her a wad of cash and his best wishes. They'd agreed that the Villa had done enough, and every day that Adele stayed was another day that put the residents at risk.

She'd packed before bed, not that she had a lot to pack. She was taking her painting supplies, though. Somewhere down the road — maybe on the coast somewhere, she'd always wanted to be by the ocean — she'd dig out her fake ID and get a job. She could be a waitress. In her off hours, she'd paint.

She took a last glance at Gilda's portrait. Folks here had been kind. She opened her suitcase again and laid the dress she'd lent Gilda on the bed. They could keep the painting, too. If Claudine was right about her work, as Gilda had said, it might earn them some money someday.

Her plan was to take a bus to the train station, then make up her mind from there. Cook would be in the kitchen prepping for breakfast. Maybe she'd give her a cup of coffee for the road.

Father Vincent was in the cafeteria. "It's time, isn't it, child?"

She nodded.

"I thought so. Wait here a moment." The priest disappeared into the kitchen and came back with a cup of coffee and a small brown bag. "I had Cook pack a lunch for you. She knows how you loved her coq au vin, so she used some of the leftovers for a nice chicken salad sandwich."

Adele swallowed the tears that threatened to rise. She hugged the priest. "Thank you so much. You've all been so kind."

"You've brought us a lot of excitement, Adele. A few scares, too. But you helped us remember what we're good at and why we're here. I thank you."

Pink — popsicle pink, the pink of a Cassat baby's cheek — punctured the sky beyond the worn chairs and back issues of *Banker's Monthly* that had become so familiar to her over the past few days. A half-built replica of the Marie Antoinette dog bed sat on a side table. Ruby would like that.

Adele rose. "I guess I'd better go. Thank you." She kissed the priest's cheek. "Tell everyone I love them." The word "love" caught in her throat. Warren. She remembered the last time she saw him. It was yesterday afternoon when he'd listened at the room's edge about her talk with Dr. Lancaster.

She slipped the lunch into her tote bag and picked up her suitcase with her other hand. "Goodbye," she said.

"Goodbye, child."

When she reached the cafeteria door, she turned. "Bye," she repeated.

"Until we meet again."

"Goodbye," she whispered as she passed Warren's dark office and went out into the cold spring dawn. "Goodbye."

So, this was what they meant by a heavy heart.

Orange infused the morning's pink, and a robin's song cut the silence. An old Volvo backed out of the carport at the parking lot's edge. Its exhaust steamed white in the chill. The car pulled in front of the Villa, and the driver's side window lowered.

"Adele?" It was Warren.

Her mouth formed the word "Yes?" but no sound came out. Her heart began to pound.

"I'm ready for adventure. For real. With you. And I'm not just quoting romance novels, either. Will you come with me?"

She couldn't speak. She set down the suitcase.

"Father Vincent checked out the car. He says we're good to go for at least another hundred thousand miles."

"What about the Villa?" She searched her brain. "The relicensing? Don't they need you?"

"The license came in the mail on Friday."

Friday. The day she arrived at the Villa. She let that sink in. He might have kicked her out long ago. He hadn't.

When she still didn't speak, he lowered his voice. "You were right, you know. Please. Let's go together."

She drew a breath. "Pop the trunk."

Afternoon sun filled the Villa's cafeteria as Gilda slid a dead dahlia into an especially elaborate floral arrangement. Her portrait stared back at her with approval. Adele must have been up half the night finishing it. Gilda had moved the painting to the cafeteria for everyone to enjoy. Whether they liked it or not.

Hank would have loved the portrait, Gilda thought. Strange, she couldn't bring his face to mind like she used to, although she still felt him right in the old ticker. "It's all good, honey. All good," she seemed to hear him say.

A handful of fried daisies added the perfect last touch to her bouquet. She loved how their leaves had dried thin and stiff like needles. Dr. Lancaster should appreciate this arrangement. At least, his wife hoped so. The accompanying card asked for a divorce. Gilda idly wondered how much it would cost to send an arrangement to Africa. She wiped off her hands and untied her apron, her gaze wandering again to the portrait.

She raised an eyebrow. "Father Vincent?"

"Hmm?" He was polishing his ratchet set near the fireplace.

"Do you have a flashlight?"

"Of course."

Together, they tipped the portrait on its side, and the priest shined the flashlight flat against the canvas. Gilda slipped on her glasses.

"There it is."

It read, "Thank you, Booster Club."

Afterword

I'm a lucky writer to belong to three supportive author groups. My critique group—Cindy Brown, Doug Levin, Dave Lewis, Ann Littlewood, and Marilyn McFarlane—is an ongoing source of support and smarts. The Think and Drink group—Lisa Alber, Cindy Brown, and Holly Franko—are brainstorming whizzes. Not the Usual Suspects—Cindy Brown (again), Kate Dyer-Seeley, and Kelly Garrett—are my marketing compatriots.

Debbie Guyol and Charlotte Rain Dixon contributed great feedback as first readers. Raina Glazener worked her usual hawk-eyed copy-editing magic. Dane at ebooklaunch designed the cover, and Eric Lancaster designed the interior.

Lightning Source UK Ltd.
Milton Keynes UK
UKHW040746020119
334844UK00001B/272/P